# *WARNING LIGHT*

---

## DAVID RICCIARDI

BERKLEY
New York

BERKLEY
An imprint of Penguin Random House LLC
1745 Broadway, New York, NY 10019

Copyright © 2014, 2018 by David Ricciardi
Excerpt from *Rogue Strike* copyright © 2019 by David Ricciardi
Penguin Random House supports copyright. Copyright fuels creativity, encourages
diverse voices, promotes free speech, and creates a vibrant culture. Thank you for buying
an authorized edition of this book and for complying with copyright laws by not
reproducing, scanning, or distributing any part of it in any form without permission.
You are supporting writers and allowing Penguin Random House to continue to
publish books for every reader.

BERKLEY and the BERKLEY & B colophon are registered trademarks of
Penguin Random House LLC.

ISBN: 9780399585753

Berkley hardcover edition / April 2018
Berkley premium edition / April 2019

Printed in the United States of America
1   3   5   7   9   10   8   6   4   2

Cover art: *Paris* by fladendron/iStock; *Young man running* by Roy Bishop/Arcangel
Cover design by Pete Garceau

quickly as CIA operative Zac Miller uses his wits to out-wit Iran's brutal Revolutionary Guards and bring price-less intelligence home."

—Alex Berenson, #1 *New York Times* bestselling
author of *The Prisoner*

"Gripping. . . . Look forward to [Zac's] further adven-tures."          —*Publishers Weekly*

"A breakneck debut thriller that Ludlum fans will de-vour."

—Grant Blackwood, *New York Times* bestselling
author of *Tom Clancy Duty and Honor*

"A fine thrill ride. . . . The writing is lean and propulsive, the characters offbeat and interesting."          —*Booklist*

"This is a fun and heady combination of suspense and intrigue. Believable and provocative, it's a tough-as-nails tug-of-war definitely worth your time."

—Steve Berry, *New York Times* bestselling
author of *The Lost Order*

"*Warning Light* is an engrossing edge-of-your-seat thriller. David Ricciardi is a perfect storyteller who cre-ates characters that resemble real-life characters."

—The Washington Bookreview

"From the well-crafted and intense story line it's hard to believe that he has not written dozens of prior thrillers. Definitely seek this one out."          —*Suspense Magazine*

*For Julie, the love of my life*

# ACKNOWLEDGMENTS

I owe debts of gratitude to a great many people for their help with *Warning Light*: James Thayer, Andrew Malkin, Betty Sheridan, Bob Morelli, Charlie Robertson, Maggie Crawford, and especially Jack Romanos; my agent at Aevitas Creative Management, Rick Richter; my editor, Tom Colgan; and the rest of the team at Berkley. And most of all, to my family—parents, brothers, wife, and children—for their unwavering support.

# PROLOGUE

THE GROUND WAS still shaking when the scientists at the University of Tehran realized that the earthquake would end in tragedy. The seismographs at the Institute of Geophysics had pinpointed the epicenter near the Dehshir Fault, under the small city of Sirjan in southeastern Iran. When it was over, the quake measured 8.4 on the Richter scale. Strong aftershocks buffeted the region for days, hampering rescue efforts and wreaking further destruction.

Initial estimates indicated more than twelve thousand dead. The injured were too numerous to count. Homes that weren't completely destroyed had been rendered structurally unsound. Collapsing buildings claimed additional victims as residents tried to rescue family members or salvage possessions. Those who hadn't been killed or hurt had lost friends and relatives, homes and livelihoods. Thousands were still missing, and their chances of survival decreased with every passing hour.

Offers of assistance poured in from around the globe. Friend and foe alike volunteered money, manpower, and supplies to help the beleaguered residents rescue their loved ones and feed their families. A U.S. Navy ship exiting the Persian Gulf offered her heavy-lift helicopters to clear wreckage and transport the injured. Expert rescue teams from earthquake-prone Japan and Indonesia were standing by, ready to arrive in-country within twenty-four hours. In a rare sign of compassion and unity, every nation bordering the Persian Gulf pledged aid to their wounded neighbor, yet Iran turned them all away.

Publicly, the government stated that it had dealt with earthquakes since ancient times and had all the resources it needed. Indeed, Iran was one of the most seismically active countries in the world and was well equipped to perform search and rescue operations. But the real reason, what the government didn't mention, was that the most secret facility in its growing nuclear complex was just minutes outside the stricken city of Sirjan, and no foreigner was going anywhere near it.

## ONE

"SPEEDBIRD 337, MAINTAIN heading one-one-five. Contact Tehran Defense Radar on 127.8. Good day."

Inside the cockpit, First Officer Edward Blake responded to the Turkish air traffic controller.

"Roger that, Ankara Center. Speedbird 337 maintain heading one-one-five. Switching to 127.8."

He glanced to his left and caught Captain Sam Allard's eyes for a moment before tuning the VHF radio to the new frequency. The British Airways flight, radio call sign "Speedbird," was closing in on Iran's Flight Information Region and needed permission to enter Iranian airspace.

"Tehran Radar, this is Speedbird 337 heavy."

"Go ahead, Speedbird 337."

"Tehran Radar, Speedbird 337 with you at flight level three-niner-zero, estimate crossing your FIR at 15:20 hours."

"Roger, Speedbird 337, squawk 0413 and proceed as filed."

The radio fell silent while the Iranian controller verified

the radar contact and flight plan that the British Airways pilots had filed before taking off from London.

In peaceful times, the flight would have followed the great circle route through Uzbekistan and Afghanistan before heading south below the Himalayas on its way to Singapore. For the past decade, however, hostilities in the area led most airlines to divert their jets to the south, over Iran. The detour added a few minutes and several thousand dollars to the cost of each flight, but it was safer than flying through a war zone.

"Speedbird 337, identified, cleared for entry. Contact Tehran Center on 133.4. Good day."

"Roger that, Radar, Speedbird 337 cleared for entry, switching to 133.4."

Captain Allard adjusted the autopilot and the six-hundred-twenty-ton Airbus A380 banked gently to the right before settling onto its new course. He scanned his instruments and cross-checked his flight computer. Underneath the wings of the Airbus, four Rolls-Royce Trent 970 engines were running smoothly, each delivering over eighty thousand pounds of thrust. The radio in the cockpit chirped sporadically as air traffic controllers directed the other planes in Sector Two around Tehran. Most of the flights were domestic, but Emirates, Air India, and other international carriers were not uncommon.

The long-haul flight was on schedule as Allard gazed out the cockpit windows. The late-day sun was starting to form shadows behind the mountains below. It was his first flight over Iran. It was more rugged and beautiful than he'd expected, but his reverie was interrupted by the copilot.

"Captain, we have a warning light on the number-three engine . . . Exhaust gas temperature is spiking and oil pressure is dropping quickly."

An automated voice in the cockpit called out another warning and a message flashed on the centralized aircraft monitor inside the cockpit. Captain Allard silenced the alarms. He was already looking at the engine data on his own monitors.

"I don't think we're going to be able to keep it running. Give me maximum continuous thrust on the good engines and let's run the engine shutdown checklist."

Blake made eye contact with his senior officer and took a deep breath. "Yes, sir, commencing in-flight shutdown on the number-three engine."

Blake pushed the button for the Fasten Seat Belt sign while Captain Allard switched to the air traffic control frequency on his headset.

"Tehran Center, Speedbird 337 requesting immediate clearance to flight level two-seven-zero. Our number-three engine has lost oil pressure and we're shutting it down."

The radio was quiet for a few long seconds. Allard and Blake shut down the malfunctioning engine and trimmed the aircraft's rudder to compensate for the off-center thrust.

"Speedbird 337, you are cleared to flight level two-seven-zero, understand number-three engine out. Are you declaring an emergency at this time?" asked the controller.

Allard looked at his copilot. "Take her down to two-seven-zero as soon as we hit driftdown speed."

"Center, 337 leaving flight level three-niner-zero for two-seven-zero. That's negative, repeat, negative on the emergency. We don't know the cause of the pressure loss yet but the other three engines are running smoothly."

"Roger, Speedbird 337. Confirm you are an A380?"

"That's affirmative, Center."

"Speedbird 337, nearest capable alternate airport is Esfahan, approximately sixty miles northwest of your position. Would you like vectors to the alternate?"

"Center, 337, negative on the alternate. We are proceeding on course, descending through flight level three-six-zero. We're going to look at restarting our number three once we reach engine-out altitude."

"Understood, Speedbird 337. Maintain heading one-two-five degrees, flight level two-seven-zero, and keep us advised of your status."

"Maintain heading one-two-five, Speedbird 337," confirmed Allard.

When the aircraft started its descent, most of the passengers felt a touch of weightlessness before their seat belts pulled them down. Flight attendants walked down the pitched aisles, waking the sleeping passengers and enforcing the seat-belt rule. Questions from the passengers were politely deflected despite the clearly elevated vigilance on the part of the crew.

Captain Allard picked up the handset for the internal public address system as the aircraft descended.

"Ladies and gentlemen, this is your captain. You may have noticed that we've slowed down and descended over the past few minutes. Everything is fine. We'll soon be leveling off at twenty-seven thousand feet, where we're going to stay for a bit. One of our engines was acting up so we decided to shut it down until we can correct the problem and get it restarted. The A380 is designed to fly quite well with only three engines and can get by with two if necessary. In the meantime, please listen to your flight attendants and remain in your seats. We will keep you apprised of the situation. Thank you."

The pilots spent a few minutes preparing to restart the idle engine but the warning lights flashed again. The mood in the cockpit remained businesslike despite the mounting problems.

Blake spoke calmly. "We've just lost Yellow hydraulic pressure."

The forces involved in moving the control surfaces on such a large aircraft were enormous. Without hydraulics to move the rudder, ailerons, and elevator, the pilots would be unable to maneuver the plane. The hydraulic systems were so critical that the A380 had two systems, Green and Yellow, to prevent a single failure from turning into a catastrophe.

"OK. What's Green system pressure and quantity?"

Blake was already looking at his monitor.

"Green is at 96 percent." He paused for a moment. "Make that 94 percent. Quantity is definitely falling. We may have a leak."

The pilots ran through a checklist to locate the cause of the problem. Years earlier, a Qantas Airways A380 had suffered a hydraulic failure after an engine exploded just after takeoff. The explosion had also been preceded by an oil-pressure loss. Only the skill of the crew, and much good luck, had allowed the aircraft to land safely.

The air traffic controller had just finished handling a domestic Iran Air flight when Blake switched his radio back to the air traffic control frequency.

"Tehran Center, Speedbird 337 . . ."

"Speedbird 337, this is Tehran Center, what is your status?"

"Center, our number three is still out, we've lost primary hydraulic pressure and are running on our secondary systems. Requesting vectors to the nearest capable alternate."

"Stand by, 337," ordered the controller before the radio went quiet.

A minute later, the controller returned. "Speedbird 337, turn left heading three-one-zero and descend and maintain flight level one-eight-zero. Prepare for landing at Beheshti International."

Allard and Blake looked at each other. The captain smiled, then shook his head.

Blake keyed his microphone and calmly said, "Center, Speedbird 337. Unable to comply."

"Speedbird 337, this is Tehran Center . . . Please say again."

The radio was quiet.

"Speedbird 337, this is Tehran Center. Please acknowledge."

There was silence from the cockpit.

## TWO

AREA CONTROL CENTER, Sector Two, was a cold, modern room dominated by computer monitors and communications equipment. The radio frequency handling Flight 337 was being broadcast over the loudspeakers and all eyes were on the air traffic controller working the flight. The veteran controller had worked planes with communications trouble, aircraft that had strayed off course, and even emergencies, but no one had ever disobeyed an instruction before. He looked over his shoulder for guidance from the sector chief.

"Why won't he divert to Beheshti?" shouted the chief.

The controller turned back to his monitor. Radar showed the British Airways flight continuing on course.

"They seem to be losing altitude and their course is oscillating."

"If they are going to avoid the restricted airspace, they must divert now. Raise them again," the chief ordered.

"Speedbird 337, this is Tehran Center. Come in."

For reasons of national security, safety, or even recreation, most countries have restricted airspace. Some parts of the sky are simply off-limits to aircraft that don't have permission to be there, and the airspace in front of the struggling Airbus was most definitely off-limits.

"Speedbird 337, this is Tehran Center. Do you copy?"

The chief became angrier as the seconds passed in silence. "I am willing to believe we have an aircraft in distress if they communicate and divert, but they cannot simply ignore us. We have to assume a possible Trojan horse. Alert Western Area Command. Tell them we have an unresponsive aircraft and an imminent violation of the airspace around Sirjan."

The turbulent politics of the Middle East had led Iran to put military officers or reservists in control of its civilian air traffic control centers, and the Trojan horse scenario was one that all of their air defense specialists had studied. With air traffic control radar unable to distinguish an A380 on a routine passenger flight from a B-52 bomber intent on attacking Iran's nuclear facilities, controllers could only establish an aircraft's bona fides by assessing the pilot's communication, behavior, and prefiled flight plan, all of which could be faked. This plane was already in central Iran and headed toward prohibited airspace, which was even more sensitive than restricted airspace. But the Iranians were ready.

With wars to its west and north, and unfriendly aircraft regularly patrolling the Persian Gulf to its south, Iran had fighter jets and surface-to-air missiles stationed throughout much of the country.

A technician in the air traffic control center picked up the third of several red phones on a console and spoke rapidly to the air force officer on the other end.

"Western Command, we have a foreign aircraft

headed toward the Sirjan prohibited area, possible Trojan horse. Aircraft is one hundred and twenty nautical miles southeast of Esfahan, heading one-three-zero, twenty-five thousand feet . . . Aircraft has ignored instructions and is not answering its radio . . ." The technician listened for a minute. "I understand. One moment."

He held the phone at his side and pointed at the map on the computer screen in front of him as he spoke to the chief of center.

"In a few minutes they will exit the SAM net around Esfahan. If they continue on this course, they won't be within range of the S-200 battery at Bandar Abbas or the HAWK battery in Sirjan for another twenty-five minutes. They're flying through a hole in our defensive net. They'll be in Southern Sector before Western can scramble fighters or launch a missile."

The chief scowled. "Raise Southern Area Command right now. Do we have any interceptors in Kerman?"

The technician spoke into another of the red phones and relayed his conversation to the chief.

"Kerman is still not operational because of the earthquake. Southern can scramble two F-14s from Shiraz in ten minutes, but their radar is down. They're asking us what to do."

The chief studied the digital map on the screen of the controller in front of him. With his finger on the screen, he traced the probable course of the violator.

"Tell them to launch the fighters and alert the HAWK battery in Sirjan. We'll coordinate from here."

The technician relayed the orders and hung up the handset. He was a patriotic man, but he knew that the aircraft in question was almost certainly a civilian airliner with engine troubles. Shooting it down would kill the hundreds of passengers aboard. He stared at the computer monitor in front of him, willing the giant Airbus to turn around.

The very real threat of an attack on Iran's nuclear facilities ensured that its interceptors were kept on a high state of alert. The fighters based in Shiraz were American-made F-14As that had been sold to Iran before the 1979 revolution. Despite its age, the F-14 was still a formidable air superiority fighter, and it would make quick work of a commercial airliner. Each of the two fighters carried a pilot and a weapons officer. In the thirty-second briefing they were given before they jogged to the flight line, the four aviators were told only that a foreign aircraft had disobeyed instructions, ceased communications with air traffic control, and was flying into prohibited airspace. No mention was made that there might be passengers aboard or equipment troubles. The fighters were to intercept the aircraft and await further orders. Typically they would force the jet to land at an airfield away from the forbidden airspace, but the fighters carried live weapons and the pilots were well trained. They would follow the orders they were given.

At the Seventh Tactical Airbase outside Shiraz, the lead fighter throttled up and lit its afterburners, sending cones of flame erupting from the engines as it rocketed into the afternoon sky. When the second fighter was airborne and formed up with his lead, the pair banked hard left and turned to their intercept course. The planes' variable-aspect wings swept back to their high-speed positions and the fighters accelerated rapidly to just under Mach 1.5. They would cover the one hundred twenty-five miles to the Airbus in less than ten minutes. The big jet would be in missile range in less than five.

While the chief and the technician coordinated the intercept of the troubled airliner, the original controller tried repeatedly to raise the British Airways flight. In addition to the established VHF radio frequency, he broadcasted over the 121.5 MHz emergency-use frequency, which all aircraft monitored. The Airbus was nonresponsive.

The controller addressed the chief again.

"Sir, the target aircraft is ninety miles from Sirjan but has slowed and lost altitude. Airspeed is down to two hundred twenty knots and altitude is erratic around flight level two-forty. Their troubles may be worsening."

"Then why are they not descending and diverting to Esfahan as ordered? They are strictly forbidden to enter this area."

The technician was on the phone again. "Sir, the fighters are fifty miles out and have the target on radar. Southern Command is not going to let that aircraft reach Sirjan."

The chief hesitated. Every muscle in his face was strained.

The technician wrote something on a strip of paper and handed it to his boss.

655

The chief scowled, then softened his expression. The two men had been just boys in 1988 when an American warship, the USS *Vincennes*, had shot down Iran Air Flight 655 over the Strait of Hormuz, killing all two hundred ninety people aboard. The men had experienced firsthand the suffering and rage that had consumed the nation in the wake of the disaster. The chief nodded slowly. He could not let it happen again.

"Give me the phone," he said. "Who is this?" he spoke calmly into the receiver.

Like all chiefs of center, he was also a senior reserve officer in the Islamic Republic of Iran Air Force. He listened to the response and replied, "This is Major Shabazz Farini of the IRIAF. Our target is most likely a British Airways A380 with mechanical issues. We had been speaking to it on civilian frequencies and tracking it normally until it developed engine trouble. Keep your weapons tight and confirm when you have visual identification of the aircraft. Understood?"

As he listened to the response, he stared at the map display as it showed the aircraft continuing on its southeast course. His breathing quickened and his face reddened.

"I understand it is a security threat, that is why *I* called *you*, but I also know that a bomber would not approach its target at two hundred and twenty knots. Do you think he's giving you time to catch up? Call me when you have visual confirmation of aircraft type!" The chief slammed the phone into its cradle.

The Iranian fighter jets slowed to five hundred knots as they approached the Airbus from its four o'clock position. The F-14s flew five hundred feet above the larger plane, giving the pilots a positive visual ID of the distinctive two-story aircraft. The fighters climbed to bleed off speed and turned hard left before rolling out on a new course behind and slightly above the passenger plane. The lead fighter moved to the left and accelerated until he was abreast of the larger plane's cockpit before descending to the Airbus's altitude. The afternoon sun made it hard for the fighter pilot to see into the passenger jet's cockpit, but he had flown to this side purposely, so the Airbus pilots could clearly see him. He accelerated again until he was a few hundred feet in front of the Airbus and rocked his wings. If the Airbus rocked its wings, it would be confirmation that the big jet was having communication problems and would follow the fighter.

But the Airbus did not rock its wings. It continued on course, slowly losing altitude. The lead F-14 pilot spoke to his commander and pulled another five hundred feet in front of the Airbus. He released three bright flares into the air. The flares were originally designed to act as decoys for heat-seeking missiles, but when used like this they were a universally understood warning to comply with instructions or face the use of force. The lead fighter banked gently to the left, indicating that the Airbus should follow, but the number-two fighter radioed his flight leader that the passenger jet was continuing on course. The leader relayed the sequence of events to his ground commander as he circled around behind the Airbus. He slotted in next to his wingman and took up firing position.

## THREE

I N THE UPSTAIRS business class section of the giant Airbus, Zac Miller, a twenty-eight-year-old American technology consultant based in London, saw the fighter plane pull alongside. It was close enough for him to read the IRIAF markings under the cockpit and see the missiles slung beneath the wings.

An elderly Englishwoman in a Chanel suit sat next to Zac with pursed lips and a furrowed brow.

"It's all right," he said as he smiled at her. With an athletic build, dark wavy hair, and dark eyes, Zac used all of his natural charm to put the woman at ease. "They do this sometimes, just for practice."

The woman lowered her chin and looked at him sternly.

"Young man, my father flew Spitfires for the RAF in the Battle of Britain. I know when a fighter is 'practicing' and when it is not."

Zac raised his eyebrows and resumed looking out the window.

"But thank you anyway." The woman smiled and gave his hand a squeeze.

Nervousness filled the cabin as the other passengers watched the fighter jet hover outside their windows, but their anxiety turned to relief when the F-14 accelerated away. Their relief was severely misplaced.

THE IRANIAN AIR traffic controllers had been working frantically, but in vain, to raise the stricken aircraft on the radio. Finally, the speakers inside the control center came to life.

"Tehran Center, this is Speedbird 337."

The center erupted in cheers until the controllers remembered the tenuous situation they still had on their hands.

"Speedbird 337, why have you not answered your radio?"

"We've been a little busy up here." The control room was silent except for Captain Allard's crackly voice coming over the speakers. "Center, Speedbird 337 is declaring an emergency. We've lost our number-three engine, all primary hydraulics, and most of our electrical backup. We only have a few degrees of control surface movement. We need to put this aircraft on the ground at the nearest straight-in approach."

The chief pointed at the red phone and started shouting.

"Tell them we've reestablished contact with the aircraft. Tell them it has hydraulic and engine failures and we are working on an alternate airport. Tell them to call off those fighters!"

The technician relayed the information to the air force

command center while the other controllers pondered the fate of the crippled Airbus. The gravity of the situation weighed on all of them.

The radio crackled again.

"Center, Speedbird 337. Our flight computer is telling us that Sirjan is our best bet. Requesting clearance for emergency landing at Sirjan."

"Speedbird 337, stand by . . ." said the controller.

The airport in Sirjan was at the center of the prohibited airspace. The controllers didn't know what was there, and they were not foolish enough to ask, though they often speculated among themselves. What they did know was that no Western aircraft had ever landed there.

The Iranian fighters were still shadowing the Airbus while their radios bristled with questions from their mission controller.

*Yes, it was a clearly marked British Airways aircraft.*

*Yes, there were passengers in view, and all its lights were on.*

*Yes, the number-three engine appeared to be shut down.*

But none of it mattered.

"Speedbird 337, clearance to Sirjan is denied. Turn right heading two-eight-zero and prepare for landing at Shiraz International."

"Center, we've got one engine out and almost no hydraulics. We're using engine thrust to turn, climb, and descend. We need a straight-in approach and we need it now. We have one hundred seventy-six souls on board and Sirjan is our only chance."

The air traffic controller looked to the chief for guidance. His body tensed as he weighed his options. He thought about national security, he thought about sovereign pride, and he thought about his career. But in the end, he decided that the lives of those aboard the wounded aircraft were worth the risks to the other three. He would not be responsible for another Flight 655. He nodded slowly to the controller working Flight 337.

"Speedbird 337, cleared to land, Sirjan runway one-four. Altimeter setting 1006, runway elevation fifty-eight hundred feet. The airport is closed at this time, so expect no runway lights or communication with the tower. We will vector you in. As best you can, turn right heading one-six-five, descend, and maintain one-zero thousand feet."

The Airbus banked slowly to the right and settled onto its new heading as it descended toward ten thousand feet. Having made his decision, the chief began barking orders.

"Tell Southern Area Command to send the fighters home and stand down the SAMs at Sirjan. Tell them I have authorized the aircraft to land and I will take full responsibility for it." After a moment he added, "I'll call the garrison commander myself. That way, he'll know who to shoot first . . ."

To another controller he added, "Raise anyone you can at the airport. Make sure the runway is clear. Sound the crash alarm. Let them know they have less than ten minutes until an A380 comes in . . . God willing."

ON BOARD THE British Airways flight, the mood was tense as the cabin crew prepared for an emergency landing. Most of the passengers sat quietly and hoped that the next ten minutes of their lives would not be their last. Zac packed up his laptop and stuffed it under the seat in front of him. He closed his eyes and breathed deeply, trying to temper the adrenaline coursing through his veins.

When he opened his eyes the old woman was looking at him again.

"This is why I only fly British Airways. Their pilots are all former Royal Air Force officers. In twenty minutes we'll be safely on the ground."

"I'm sure you're right," Zac said. He admired the woman's character.

"But I'll never understand how these people live in the middle of the God-forsaken desert without gin and tonic," she added.

BY THE TIME they were eight miles out, Allard and Blake had lined up the giant Airbus on the runway heading and descended to eighty-five hundred feet. Mercifully, the landing gear lowered and locked into position on the first attempt. Without approach or landing lights on the runway, the pilots relied on their GPS and air traffic control to orient the plane and coordinate the speed, altitude, and attitude of the aircraft for touchdown. A computerized voice in the cockpit called out altitude and speed measurements every few seconds.

The accumulated system failures and thin air at the high-elevation airport required the Airbus to fly faster than normal over the ground when it landed, but Captain Allard had erred too far on the side of extra speed, and at one mile out the plane was traveling too fast to land. With one hand on the yoke and one hand on the throttles, he pitched the nose up and cut the engines, but they were still too fast. Touching down at this speed and weight could blow the tires and send the plane out of control. The Airbus soared past the touchdown point, flying fifty feet above the ground as it bled off speed. The first quarter of the runway passed by.

The giant aircraft reached the point of no return as it approached the middle of the runway. If it didn't land now, there would be no second chance. Allard pushed the nose down. The plane dropped, slamming the landing gear onto the runway and sending smoke billowing from the tires. Automatic spoilers deployed to reduce lift.

More smoke poured from the main landing gear as the antiskid braking system worked furiously to slow the big jet. The end of the runway approached quickly. Captain Allard used maximum reverse thrust on the remaining inboard engine but the Airbus was still making over one hundred knots with three-quarters of the runway behind it. Shuddering and swaying, the massive aircraft slowed gradually until it finally came to a halt, seventy-five feet from the end of the runway.

# FOUR

PPLAUSE FILLED THE cabin as the plane finally stopped. Passengers smiled and laughed nervously, relieved to be safely on the ground. One young mother was in tears, clutching her daughter, but most of the fliers were not terribly alarmed. The preparations for the emergency landing had been far more frightening than the landing itself. Zac looked at the Englishwoman seated next to him. She sat reading a book with an Hermès bag on her lap and a frown on her face. She caught his gaze.

"You can be quite certain that this is going to be unpleasant," she said in her upper-class accent. "This place has gone to the dogs ever since the revolution."

"I'm sure it's changed since then. Hopefully we'll be out of here in a few hours," Zac said.

The woman formed her tight-lipped smile again.

"You are either very kind or completely daft. I sincerely hope it's the former. They simply hate the British and the Americans here. They'd still be making carpets and living in tents if they hadn't inherited all that oil."

Zac sized up his seatmate. "Inheritances often bestow power and treasure upon the undeserving."

The woman regarded him warily.

He smiled and said, "Just look at the English aristocracy."

"Touché," she said, and promptly returned to her book.

Zac looked intently out his window on the left side of the plane. To most Westerners, the Middle Eastern desert conjured up images of endless sand dunes, but this part of Iran was rugged country. The view was of hard, lifeless soil; steep, rocky mountains; and a landscape baked by the sun. Except for a small cluster of buildings a mile away, it was completely devoid of any sign of civilization. It was so remote, so desolate, that the moving map display inside the cabin didn't even have a name for the place where they'd landed. A calm voice came over the intercom system.

"Ladies and gentlemen, this is Captain Allard again. Our faulty engine triggered a second warning light up here in the cockpit, so out of an abundance of caution, we decided to make this unscheduled landing here in Sirjan, in the Islamic Republic of Iran, to have the aircraft repaired and inspected. Please remain in your seats while we work to get the aircraft to the terminal. Thank you for your patience."

As Allard spoke to the passengers, an old Mercedes-Benz fire truck rolled up the center of the runway. Four men stepped out and looked up at the left side of the plane. One of the firemen spoke into a handheld radio while the others simply stood in awe of the giant Airbus.

Three heavy trucks with military markings arrived a few minutes later. A pickup truck with stairs attached followed close behind. The driver of the stair-truck maneuvered carefully until the stairs were aligned with the plane's cabin door. A squad of soldiers climbed out of their vehicles and loosely encircled the aircraft while their officer ascended the stairs. Allard invited the young Iranian captain into the aircraft, where they spoke in English for a few minutes.

The army officer explained that the small domestic airport had been damaged by the recent earthquake and was ill-equipped to deal with its unexpected guests, but would do its best. The airport did not have a tug to tow the big jet off the runway so the passengers would have to walk the two kilometers back to the terminal. One of the army trucks would ferry those unable to make the walk. Given that formal immigration procedures could not be followed, no one would be permitted to leave the airport but, the officer explained, it was inhospitable country and the area boasted little to see anyway. He asked that Allard convey this information to the passengers before they deplaned. Allard agreed and told the officer that, on behalf of himself, British Airways, and the passengers, he appreciated the assistance and the hospitality. The conversation was cordial and both parties seemed to be relieved that a potential disaster had been averted.

Though the passengers were grateful to be safely on the ground, human nature was such that many soon began to think about missed meetings, delayed vacations, and the minor inconveniences that seem so calamitous when lives are planned down to the minute. Dozens of passengers tried their mobile phones but none could get a signal.

When Zac heard the deplaning announcement he fished out his U.S. passport, grabbed his carry-on bag, and followed his elderly seatmate down to the lower level of the aircraft and the open door. He felt the hot, dry air on his face as he looked out over the vast Iranian countryside. Sunset was not far off. A small housing development occupied the flatlands next to the airport, but a spectacular mountain range stood off in the distance, filled with cragged peaks and deep gorges. The sun bathed the land in soft pink light, making for a striking contrast with the deep blue sky.

His seatmate was in line in front of him, hefting a rolling suitcase toward the stair-truck.

"May I carry your bag for you?" Zac offered.

"That would be nice, thank you." She proffered her hand. "I am Celia Parker. *Lady* Celia Parker," she said with a mischievous smile.

"I suspected as much," Zac said with a grin before introducing himself. "Didn't you check a bag?"

"Not at my age. I can't waste two hours waiting for my luggage in the off-chance they don't lose it."

The line on the stairs moved slowly and Zac took several photographs of the scenery with his mobile phone while he waited.

A frown crossed Celia's face.

"I would be careful taking pictures round this lot. My husband was nearly arrested in Moscow in 1982 for taking a picture of the outside wall of the Kremlin. Can you imagine? The complex was in every Intourist brochure and on the BBC twice a day. It was one of the most photographed places on Earth."

Zac glanced at the old woman. "That's probably good advice, but I've spent a lot of time in the mountains and that's one of the nicest sunsets I've ever seen."

"They took his camera right there on the street. We lost all of our photos from the Hermitage up in 'Leningrad,'" she said with contempt. "Barbarians."

Twenty minutes passed before Zac's passport was checked and he was in the line of passengers walking slowly toward the terminal. He'd suggested to Celia that she catch a ride on the army truck, but quickly surrendered to her withering gaze. Despite her age, she was proud, stubborn, and able to make the walk at a slower pace, which suited him just fine. Hues of pink, blue, and white tinted the sky as the sun continued its descent. He took a few more pictures while they walked.

"Are you traveling for business or pleasure, Mr. Miller?" Celia asked.

"Business, and please call me Zac. I work in London but I have some meetings in Singapore."

"I used to live there. Singapore, that is. My late husband and I spent a decade there. Wonderful place for expatriates. Well, I suppose London is too, isn't it?"

"It is. My job keeps me busy, but I bought a motorbike that I use on the weekends. I often ride up north with a group of friends. I've even taken it all the way to Edinburgh."

"It must be a lovely trip. Do you get home often to see your family?"

Zac hesitated just long enough for Celia to pick up on it.

"Wrong subject? Sorry, I didn't mean to intrude," she said.

"It's fine. My parents passed away when I was fourteen. Their car was hit by a drunk driver. I was raised by my aunt and uncle, but they sent me off to boarding school and we were never very close."

Celia nodded. "A tragedy on many levels. My condolences."

The terminal building looked as if it had been through a war. The earthquake had shattered more than half of the windows and many of the doors hung unevenly on their hinges. Fortunately, the simple interior, with linoleum floors and hardwood furniture, had been spared much of the devastation that had befallen the exterior. The men were directed to one area of the airport and the women to another.

"Segregation by sex?" Celia piped up. "Dear God, I'm not sure I even remember how to spell the word. Well, Mr. Miller. It's been lovely meeting you. I hope when this Kafkaesque ordeal is finally concluded we will fly the rest of the way to Singapore together."

"I hope so too, Lady Celia."

All the signs inside the terminal were in the Persian language, but a few airport employees had arrived and were gesturing to the seating areas and bathrooms, all of which instantly became overcrowded.

Zac sat on a bench and worked on his laptop until the line for the men's room finally disappeared. He took his carry-on bag and turned down the hallway. One of the airport employees, who was speaking into a handheld radio, motioned him to the door on his right. Zac entered and was surprised to see the army captain who had met the plane seated at a table. Zac assumed he had entered the wrong room until the door closed behind him. There were three other soldiers there.

"Your passport, please," the officer said to Zac in surprisingly good English.

"Sorry, I think I have the wrong room. I was looking for the toilets."

"This is the right room. Your passport, please."

Zac handed him the document.

"What were you taking photographs of earlier?"

Zac thought for a moment. "Just a few pictures of the sunset on the mountains. It was very scenic."

"May I have the camera, please?"

Zac realized that it was not an accident that he'd been directed to this room, and neither was the timing. They had waited for him to go to the bathroom. They wanted to separate him from the other passengers without making a show of it. He thought of the Englishwoman's warning.

"Yes, of course. It's in my pocket."

The soldiers watched closely as Zac set down his carry-on bag and removed his phone. One of the men took the device and left the room. The captain asked if Zac had been to the Islamic Republic of Iran before, what he did for a living, and general questions along the same line. There was a period of uncomfortable silence while the soldiers stared at Zac and he stared at the floor.

"Have I done something wrong?" he finally asked.

"What makes you think that?" asked the captain.

"Are you questioning all the passengers like this?"

Silence.

The soldier who'd taken the phone returned after twenty minutes and had a whispered conversation with the captain.

"This should be cleared up soon. I will be back shortly," the captain said before stepping out of the room. He returned an hour later and spoke briefly with the soldiers before turning to Zac.

"Time to go."

The captain motioned toward the hallway. By the time Zac turned toward the door, he felt a sharp prick in his neck. By the time he hit the floor, he felt nothing at all.

## FIVE

Z AC AWOKE TO a powerful throbbing at the base of his skull and coughed weakly as he tasted the stale, rank air. With great effort, as if rousing himself from a dream, he opened his eyes. He was seated on a chair above a grimy and uneven floor and his traveling clothes were gone. Someone had dressed him in frayed canvas work pants and a faded denim shirt. He thought back to the room with the soldiers. He remembered getting ready to leave, but nothing else.

It required deliberate effort to lift his head. To his right sat a soldier in a chair, but it wasn't one of the men who had apprehended him. This one wore a different uniform and a black beret. He caught Zac's gaze for a moment and walked out of the room.

Zac tried to stand but his arms and legs would not respond. His ankles and wrists were bound. The room was an office like one might find in an old factory or a warehouse. It was Spartan, with off-white paint, a table, and a few chairs. He wondered how long he'd been unconscious.

The soldier returned and resumed observing his prisoner.

"Do you speak English?" Zac asked.

"No, Pashto and Arabic, and Persian, of course," responded the guard in thinly accented English.

"Why am I here?"

"No English, sorry."

The guard was toying with Zac, so the two men simply sat in silence until three more soldiers entered the room. The second man through the door was older and wore a crisp, khaki-colored uniform more suited to a desk than to combat.

*Probably an officer,* Zac thought.

The man spoke quietly with the original guard in Persian, or at least Zac thought it was Persian. He couldn't speak a word of the language, but they obviously thought he could. He watched the officer's profile as he spoke. The man radiated determination and intelligence. His dark, deep-set eyes locked on to the other soldier as they spoke, but Zac recoiled when the officer turned. The left side of his face, from his neck to his hairline, was a glossy mass of purple and brown scar tissue. There was no recognizable shape to it: no eyebrow, no facial hair, no form at all. The only human quality was his perfectly functioning eye. Like a black hole, it took in everything and revealed nothing.

"I am Colonel Arzaman of the Revolutionary Guards." His voice was calm but forceful. "Tell me, why have you come to Iran?"

Zac opened his mouth to speak, but nothing came

out. His eyes danced over the man's face, wondering what could have caused the horrific scarring.

Eventually he spoke, barely above a whisper. "I never meant to come here. I was on my way to Singapore. Our plane had engine trouble and we had to make an emergency landing."

Arzaman's expression remained impassive. He sat across from Zac and folded his arms across his chest. His left hand had been burned as badly as his face. The fingers were crooked and small. His eyes never left Zac.

"Tell me what you did after the plane landed." He raised a cautionary finger. "Do not leave anything out."

The circumstances, the man's scarred face, and his sharp gaze made Zac look down at the floor again. He realized now that the brown grime on the tiles wasn't dirt. It was dried blood. His breath quickened. He looked Arzaman in the eyes and answered carefully.

"After we landed, I took a few pictures while I waited for my passport to be checked. A soldier wrote down my information and I walked to the terminal. I worked on my laptop for a while then went to the bathroom, when I was . . . met by the soldiers."

"And what did you take pictures of?"

"The sun setting on the mountains. As I told the others, I've never been to the Middle East and was trying to make the best of our unexpected stop."

Arzaman was silent for a moment, his black eyes unmoving.

"What else did you photograph?"

"Just mountains and rocks."

Arzaman scowled. A look of profound disappointment spread across his face.

"This process will be less difficult, especially for you, if you do not waste my time."

"I swear I didn't take any pictures of the soldiers, the airport, or anything else. There wasn't anything else to take pictures of. Just desert, mountains, and sky."

Arzaman said nothing, so Zac tried another tack.

"Look, I took those pictures with my phone. If I were intentionally taking pictures of something . . . unusual, don't you think I'd use a better camera?"

"An excellent point. One of the first things we did was examine your phone. We discovered that it is quite advanced. Not only does it have a high resolution camera and GPS device, but a sophisticated password and encryption system as well. You took photos of some very sensitive areas."

Zac's chest tightened. Whether it was to stoke nationalism at home or simply poke its enemies in the eye, Iran had a well-known habit of arresting foreigners and holding them as spies. The list included hikers, tourists, and businessmen. Some had been held for years on trumped-up charges before being released, and those were just the ones Zac knew about.

He looked nervously at Arzaman. "All phones in the U.K. have cameras, GPS, and passwords. I bought it off the shelf at a wireless store. It's a regular phone."

"Please. I am well acquainted with Western technology. This is extremely sophisticated equipment. You would have me believe that all cell phones in the West are like this? We have not yet decrypted the data on it, but we will, so do not lie to me. You will only make things more difficult for yourself."

Zac pleaded, "Bring it back. I'll give you the passwords. I'll show you every picture. It's nothing special. I just have the encryption software because I use it for work."

"Another good point. Let us talk about your work for a moment. We will return to the phone later." Arzaman spoke with the formality of an educated man who'd learned a foreign language later in life. "And for whom do you work?"

"E.A.D."

"What does this mean, this E.A.D.?"

"Electronic Architecture Development. It's a technology consulting company. That's why I have the high-end phone and laptop. We buy the newest equipment to evaluate it. Please, call my office. They'll vouch for me."

"Of course they will. I would expect nothing less. Your passport says you are American?"

"Yes, but I live in London."

"Your name?"

"Zachary Miller."

"I can read your passport. What is your real name?"

Not knowing what to say, Zac said nothing.

"What were you going to do with the photos?"

"I wasn't going to do anything with them. I'll delete them. I'll give you the password to my phone." He spoke quickly, desperately. "Look, we made an emergency landing. It's a one-in-a-million chance that I'm even here. I was staying at a friend's apartment in Paris while he's out of the country. When I learned that I had to go to Singapore, I just grabbed my bag and left. This is a huge mistake."

Arzaman sat in silence for a minute that seemed like a year. He looked at Zac, but the Iranian's mind seemed to be elsewhere when he began to speak.

"Many years ago, during the Holy Defense War with Iraq, I was a young lieutenant in command of a tank company. We had been ordered into rain-soaked Dezful, in western Iran, to drive back the invading Iraqis. I arranged our eighteen tanks into a wedge formation, with my own Chieftain in the vanguard, and attacked over a dry stretch of ground. We quickly destroyed one of the enemy tanks and disabled three more. The defenders fled like dogs in their Soviet-built T-62s. They simply did not have the will to fight. We pushed through the center and drove up the middle of the valley to finish off the enemy and secure our gains. But on the other side of a ridge was a battalion of Iraqi T-62s, dug-in and waiting. They opened fire immediately. We had been led into an ambush. Our crew worked furiously to escape, but the underpowered Chieftain turned slowly. Its engine struggled with the heat and mud until a deafening explosion filled our tank. We rocked violently onto our right track and crashed to the ground, disabled and ablaze."

Arzaman turned and stared into Zac's eyes.

"I opened the hatch and had begun to pull myself out when our external fuel supply burst into flames. A fireball of burning diesel engulfed my left side. My flame retardant suit shielded my body, but the heat fused my hand to the surface of the burning tank."

He rotated his disfigured hand as he stared at it.

"Faced with certain death or excruciating pain, I ripped the skin from my hand and leapt from the tank. A few seconds later, the burning fuel flowed into the open hatch and ignited the cordite we used to fire the main gun. The turret, with my crew still inside, spewed flame like a volcano."

Arzaman spun on his feet and faced Zac. The volume of his voice rose with his anger.

"I tell you this because I learned that day, in a very literal way, that pain and suffering can set you free; that we must endure hardship if we want to survive. I learned that everything is not always as it appears. I would not trade that experience for anything, so do not lie to me, do not insult me with your feigned innocence. I do not believe for one second that you are here by accident."

Zac looked at the enraged Iranian, at the soldiers staring down at him, rifles in hand. This couldn't be happening. Any minute now he would awaken from the nightmare. He looked up at the colonel.

"I want to talk to someone in the U.S. embassy."

The nearest soldier smashed the butt of his rifle into Zac's stomach. He doubled over in the chair and gasped for breath.

Arzaman began shouting. "Do not lie to me! Do not tell me you are taking pictures of the sunset. Why do you treat us like fools? Look at me. Do you think this is a game? Do you think anyone even knows you're here?"

Arzaman grabbed Zac around the throat and pinched his carotid arteries. The Iranian squeezed harder and Zac felt light-headed. His vision began to cloud. He thrashed about in the chair, trying to break free. The Iranian loosened his grip and smirked. He pushed Zac back until the chair was balanced only on its rear legs.

Arzaman whispered, "One last chance. Who are you working for? Who sent you here?"

"No one sent me. I'm telling thc truth."

The Iranian flung the chair backward and Zac's skull struck the floor. Warm blood flowed into his hair.

"Who sent you here?" Arzaman screamed.

He kicked Zac in the ribs with the steel toe of his boot.

"Who else was with you on the plane?" Another kick, this time to the head. "Who is your contact here?"

Zac's eyes darted about as he thrashed in vain against the ties that bound him to the chair. He tried to speak but nothing came out. One of the soldiers struck again with his rifle while the other hit him in the ribs. The beating continued for twenty minutes until Arzaman looked down in disgust, spat on the American, and walked away.

## SIX

Z AC LAY BLEEDING on the floor, drifting in and out of consciousness. His thoughts wandered from the present to the past, to a point in time just days earlier. He'd been in Paris, staying at the apartment of a college friend and having lunch with a beautiful French-woman.

He'd arrived at the restaurant early and ordered an un-pretentious bottle of Burgundy that was decanted at the table. Genevieve arrived ten minutes later, just as she was finishing a conversation on her mobile phone. She and Zac greeted each other in English.

She sat at the table and promptly pointed out that she didn't drink red wine. Zac retorted that he'd ordered it for himself anyway. They looked at each other for a moment, and she reached across the table for the carafe.

"This could be a long afternoon," she said as she poured herself a glass of wine.

"I certainly hope so. I've been looking forward to it for months."

"I'm sure you have," she said as she filled his glass.

He smiled. "Is it going to be like this all day?"

"Oh, no. It's going to get much worse." She pursed her full lips for a few seconds, then flashed a wide smile and raised her glass. "*Santé*. That's what we French say instead of 'cheers.'"

"*Santé*," Zac repeated.

They clinked glasses and sipped their wine.

"So what brings you to Paris?" Genevieve asked.

"You," he answered matter-of-factly.

Genevieve opened her menu and began to read it.

"Crossing the English Channel for a lunch date reeks of desperation," she said, her eyes surveying the list of appetizers.

"In your case I prefer to think of it as noblesse oblige," Zac said, reading his own menu.

Genevieve choked back a laugh. "Do you see anything you like?" she asked.

Zac looked up at her and paused. "Everything looks great," he replied.

"Hmm . . ." she said, her eyes still glued to the menu. "I'm leaning toward the raclette or the beef."

"I'm impressed. Most of the women here seem to be eating a few forkfuls of lettuce."

"Life is to be lived, not survived." Genevieve locked eyes with him. "Besides, my body is young and strong, and I enjoy working off the calories."

Zac returned his gaze to the menu. "Then maybe we should order one of each."

The waiter returned to the table a few moments later and Zac ordered for both of them in fluent French.

"So you speak French?" Genevieve asked, slightly perturbed.

"A little," Zac lied. "I picked up a travel dictionary on the way to the restaurant."

Genevieve leaned back on the banquette and eyed him skeptically. "That would explain why you didn't think to mention it during any of our conversations . . . Did you overhear what I was saying on the phone when I arrived?"

"You mean when you told your friend Natalie how excited you were to finally be getting together with the American man you'd been telling her about? No. I didn't hear any of that."

Genevieve balled up her napkin and made as if to throw it at Zac, but instead tossed back her head and laughed.

BY THE TIME their food arrived, Zac had stopped trying to keep the telltale grin off his face and Genevieve's eyes were lingering on him long after he'd finished speaking. Her long, dark hair cascaded across her shoulders when she laughed and he felt himself falling for the elegant, sophisticated Parisienne.

She'd just ordered a second bottle of wine when Zac's mobile phone rang.

"I'm sorry, I have to take this call. It's my boss."

"I understand. I have the same type of job."

Zac stepped outside the restaurant and into a crisp autumn afternoon in Paris.

"Hey, Peter," Zac answered the phone.

"Can you talk?" asked Peter Clements.

"Yeah. I'm out on the sidewalk. What's up?"

"I'm in my office with Ted Graves. I've got you on speakerphone. We just got some bad news. We're scrubbing SNAPSHOT. I wanted to tell you now so you don't rush back tomorrow."

The warm glow Zac had felt inside the restaurant vanished.

"What do you mean you're scrubbing it?"

Ted Graves spoke up. "The officer we tasked for the mission is known to the Iranians."

"What do you mean he's known? How do they know who he is?"

"We're not exactly sure. He was Army Special Forces before he came to CIA. It's possible that he crossed paths with some senior Qods Force operatives back in Iraq. We have reason to believe his legend won't hold up."

"I'm sorry, Zac," Clements said. "There just isn't time to train someone else. You said yourself the window was probably only seventy-two hours before the Iranians put everything back together after the earthquake."

"I can't believe you're giving up on this knowing what's at stake. This is ridiculous."

Graves shot back, "Easy, Miller. It's not your ass that's going to be on the line out there. Do you know what the Iranians would do to this guy if they made him? Rotting in Evin Prison would be paradise by comparison." Graves worked for Clements too, but he ran clandestine operations out of London. All of the field spooks reported to him.

"Send me," Zac said.

"No way," Graves responded. "Zac, you're a strategic weapons analyst. What did you do, spend four weeks at The Farm when you signed up? You've got no tradecraft, no language skills, and no legend. You'd be a sitting duck out there."

"Zac, I have to agree with Ted on this. The officer we selected spent his whole career in the Middle East. He speaks Persian, Arabic, and Dari. If something went wrong, he could've handled it. Your dedication is admirable, and you're one of the best at what you do, but you're not qualified for this."

"Peter, you know how important this is. We don't have any assets in-country who have the training or the equipment to do it. If we let this opportunity slip by, you might be standing in front of a congressional committee one day explaining why CIA 'missed another one.'"

"That's bullshit and you know it," Graves snapped.

Zac dialed back the volume. "Send me, Peter. I'll only be on the ground for six hours, surrounded by Westerners and watched over by the pilots. I won't need all those skills. Hell, I'm supposed to look like a Westerner, wandering around taking pictures. I know how to use the camera and I know better than anyone what to look for. I trained Ted's guy."

Graves began to speak but Clements interrupted him.

"OK. Get back here now. You don't have much time to . . ."

"Peter, this is crazy," Graves said. "He'd be going in naked. You can't really be . . ."

"Ted, this is my call and your objections are noted for the record. Zac, swing by your flat and grab some clothes, then get to the office. We'll have everyone assembled here to get you ready."

"I'm leaving now. You won't regret this."

Zac ended the call and strode back into the restaurant. Genevieve's warm smile disappeared when she saw the look on his face.

"Problem?" she asked.

"I have to go to Singapore and I have to leave right now. I'm sorry, but my boss insisted." Zac placed a hundred euros on the table.

"You can't finish lunch? Why don't you leave from here?"

"I would like to, but I have to pick up a few things at the office first."

Genevieve folded her arms across her chest and pursed her lips. Zac couldn't help but smile. He reached for her hand and she stood to face him.

"My friend's apartment will be vacant for a few more weeks," he said. "I'll buy you dinner as soon as I'm back."

"You'd better."

They kissed on both cheeks. Genevieve's soft hair brushed across his face as he inhaled her perfume . . .

ZAC REGAINED CONSCIOUSNESS on the cement floor. He looked at the blood that had pooled around his face and recalled his appeal to Peter Clements.

*"Send me, Peter. I'll only be on the ground for six hours . . ."*

What an idiot.

## SEVEN

D ESPITE THE BEST efforts of the airport staff, the earthquake-ravaged terminal at Sirjan was strained beyond its capacity to serve the stranded passengers. Sore backs, full bladders, and disrupted schedules soon took their toll on everyone's patience. The one available telephone line was unreliable, in high demand, and soon became a source of tension among the fliers. They were tired, uncomfortable, and eager to get on with their lives.

The Iranian staff refused to answer questions for several hours, so when an airport employee climbed onto a table between the men's and women's waiting areas and called for attention, everyone's hopes rose for a speedy departure.

"Attention everyone," he began in English. "Unfortunately, your airplane is being grounded for repairs and inspection. Since Iran Air does not fly this type of aircraft, British Airways has to fly a repair crew here to fix your plane. Furthermore, since we are unable to move your aircraft off of our runway, the second plane will be landing in the neighboring city of Shiraz."

A chorus of groans and mutterings interrupted the speaker.

"Quiet, please. And now for the good news, the second plane will also be taking all of you on to Singapore. So please pack up your belongings and listen for further announcements. The buses should be here shortly."

A few hours before dawn, the passengers and their luggage were loaded aboard four late-model Volvo buses. For five hours, a pair of military trucks escorted the small convoy west through the mountainous desert to Shiraz. Shahid Dastghaib International Airport was relatively modern and well equipped, and after a quick trip through immigration, the passengers were led to a waiting British Airways 777.

The London-based flight crew eagerly helped their stranded customers aboard. While there were no boarding passes, smiling flight attendants checked passengers' passports against a manifest and a seating chart that had been compiled by the Iranian airport workers.

Zachary Miller settled comfortably into seat 11A in business class. The women boarded after the men, and Lady Celia Parker had been upgraded to first class. She attempted to turn around to see where Zac was seated, but the wide first class seats blocked her view.

The 777 taxied past rows of fighter jets and attack helicopters that occupied the tarmac around the mixed-use airport. Though the Iranians had been hospitable, the constant military presence during the ordeal had kept everyone on edge. Most passengers simply gazed out the windows or closed their eyes. The big jet turned onto the active runway and accelerated quickly. The moment its wheels left the ground, a chorus of cheers erupted from the passengers.

After a few minutes the pilot came on the public address system.

"Ladies and gentlemen, this is Captain Lincoln. I certainly hope you've all enjoyed your complimentary excursion to the Middle East, courtesy of British Airways. But, just in case you haven't, BA has offered each of you a free international ticket, a first class meal, and, once we've left Iranian airspace, a glass of our finest champagne . . ."

Another round of cheers drowned out the rest of the captain's address, but the passenger in seat 11A would not be taking advantage of the airline's hospitality. He reclined his seat and closed his eyes as a smile crept across his face. He was grateful that seat 11B was vacant, for today he had no desire to make idle chitchat. Indeed, even though they looked remarkably alike, the man in seat 11A knew almost nothing about the man he was impersonating.

## EIGHT

THE IRANIAN PRESIDENT and the minister for Intelligence and Security were having an animated conversation about the country's nascent ballistic missile program, when two men in dark suits entered the conference room and took up positions on either side of the doorway. The discussion stopped mid-sentence and everyone stood. Grand Ayatollah Amin Khorasani, the supreme leader of the Islamic Republic of Iran, entered the conference room in flowing camel-hair robes and the black turban that marked him as a direct descendant of the Prophet Muhammad. He paused at the head of the table before taking his seat.

"May Allah's peace, mercy, and blessings be upon you all."

"And upon you, peace," responded the group in unison.

It was unusual for Khorasani to attend a meeting of the Supreme National Security Council, and no one took it as a good sign that he had chosen to do so today. The assembled officials included not only the president, but the heads of the main branches of the government and the military. They were the dozen most powerful men in the nation and they waited in silence as the white-bearded cleric conferred privately with his representative on the council, Admiral Gharamani.

For several years, Gharamani had handled negotiations with the West regarding the scope and intent of the Iranian nuclear program. Constructing its numerous facilities around the country had come at an enormous cost, not only in terms of building expense, but in economically punitive sanctions imposed by the Western powers. Fortunately for Iran, the West never appreciated the magnitude of the sacrifice made by the nation, or understood its significance. Despite having the third largest reserves of oil in the world, Iran had willingly subjected its citizens and its economy to decades of deprivation. No nation with such enormous resources would have done so without a clear goal in mind.

Gharamani had won many important victories over his Western counterparts whose desperation to sign any deal had forced them to make important concessions on key strategic issues. Iran had since secured military deals with Russia, China, and North Korea, and crossed a critical threshold in safeguarding itself from any foreign power. Its reserves of hard currency had been unfrozen, allowing it to expand its nuclear facilities to the point that many were now impervious to destruction or even detection. The atomic genie could not be put back in the bottle.

It was one of these secret nuclear facilities that had drawn the supreme leader to today's meeting. In his morning security brief he had read a single line about a foreign aircraft landing inside the Sirjan prohibited area. The brevity of the notation and its position toward the back of the eleven-page brief indicated that his national security team did not feel that the incident warranted much of a response.

He was here today to show them the error of their ways.

The supreme leader looked across the table with cold, hollow eyes as he began to speak.

"For five thousand years our ancestors have traveled this land. It was the birthplace of civilization, the home of the prophets, and now it is ours. Since those early times, technology has been a source of prosperity and security, science has been a source of enlightenment and a sword of defense. From stone tools to iron plows, from arrows to gunpowder, our forefathers fed and defended themselves with inventions and innovations."

His eyes moved methodically from man to man as he spoke.

"The journey has not been easy. Moving forward on the path of righteousness has required sacrifice in treasure and in blood. For most of you, your payment of the zakat each month is the closest you come to knowing true sacrifice. Yet we demand more from the average citizens of the republic. We have commanded them to go not only without luxuries, but without necessities as well. We have forced them to forgo the present for the future. And the sacrifice required by those in our nuclear program has been even greater. Our generals have been kidnapped. Our scientists have been poisoned, shot, and murdered with bombs. Five of our Russian partners died in a mysterious plane crash. Our shipments of exported arms seem to explode prematurely whether traveling by plane or truck. Computer viruses attack our centrifuges, and the list goes on. How many of *you* are forced to wonder if a magnetic bomb will be slapped to the side of your car door every time a motorcycle passes by?"

Several of the men in the room looked away.

The leader stood from his chair, raising his voice with every sentence.

"So why did we build twenty-nine nuclear facilities around the country? Why did we forgo a hundred billion dollars of oil and trade revenues? We did it because one day our nuclear weapons will allow us to unite the world under Allah, the one true God!"

The leader slammed the handle of his walking stick against the table and glared at the minister for Intelligence and Security, whose office had prepared the morning brief.

"But how can we do this when an enemy aircraft lands next to our most strategic nuclear facility and you do not investigate? How can we ask our people to sacrifice so much for so long and yet you neglect their basic security? How can we achieve our goals when you fail to do what is necessary?!"

The room became uncomfortably still. The grand ayatollah was known to occasionally lash out at his ministers and military chiefs, but few had ever seen him so angry. He sat in his chair and waited, as if daring his subordinates to speak.

"Leader, if I may," offered Major General Behzadi,

the commander of the Revolutionary Guards. "We have taken control of the situation and detained a foreign national."

"Go on."

"The plane claimed to be having engine trouble and refused orders to land elsewhere. We ran the passengers through the Guardian system for anything suspicious and are now examining the aircraft."

"What is the status of the Sirjan facility?"

"There is some superficial damage due to the earthquake, but it is at least 85 percent operational."

"There have been no alerts?"

"There were, but they were investigated and attributed to aftershocks. There have been no alarms since the British plane landed."

"What of the man you have in custody?"

"He's an American, traveling alone. He was undertaking surveillance of the base."

"He admits this?"

"He claims he was taking pictures of the sunset, but it is a lie of course. We have asked the pilots and crew to stay behind, ostensibly to look after their aircraft, but we are interviewing them carefully. We sent the rest of the passengers on their way early this morning to avoid arousing suspicion. You see, no one is aware that we have the American in custody."

The supreme leader addressed the minister of Foreign Affairs. "Have we heard anything from the British or the Americans about this?"

"Only a thank-you and offer of payment from the

British Foreign Office for accommodating the plane and passengers. Nothing direct or back channel from the United States."

"Excellent work, General Behzadi," the leader continued. "I am glad to see that someone is paying attention. Please update me personally on your investigation. Leave nothing to chance. We must know what this enemy agent has discovered and what he has done with the information."

"Yes, Leader. I have my top counterintelligence man on it, a Colonel Arzaman. He is a decorated veteran of the Holy Defense War."

"Arzaman . . . I know of this man. He is both relentless and ruthless. He has my blessing to do whatever he must to protect the republic. And, General, if you confirm that this American has put our security at risk, or attempted to put our security at risk, I want him to feel the pain of a hundred thousand deaths, and may Allah have mercy on his soul."

NINE

THE BIG BOEING jet touched down gracefully at Changi International Airport in Singapore and another batch of world travelers was returned to the twenty-first century. Before the jet had even turned off the runway its passengers had switched on their mobile phones to call hotels, reschedule meetings, and book new connecting flights.

Inside the airport, the Iranian agent posing as Zac Miller approached Singapore Immigration and Checkpoints and handed his passport to the officer behind the desk.

"Welcome to Singapore, sir." The officer scanned the passport and typed on his computer. He glanced at the traveler. "You listed your departure point as the U.K. but the computer shows you coming from Iran."

The Iranian forced a smile. "Yes, we made an unplanned stopover. I wasn't sure what to write down."

"Right, you're with that British Airways flight. I should have recognized the flight number. I've had a few of you through here already." The agent typed into his computer again, asked a few questions about the nature and length of the visit, and handed the passport back.

"Enjoy your stay."

"I am sure I will."

A gray-haired woman in an expensive suit tugged at the Iranian's elbow. He turned around quickly and his eyes bored into hers.

The woman recoiled slightly. "Oh, I'm terribly sorry," she said with a posh English accent. "I thought you were someone else."

"Not a problem," said the Iranian. "It happens all the time."

He excused himself and walked toward the baggage claim hall, wondering if the encounter with the old woman was something he should be concerned about.

He quickly retrieved his luggage and caught a taxi. On the ride to his hotel the agent dismissed the English-woman as a threat. He hadn't seen her at the baggage carousel and her old eyes probably weren't that sharp. Besides, he had more important things to think about. It was almost nine o'clock in the evening and his workday was just beginning.

Imprints of Zac's hands had been taken while he was unconscious and a special set of latex gloves had been formed just hours before the flight left Iran. Wearing the nearly transparent gloves, the imposter unpacked Zac's suitcase and touched the phone, toilet, faucets, and several other items in the hotel room, leaving a trail of false fingerprints. He left Zac's passport atop the dresser and by nine thirty he was downstairs in the lobby speaking with the female concierge. She politely deflected the agent's pointed questions about Geylang, an unsavory area known for entertainment that occurred on the fringe of the law or well outside it. Five minutes later he was in a taxi and on his way.

Over the course of the next two hours, the agent used Zac's credit cards to buy drinks at several seedy bars. Though he discreetly poured most of the cocktails onto the floor, by midnight he was acting quite drunk and making a spectacle of himself, salaciously asking every bartender and many of the patrons where he could find a good young girl. Though prostitution was legal in Singapore, criminal gangs were active in the sex trade and ran many of the brothels. He would avoid those places. Where there were money and criminals, there would be guns. He didn't want armed men around for the job he was to perform tonight. He needed a soft target.

The streets were surprisingly busy for the late hour. Taxis dotted the road, dropping off and picking up all manner of men and women. The hot and humid night air was filled with spicy aromas emanating from the neighborhood's numerous open-air restaurants. The agent cruised the area on foot and soon realized that selecting his prey would not be difficult. There were many streetwalkers about. Heavily made-up and barely clothed, they chatted in small groups while marketing their wares. These independent contractors operated outside the law.

As he surveyed the scene, he decided that such immodesty was unfair. It was designed to arouse him, after all, and he could not be responsible for his actions when confronted with such brazen sexuality. One girl in particular, waif-thin and barely clothed, caught his eye. He guessed she was at most fourteen years old. She would make a nice bonus for such a strange mission. Besides, Allah would not object, for the Prophet Muhammad himself, *peace be unto him*, had once taken an even younger bride.

It took less than a minute to negotiate a price, and the girl led him to an unmarked doorway among the dilapidated buildings. The tiny room that passed for a lobby was dark and filthy, and a rough-looking man behind a broken table handed over a room key. The Iranian studied the girl's body as he followed her up the stairs.

He had admired her lean figure when they were outside, but now as he looked more closely he thought that her thin legs were perhaps too thin, maybe from drugs or even hunger. She wore heavy makeup, but some of it had been applied over deep bruises. A sliver of conscience began to wedge itself into his mind. As they climbed to a third-floor room, he remembered that Muhammad had indeed married Aisha when she was very young, but that had been nearly fourteen hundred years ago when an old man lived to be twenty-five or thirty years old. In his heart, the agent knew that Allah would not forgive him for everything he did in His name. The Iranian would complete his mission tonight, but the poor girl would not have to submit again before she left the world.

Ten minutes later, he climbed down the fire escape and stripped off the bloody gloves that had left Zac's fingerprints in the room and on the knife. He placed an anonymous phone call to the police to complete his distasteful mission.

By sunrise the agent was flying to Hong Kong on a forged Omani passport. Fatigued, but unable to sleep, he had several stiff drinks, wishing he could close his eyes and clear his conscience of what he'd done. He was not a killer. He was a cryptographic analyst who'd been drafted into this hellish assignment only because he spoke English and looked like the American, Zachary Miller. After two more drinks the agent finally drifted off to sleep, unaware that he was about to experience the first of many nightmares that would haunt him for the rest of his life.

## TEN

H ALF A WORLD away from Singapore, two deliverymen in matching jumpsuits exited their van and let themselves into a five-story apartment building in the sixth arrondissement of Paris. The pair struggled as they carried a large trunk up to the apartment of Zac's college friend. After they let themselves in and locked the door behind them, the men donned gloves and opened the trunk, carefully removing a large rubber bag. They looked at each other and prayed silently for forgiveness for what they were about to do.

The men carried the rubber bag into the master bedroom before removing the corpse of a young woman. Though she had been beaten and violated before being stabbed to death, the men moved the body delicately onto the unmade bed, careful to avoid marking or bruising it in any unintended way. She had been dead for many hours, yet the body was warm, almost feverishly so. It had been heated to accelerate decomposition and make the time of death appear to coincide with Zac's stay at the apartment.

The men removed sealed glass vials from their jumpsuits. The first contained bodily fluids from the victim. The second held blood taken from Zac's arm while he was unconscious. It had been flown in just hours ago in a diplomatic pouch from Iran.

Each man had been carefully instructed by a forensics expert on how to create a convincing crime scene. The blood and fluids were applied to sheets, clothing, and the victim's body. A third vial containing skin cells scraped from Zac's body were pressed under her fingernails and several of his hairs were scattered about the room.

Satisfied with their work, the men returned the empty trunk to the van and rejoined their driver, who had been watching the building's entrance. The trio rode in silence for several minutes through downtown Paris until the driver made a brief call on a prepaid cell phone. He spoke to his accomplices when he'd finished.

"I just made an anonymous tip to our man in the *police judiciaire*. He assures me that by tomorrow the murder will be the lead news story in all of Europe, and we will have used our enemy's hand to catch a snake."

## ELEVEN

ZAC STRUGGLED TO comprehend where he was. Only when he saw the bloodstains on the floor did he recall the beating he'd suffered at the hands of Arzaman's goons. There was a guard on the other side of the room, but he walked out as soon as they made eye contact. Zac's body ached as he rolled onto his back.

Even though his career track at CIA was to be behind a desk, Zac had spent a month at the Agency's clandestine operations training facility at Camp Peary, Virginia, when he'd first joined. The experience was designed to give analysts a better appreciation of the realities and limitations of human intelligence gathering. While there, Zac had learned some basic hand-to-hand fighting techniques and, much to his surprise and the surprise of his instructors, he had a natural talent for it. He'd studied Brazilian Jiu-Jitsu when he'd finished at Peary, using his natural speed and athleticism to augment the time-tested techniques of the martial art.

Zac saw an opportunity when the guard returned and began to untie the ropes from his wrists and legs. He knew that if he could reach the guard before the man could get his weapon out, Zac could take him down.

But all thoughts of hand-to-hand combat vanished the moment he tried to stand. The beating had left him barely able to move his arms and legs, much less overpower the guard. The two men walked slowly to a bathroom, where Zac ran his head under the faucet. He rubbed his face and rinsed his hair as he tried to wash away the harsh new reality.

Arzaman was waiting back in the room with two burly soldiers. They grabbed Zac by the arms and forced him into a chair.

"When can I go?" he asked.

"When will you tell us the truth?" Arzaman countered.

"I told you everything I know."

"Why don't I believe you?"

The circular questioning went on for several minutes until Zac could no longer contain his anger. He leapt from the chair and lunged at Arzaman. The two soldiers caught him and shoved him back down. This time they handcuffed him.

"You think I'm a spy? My plane was going to Singapore. It nearly crashed. Then there's some top secret facility right next to the airport? Don't all those coincidences seem a little ridiculous?"

"I do not believe in coincidences."

"This is some game that you're playing, isn't it? You're setting me up. You don't listen to anything I say and keep accusing me of photographing some secret place that I couldn't even see. Why would you even put a secret facility next to an airport? Who would believe that?"

Arzaman ignored him. "Do you know what I find odd?"

Zac shook his head, knowing there was no right answer.

"Do you know what a 'flight data recorder' is?"

Zac considered ignoring him for a moment, but the question was easy.

"That's the black box, right? It records all the information on the plane in case it crashes."

"Correct. It records the instrument readings, the positions of all the controls, and even the voices of the pilots. It is a very robust piece of equipment, as you said, designed to withstand even the crash of an airplane."

Zac said nothing.

Arzaman spoke again. "Since the emergency occurred on our soil, we requested to see the data from your flight. The recorder on your plane was completely blank. None of the data was retained. Absolutely nothing. Only the voice and radio communications were recorded. Do you know how rare that is?"

"I have no idea. I was a passenger. How many flights have you been on when they've asked you to test the black box?"

"But it's curious, isn't it? We asked the repair crew for a copy of the tape when they started working and they told us it was blank."

"So the repair crew is here? Please keep the phone, keep the laptop, just let me leave."

"I am afraid that is no longer possible. You see, the other passengers from your flight are already in Singapore. They left eighteen hours ago on another aircraft. In fact, your plane surprisingly required only minor repairs and departed about six hours ago."

"They wouldn't have left without me. They checked everyone's name when we got off. They'd be looking for me."

Arzaman leaned forward and spoke just above a whisper. "Ah, but they are not looking for you." He smiled. "And even if they were, they would never find you, for you have vanished like a ghost; a sad, pathetic, lying little ghost."

Arzaman walked toward the door and paused as he crossed the threshold. He looked back over his left shoulder until the scarred side of his face was all that Zac could see.

"Good-bye, ghost."

The colonel had barely left the room when the two soldiers wrenched Zac out of the chair and tied a burlap sack over his head. They led him into the hallway and one of the Iranians shoved Zac from behind, sending him to the floor. The soldiers laughed and yanked him to his feet. The muzzle of a rifle prodded him in the back as he walked.

The trio turned into another room and the soldiers tied a rope to Zac's handcuffs. Looping the rope through a pulley attached to the ceiling, they hoisted his arms high over his head, tugging on the rope until the metal cuffs dug into his wrists. Zac raised himself up onto the balls of his feet to ease the pain. One of the soldiers said something in Persian, but Zac didn't understand. The soldier repeated what he'd said. The other soldier stepped closer and began shouting.

Zac protested that he didn't understand, but the two soldiers only yelled louder. One of them punched Zac in the stomach. The other soldier struck Zac's thigh with a heavy object and his legs gave out. He hung in the air, the steel handcuffs cutting into his wrists as they supported his entire weight. Blood trickled down his forearms and the butt of a rifle smashed into his kidney. Zac vomited inside the hood as the soldiers left the room.

He dangled from the ceiling for several minutes with the wind knocked out of him, concentrating on each breath, forcing the foul air into his lungs. But he could ignore the pain in his wrists no longer. The handcuffs were going to tear his hands from his body. He cried out as he stretched the knotted and bruised muscles in his legs, but the relief to his wrists was palpable as his toes reached the ground.

Eventually his calves could no longer support his weight and Zac forced most of his weight back onto the handcuffs. He stood there until the pain in his wrists again became unbearable. Every few minutes he would shift his position up or down by an inch or two, trading one agony for the other.

The cycle of hell continued for what seemed like hours. When the soldiers finally returned, they released the rope and Zac collapsed in his own filth, trembling on the ground until he passed out.

# TWELVE

THE TWO SOLDIERS had removed the hood from Zac's head after he'd passed out, but several hours later he was still lying motionless on the floor. One of the men kicked him in the ribs and Zac mumbled something. The soldier kicked harder and Zac sat up, trying to make sense of what was happening. It came back to him as he looked around the room.

One of the soldiers motioned with his rifle for Zac to get to his feet. Everything hurt as he raised himself off the floor. The two soldiers regarded him coldly as he regained his balance.

"The *farangi* still has some life in him," said the first one.

"That will change soon enough," said the other.

The three men left the room. In keeping with Middle Eastern tradition, the barrel of an AK-47 showed the way. With one soldier in front, and the one with the rifle behind him, Zac was guided down a long, windowless hallway. They might have been taking him for another interrogation or maybe his execution, but one thing was certain—they weren't about to release him. Sooner or later he would die in Iran and no one would know for sure what had happened. His family and friends would believe whatever scheme the Iranians had invented, and Zac would get a star on the Memorial Wall back at Langley.

Among all of the unknowns, there were two things that were perfectly clear. Zac's country needed him to survive; and if he wanted his freedom, he was going to have to take it.

HIS MIND-SET CHANGED as he walked along the dusty floor. He noticed the physical security around him and considered how he might defeat it. His hands were still cuffed, but they were in front of his body, where he could use them. The building wasn't a jail. It looked more like a warehouse and it was mostly deserted. They'd passed only one other person as they walked, another soldier. Doors lined the hall, but most were hollow with light-duty hardware. Interior doors. The lead guard had handcuffs and a pistol on his belt, but the most immediate danger was from the rifle carried by the guard walking behind Zac. He would have to get control of it if he wanted to survive any escape attempt. He'd only fired an AK-47 once before at The Farm, but he had grown up hunting. If he could get his hands on the rifle, he knew enough to use it.

They walked until Zac noticed a door down a side hall. It was wide and metal, with a well-worn push bar for a handle and the familiar graphic of an Exit sign above. A way out. A plan began to take shape. He visualized it in his mind a few times. It was risky, but he didn't know how long he had to live. It was time to act.

Zac spun to his left and faced the guard behind him. With his cuffed hands, he yanked the barrel of the rifle until the muzzle was past his hip. The soldier yelled for help and held on to his weapon, but Zac gripped the barrel tightly and rammed his knee into the man's groin. The soldier instinctively pulled the trigger, sending several rounds into the lead guard just as he was reaching for Zac. The dying man fell to the ground. Zac continued to wrestle with the rifle, repeatedly driving his knee between the soldier's legs. The soldier finally moved his hands to protect his crotch and released his grip on the AK. Zac flipped the rifle around and, with both hands on the pistol grip, sprayed several rounds into the soldier's chest.

Zac found the handcuff keys on the lead guard's belt and unlocked himself. He stuffed the pistol in his pants, grabbed the rifle, and ran. The bright desert sun blinded him the instant he opened the outside door. He heard men shouting inside the building and the unmistakable sound of running boots.

Zac stepped back inside and closed the door. He dropped to one knee and aimed the rifle toward the sound of the approaching men. Two soldiers ran around the corner with their own AK-47s. Zac fired late, missing with the first few rounds but making contact with the next several. Both men collapsed on the ground. Zac grabbed a fresh magazine from one of the wounded soldiers, took the boots from the other, and bolted for the exit.

He opened the door a second time. This time it was the heat that stunned him, but he kept going. There were several small industrial buildings in the area, but no people. To the left was a dirt road and some railroad tracks. Ahead was a steep mountain range covered with scrub brush and rock, and down in the valley was a small town. The airport was nowhere in sight.

A small sedan and a dusty Toyota Land Cruiser were parked in front of the building he'd just left. The truck would be the perfect escape vehicle if only he knew where he was or where to go. Plus, the road led to town and right now survival meant staying away from people. He needed time to make a plan. The mountains were steep and inhospitable. They were in the opposite direction from civilization; away from food, water, and transportation. Surviving up there would be difficult if not impossible. The mountains were his only chance.

He walked briskly to the next building. It was deserted. There were no vehicles and no signs of activity. Most of the buildings looked like warehouses. It was a strange place to keep a prisoner. Maybe they were planning to execute him here or they just wanted to get him away from Sirjan. Had someone betrayed his mission or blown his cover? His mind was moving in a hundred different directions.

*FOCUS, dammit. None of that matters if you're dead.*

He darted into the scrub brush. His body hurt from the beatings. Only adrenaline and his will to survive kept him moving. His first priority was to put some distance between himself and the four dead soldiers. It was just a matter of time until one of them failed to report in, or a phone went unanswered, or a wife called headquarters wondering why her husband wasn't home.

The dusty and rock-strewn ground required his constant attention as he ascended into the mountains. Twisting an ankle or breaking a leg out here could be fatal, but the severe terrain and sheer enormity of the desert also gave him a fighting chance to escape. He hiked for a few hours until the mountainside became so steep that he could barely step toe to heel. There was little vegetation at the higher altitude and the land around him turned from shades of desert tan and sage green to a rocky gray. Snowcaps dotted the horizon and scree fields littered the ground. Movement over the loose rocks was perilous, and Zac slung the rifle across his back to use his hands for climbing. The ridges and valleys of the mountain range soon took him out of sight of the warehouse.

He paused atop a long scree field. Even in the mountains it was close to one hundred degrees and the heat seared his lungs as he struggled to catch his breath. His legs were sore, his ribs ached from the beating, and he hadn't seen any water. He sat atop the loose rocks and wondered how he would make it out of Iran alive.

# THIRTEEN

TED GRAVES SAT in his office reviewing the overnight intelligence bulletins. As CIA's London chief of operations, he supervised the local officers who were part of the Directorate of Operations, the field personnel most people envisioned when they thought of the Central Intelligence Agency.

It seemed to Graves as if most of the fundamentalist religious groups wreaking havoc around the world these days were nothing more than anarchists looking for an excuse to return the world to the Middle Ages. Sometimes he was tempted to just let them fight it out among themselves; then the Agency could kill the last man standing and be done with it.

But the terrorists had too much money, too many weapons, and enough barbaric ideas to be a real problem. They weren't content to blame the West for the failed ideologies that had destroyed their own countries; they wanted to destroy the West too, and Ted's job was to make sure that didn't happen. His frustration level was already high when Peter Clements walked into his office.

"Good morning, Ted. Have we heard anything on SNAPSHOT?"

"No. Miller never made the uplink or the check-in. I had Kirby call his mobile and e-mail him but there was no response. I also checked with the aircrew. They said Miller was on the flight out of Sirjan, and the hotel in Singapore said he checked into his room."

"So what do you think?"

"I think you never should have sent him."

"I'm aware of that. What do you think we should do now?"

"Peter, if this were one of my men, he would have had a plan, language skills . . ."

"Ted, I get it, but the fact is we have an officer out in the field and we don't know if he's all right or in trouble. Tell Kirby to look wider and dig deeper."

Graves nodded and picked up the phone as Clements walked out of his office.

"I need you up here now," Graves said into the phone.


TWO MINUTES LATER, the West Point graduate and former helicopter pilot walked through his door.

"What's got you so excited?" she said as she pulled up a chair and shook out her strawberry-blond hair.

When they'd first started working together, Christine Kirby's physical attractiveness and fondness for speaking in double entendres had distracted Graves to no end, but now that he knew her little game, it only sidelined him for a few seconds. He motioned for her to close the door.

"Anything back from Miller?" he asked.

"Nothing."

"OK. Then we're going to have to look a little harder. As of now, I'm reading you in on Operation SNAPSHOT. Zac Miller was performing surface-level reconnaissance on an objective inside Iran, then departing on a commercial airliner for Singapore. Right now his status is unknown."

"I thought Miller was an analyst."

"That's right."

"Then why was he performing surface recon inside Iran?"

"Great question. Why don't you ask Peter Clements?"

Kirby grinned. "No, thanks. I like my job."

"What we know is that Miller flew into and out of Iran, but he missed a satellite uplink on the ground and never checked in from Singapore. This has taken on extra urgency. I want you to work with NSA to verify his immigration status in Singapore. When did he enter? Did he exit? Get someone over to the hotel posing as his mother to find out if anyone actually saw him. Give the legal attaché at the embassy a list of twenty names with Miller's on it and see if anything hits with the local police. You know the drill. SNAPSHOT is a high-profile mission within the Agency."

"They should have called it Operation SNAFU."

"I wouldn't mention that again if you really do like your job."

"Roger that." Kirby stood to leave. "Should I keep Peter in the loop on this too?"

"Let's keep it between the two of us until we figure out what the hell is going on."

Kirby nodded, then turned toward the door.

"Wait," Graves said. "There is one more thing. Assemble a four-man security team in Singapore. If we get a lead on Miller's location, I want him brought in."

"What if he refuses?"

"That's not his call."

## FOURTEEN

B EFORE ZAC HAD left London, he'd asked the oper-
ations staff about his options if he were to find
himself in the situation he was in now. A former
Army Special Forces officer had told him to forget about
Afghanistan or Pakistan. His chances of survival as an
American in either of those countries might be worse than
if he stayed in Iran. His only possible escape would be to
hike through the mountains of southeastern Iran to the
Persian Gulf. Coastlines were notoriously hard to guard.
Maybe he could stow away on a ship or steal a boat.

Zac watched the sun move lower in the sky as afternoon approached.

*If the sun is over there, then that must be west.*

He realized that he'd been traveling northeast; away
from the Persian Gulf. It was unfortunate, but it had
been his only choice at the time. Heading south would
have brought him near the neighboring town and all of
the dangers it would have entailed. Like never before he
craved the arrival of darkness and the concealment it
would bring. He resolved to head east until nightfall before turning south.

Zac found a stretch of level ground along the side of a ridge and made good time as he wound his way through the widely spaced scrub brush. At the end of the ridge the ground descended steeply into a valley. A road lay at the bottom. Crossing the pavement would take just a few seconds, but traversing the valley walls would leave him exposed for several minutes.

He crouched behind a sagebrush to watch for vehicles, but none came. He considered waiting a few more hours until it was dark, but his gut told him that he needed to spend every second putting more distance between himself and the warehouse. He descended into the valley, watching carefully for any vehicles, and sprinted across the road.

He'd hiked barely twenty feet up the other side when something made him freeze. There was a noise to his left, and it was coming closer. Zac unslung the rifle and knelt on the ground behind a small boulder. After staring intently at the road, he looked up to see an airliner painting coral-hued contrails across the darkening sky. The sound he'd heard was only the faint noise of a jet, miles above him, its passengers flying safely to their destination. Zac sat there, the breeze in his face, watching the jet fly away.

He knelt on the hard ground, dejected and deep in thought, and noticed movement in his peripheral vision. He looked carefully but saw nothing. His heart pounded in his chest as he moved the rifle left, then right. After a few seconds, a wild goat emerged from behind some brush about a hundred yards off. It moved slowly uphill as it picked its way along the rocky surface. Zac found the goat in his sights. A hundred yards uphill in poor light was not an easy shot. Though the AK-47 was a reliable rifle, it was not a particularly accurate one.

He knew he should stalk the goat, but he was hungry and running for his life. He didn't have time to circle downwind and close in for a perfect shot. He fired. The round struck the hill a foot above the goat and it scampered away. Zac fired again, and a third time, but the goat kept running until it disappeared over the top of the hill.

He stood staring at the empty hill and listening to the report of the rifle reverberate through the valley. As the sound faded, it was replaced by the noise of a vehicle. Zac turned back to the road to see a truck speeding toward him. It was a Land Cruiser, like the one he'd seen outside the warehouse. The rifle shots had masked its approach and now it was only a few hundred feet away. The late-day sun was lighting him up like a searchlight. The Toyota driver would have to be blind not to see him. Zac bolted up the hill.

Squealing tires and slamming doors echoed through the valley. Within seconds someone opened up with an automatic weapon and bullets were flying past his head, ripping through the air at supersonic speed. He dove onto his stomach, his knees and elbows crashing onto the rocky ground. The soldiers were below the ridge. He couldn't see them, but he knew they would come. He turned toward the road and raised his rifle.

He saw the head of a man coming up the hill, but held his fire. Zac's senses became hyperalert. Everything seemed to move in slow motion. Even his pounding heart seemed to slow. He felt the grains of dry mountain sand on his hands as he held the wooden grips of the AK-47. A second soldier appeared beside the first one. The pair was vigilant, holding their rifles in tight and scanning one-hundred-and-eighty-degree arcs from front to back. Zac slowly moved the iron sights of his own rifle to the chest of the first man, but this wasn't a defenseless goat. This time Zac waited.

When the second soldier turned to check his flank, Zac squeezed the trigger.

The first soldier staggered on his feet, blood leaking from the hole in his side. The two Iranians dropped behind cover before Zac could switch his aim. He crawled sideways, beneath the ridge, and seated his spare magazine in the AK. When he rose to his feet, the soldiers were gone.

Zac had to stop them before they reached their truck and radioed for reinforcements. A shot rang out, and then another as he ran toward the Land Cruiser. Bullets cracked through the air, smashing into the ridge behind him. Another burst of fire came his way and something stung his left shoulder.

*Son of a bitch!*

But the gunfire also gave away the position of the shooter. Zac saw the two men, fifty yards off, hidden behind some scrub. He dove to the ground and fired several rounds toward the brush. He received several rounds in return, but they all flew over his head. Zac glanced at his left shoulder. It was bleeding, and it stung like hell, but it was just a surface wound—maybe even a ricochet. When he looked back, the men were gone. Zac rose to his feet and caught a glimpse of one soldier supporting the other before the two Iranians disappeared down the steep grade.

Zac sprinted along the ridgeline until he could run down to the road without being seen. The soldiers' truck was parked on the near side, a tall whip antenna mounted to its rear bumper, but the men were nowhere in sight. He crossed to the opposite side of the road and saw them moving tentatively down the hill. It was getting dark in the valley, and Zac was able to crawl unnoticed in the shoulder. He stopped across the road from the Land Cruiser and hid.

The driver helped the wounded soldier into the backseat, then walked around to open his own door. Zac opened up with a burst of rifle fire. The bullets pinned the driver against the truck. Streaks of blood trailed down the sheet metal as his body slid to the ground.

Zac rose to his feet and walked toward the Land Cruiser. The wounded man in the backseat searched weakly for his weapon. Zac raised his rifle and fired. Half a dozen bullets punctured the door and shattered the window before finding their target. The dead man slumped in the backseat.

Zac opened the driver's side door. He could make good distance behind the wheel, but the Land Cruiser was filled with blood, bullet holes, and broken glass. Any passing motorist would be alarmed by the sight of it and Zac probably had half of the Iranian army looking for him already. He didn't need to advertise his location. He ransacked the truck. There were fresh magazines for the rifle plus a parka, a canteen, and a knife. He donned the parka and stuffed the rest of the gear in his pockets.

Zac dragged the driver's body off the road and trudged halfway up the valley before he paused to look back at the shot-up truck. All he could do was shake his head and curse.

## FIFTEEN

NIGHT DESCENDED UPON the region as the last light faded from the high mountain peaks. The clear desert air and a thin crescent moon made for excellent visibility as Zac put more distance between himself and the shot-up Land Cruiser. He headed east and made good progress for nearly an hour until his knees buckled and he collapsed onto the ground.

He began to shake. He'd never shot anyone before and now he'd just killed half a dozen men. He could rationalize the four soldiers in the warehouse. If he hadn't shot them, he would either be dead himself or back in confinement. But the last two . . . he'd ambushed them as they'd tried to escape.

Yet, he'd felt no pangs of conscience, no hesitation, no emotion whatsoever as he'd pulled the trigger. He hadn't second-guessed himself; hadn't paused to reconsider. He'd seen nothing except the enemy. He didn't even remember hearing the sound of his own gunfire. But as the panic began to subside, he was grateful that he'd suffered no indecision. Hesitation might have gotten him killed, and when it came down to it, his ultimate goal was survival. He could live with the decisions he'd made.

Zac stood and immediately discovered that pain had returned to his body. He pulled off the parka and looked at his left shoulder. The wound was still damp and stuck to his shirt. With a grimace he separated the shirt from the wound, drawing a trickle of fresh blood. It was a deep scratch, but at least there wasn't a bullet lodged in there. He took a few sips of water from the canteen and set off to the south. For the first time since he'd escaped, he was heading for the Gulf.

The air cooled quickly after sunset and soon became cold. The extreme swing in temperature was unlike anything he'd ever experienced. Miles passed underfoot, but even in the cold of night, the lack of water was a problem. The canteen he'd taken from the truck was already empty, and he'd barely been sipping enough to keep his mouth moist; so his spirits rose when he crossed a small stream running down the north side of a hill. The water had a metallic taste to it, probably from contaminants in the land around it, but he didn't have hours to search for another source. He drank his fill and topped off the canteen.

He walked for half an hour until his gut erupted in pain. He looked down, thinking maybe he'd been shot. He doubled over, then fell to his knees. Within seconds he broke into a heavy sweat and was throwing up what little was in his stomach. It took hours for his body to purge itself of the impure water. Shivering, he lay down upon the dusty earth, rolled onto his side, and pulled his knees to his chest.

It was another hour before he struggled to his feet and began to shuffle over the ground. He was lucky to find a small cave after a few miles. It wasn't much more than a crevice in some stratified rock, but when he curled up he could get his entire body inside. He poured the contaminated water out of his canteen and clasped the rifle across his chest. The cold air and his chattering teeth kept him from the sleep he so desperately needed.

Alone in the dark, Zac's mind began to wander. He tried to steer his thoughts in a positive direction. He thought of his colleagues at CIA, bright, dedicated people who were undoubtedly searching for him after he'd failed to check in. He remembered his friends from London, a close-knit group who would wonder about his long absence and miss him. He contemplated a pleasant future with Genevieve. But despite his best efforts to stay positive, his thoughts kept drifting back to the traumatic event that had changed his life.

ZAC HAD BEEN just fourteen years old when his parents had driven into Philadelphia one evening for dinner, leaving him alone in the house. The ringing of the home telephone awakened him just after midnight. His voice was hoarse from sleep and a state police officer, unaware that he was speaking with a teenage boy, informed him that Mr. and Mrs. Andrew Miller had been killed that night when a drunk driver had struck their car, sending it skidding off the road and into a concrete bridge support. Zac hung up the phone and cried for hours until he finally fell asleep, curled up in the fetal position on the kitchen floor.

His father's older brother and his wife had no children of their own and quickly adopted Zac. His uncle Alfred came to Pennsylvania to close up the house and drive him to his new home in Connecticut. His uncle indulged Zac as he walked numbly through the house one last time, sitting for hours in his parents' bedroom, where he used to get dressed with his father, and at the kitchen table, where he'd done his homework while his mother made dinner.

Something changed inside Zac the next morning and he announced that he was ready to leave. He kept only his father's briefcase and motorcycle helmet, and the engagement photo of his mother that had been in the newspaper. His uncle had everything else put into storage and Zac left his childhood home forever.

Before his parents' death, he had always looked forward to their visits to Connecticut. Zac's father and uncle were avid sailors, and the three of them spent hours on the water each day, especially if the weather was windy and rough. He proudly remembered watching the two grown-ups smile as young Zac steered the big boat through the heavy seas.

Sailing regularly with his uncle was one of the few things that he was looking forward to after his parents' death, but Zac was barely settled into his new home when his aunt and uncle informed him that he would be attending boarding school in the fall.

Zac was devastated. First his parents were snatched

away and now his aunt and uncle were abandoning him in his time of greatest need. He hadn't known that his aunt Liz was seriously ill, having recently been diagnosed with cancer. Bitter and alone, Zac had decided then that he could rely on no one but himself.

THE SUN ROSE over the Iranian countryside and a warm breeze blew up the hill, returning Zac's thoughts to the present. He knew that relief from the cold would be short-lived and he would soon be wishing for cooler temperatures again. But his victories here were small, and he was learning to cherish every one of them lest the more numerous hardships break his will. Before he fell asleep, the faintest of smiles emerged on his face as he thought, if it came down to it, he wouldn't let the bastards take him alive.

## SIXTEEN

CELIA SMILED AS her car turned into the driveway of the Raffles Hotel in Singapore. A bastion of a bygone era, its colonial architecture and impeccable white facade made her feel instantly at home. And a home away from home it was. Her late husband's merchant banking career had relocated them to Singapore for nearly a decade, and their band of mostly British expatriates used to gather at the hotel each day for afternoon tea.

Many years had passed in the interim. Spouses had died or been divorced, families had returned home or moved on, and individuals had simply drifted away. But the remaining members of this affluent and worldly group had made a concerted and successful effort to reunite at the Raffles once every year to relive bygone days and catch up on the present. Along with Celia's visits with her two daughters and their families, the annual gathering was one of the highlights of her life.

A uniformed Sikh doorman opened the door of her car as she returned to the hotel, having spent the day at the National Orchid Garden. It was nearly nine in the evening by the time she walked into the Grill. She was the last to arrive.

There were eight of them this year, down two from the prior year due to an illness and a death. As the maître d' walked Celia to the table, one of her companions spotted her and the whole table stood to welcome her.

One of the gentlemen, Sir James Houghton, was a former British diplomat. Dressed immaculately in a gray double-breasted suit, he bowed slightly as she approached.

"Good heavens, Celia. You've elevated the concept of fashionably late to haute couture."

"So sorry to keep you waiting, James. Has the restaurant run out of single malt whiskey yet?"

"Speaking of which, where is our waitress? I'd wager you could use a drink yourself."

"She's probably in hiding since you've been leering at her all night," chimed in one of the other guests.

"I'll leave you to admire the Old Masters, Geoffrey. I prefer my works of art to be three-dimensional."

"Ah, well, when you put it like that, I'm sure she'll be positively flattered."

The good-natured ribbing continued as everyone finished their greetings and took their seats. Sir James ordered four bottles of vintage Petrus Pomerol and had them decanted at the table.

"Celia, how are you? We just arrived this afternoon and James told us about your ordeal," said Katrina Reinhold, who, with her husband, Hans, was one of the two married couples in attendance.

"Well, I won't lie to you. It was a difficult trip, but I've

spent the last two days resting and taking in the sights.
I'm feeling much better now, thank you."

"How was Iran? It must have been nerve-racking for
a Westerner," added Hans.

"It was very much like this," Celia said with a straight
face as she gestured to the opulent surroundings, "except
I sat on a wooden bench for twelve hours and had to
queue up for twenty minutes to use the lavatory."

"Where exactly were you?" asked Sir James.

"A small city called Sirjan. It's quite remote."

"Goodness, that was a spate of bad luck," James said.
"There was an earthquake there just a few days ago."

"Indeed. The airport was a mess; doors broken, windows shattered. They had almost no services at all. It
must have been devastating to the local population. It
looked like a very poor area."

"It was a frightfully powerful earthquake," James
said. "Landslides in those mountainous regions cause a
terrible amount of destruction. Magsie and I passed
through Sirjan a few times when I was assigned to Tehran. It was just a village back then."

"I thought of you and Magsie many times while I was
there. We were segregated by gender in the airport since
none of the women were wearing the Islamic version of
proper clothing. I felt as if I'd set my watch back fourteen
hundred years when I got off the plane. It must have
been horrible for her."

"Actually, Tehran in the early 1970s was a wonderful
place. The shah was receptive to Western ideas. Women
were liberated and had access to education, and the Mo-

hammedan fundamentalists had all been expelled. It wasn't Vienna, but Tehran certainly wasn't a hardship posting. We both loved it."

"Well, what happened?" Celia asked. "Their attitudes toward women are positively medieval now."

A scowl crossed James's face. "The revolution's fuse was lit twenty years before we arrived, but it burned slowly. Back in 1951 one of their parliamentarians, a fellow by the name of Mohammad Mosaddeq, became prime minister and nationalized the Anglo-Iranian Oil Company. It was a terrifically popular move with the people, but Britain considered it theft. Mosaddeq subsequently dissolved parliament and was on his way to becoming dictator until two years later, when MI6 and CIA spent a million U.S. dollars to engineer a coup and restore the shah to power."

"One million dollars? You can't buy a flat in London for that today," interjected a rather intoxicated Geoffrey.

"Quite so," said James. "For the next twenty years the shah opened up the country to the West again, the Mohammedans were kept in check, and life was basically good. But as more and more Iranians became educated, they grew dissatisfied with their lot in life. There was a sense of entitlement or, perhaps more correctly, an expectation that their lives would improve. However, the economy was stagnant and there were few job opportunities. Meanwhile the shah was lining his pockets and living quite lavishly for all to see. By the mid-1970s, the people had turned restive again. Magsie and I left in 1976, just as things started getting interesting."

"What year was the revolution?" asked Geoffrey.

"The shah's secret police suppressed most of the dissent until 1978, when students started taking to the streets. The protests soon became violent and the two sides eventually fought to a standstill. At that point, everyone was waiting to see what the army would do. You see, the chief of the army had been elevated to prime minister upon the shah's return, but he'd passed away by the time the trouble started. When his successor announced that the army would remain neutral in the whole affair, the country was suddenly up for grabs."

"But if the protestors and the secret police were evenly matched, and the army was out of the fight, what tipped the balance?" Katrina asked.

"It's really *who* tipped the balance," James said. "It was a religious leader by the name of Ruhollah Khomeini. He'd been allowed to return to Iran in 1979 on the condition that he only set up a small religious enclave in the south, but I'm afraid his plans were a bit grander. His supporters co-opted the students' revolution and made it their own. They preached that fundamentalist Islam was the answer to the corruption of the shah and to all the country's other problems as well. The revolution suddenly became the Islamic Revolution, the American embassy was stormed, and those poor hostages began their ordeal."

"And Ruhollah Khomeini became 'Grand Ayatollah' Khomeini," Celia added with a touch of scorn.

"Exactly. The Iran that you visited was quite different from the Iran we inhabited in the seventies. It was the same place, separated only by time."

"Thank you, Herr Einstein," Geoffrey mumbled.

"It sounds horrible," Katrina said.

"Unfortunately it became much worse after 1979," Sir James continued. "To safeguard the revolution and to prevent the army from becoming the arbiter of future governments, a second army was created, the Islamic Revolutionary Guards. It spread its tentacles throughout the military, the economy, and the political culture of the country. They even established a division called the Qods Force. It literally means the 'Jerusalem Force,' and through it Iran has expended considerable time and money supporting disruptive and destabilizing organizations throughout the world. Its mandate runs the gamut from providing weapons and intelligence to Hamas, Hezbollah, and Islamic Jihad, to running training camps for terrorists. Qods taught anti-coalition forces in Iraq and Afghanistan how to form roadside bombs and conduct suicide missions. They're very bad actors, I'm afraid."

"Celia, were you scared?" Katrina asked.

"Nonsense. Celia's never been scared of anything in her life," Geoffrey added. "She'd probably stare down the devil himself."

"Thank you for that, Geoffrey. I wasn't actually afraid, but I was uncomfortable, and not just physically. There were soldiers everywhere and you could see the contempt in their eyes when they looked at you. They seemed to be suspicious of everyone, constantly walking through the airport and watching our every move. We had to take buses to another airport before we flew out, and we had a military escort the entire way. It was very disconcerting . . ." A frown crossed her face.

"What is it, Celia? You look troubled," asked Sir James.

"Well, there is one thing that still distresses me. I sat next to a lovely young American man on the first leg of the flight, but I didn't see him on the flight here. I was up in first class, so I didn't think much of it until we landed. We were going through immigration and I thought I saw him from behind . . ."

"Oh, Celia, you tart!" interrupted Geoffrey, who'd finished at least a bottle of the Petrus by himself.

"As I was saying," she continued. "He was dressed exactly like the American and he even had the same type of carry-on bag, one of those awful laptop-backpacks. But when I approached him to say hello, it wasn't him at all. The whole situation was very upsetting."

"It's probably just a coincidence, Celia. I'm sure BA wouldn't have left without your friend," said Hans.

"Do you remember the name of this American chap, dear?" asked Sir James.

"Yes, of course. He introduced himself as Zachary Miller, and he'd been taking pictures of the countryside when we landed."

## SEVENTEEN

ZAC WAS STIFF, sore, and perilously thirsty. He spent the day in the cave, out of the sun and out of sight. With the approach of sunset, he was ready to get moving. He oriented himself to the south and set off toward a distant mountain peak and several stands of trees. If vegetation could grow in such an inhospitable environment, then there might be water there too.

Mile after mile his thirst, his aching muscles, and the extremes of temperature attacked his resolve. He could push through the pain, but it was his mind that was his true enemy. It was telling him that the odds of successfully escaping were overwhelmingly against him, that it was nearly impossible to survive and evade recapture. He tried to estimate how far he had walked the prior day and night. Maybe fifteen miles, maybe twenty. As the steps blended together in the darkness, he couldn't believe that he was trying to walk to freedom. Lost in the middle of a hostile foreign country, he was guiding himself by the rising and setting of the sun. In an age when a GPS system was in every car, boat, and phone, he was estimating the cardinal points of the compass. The margin for error was enormous.

And when he found the Persian Gulf, then what? Call for help? Maybe stow away or steal a boat? And if he did manage to steal a boat, how would he cross the Gulf and where would he go? Saudi Arabia? He knew how to sail, and he'd spent his summers racing with friends on Long Island Sound, but crossing a sea full of hostile warships was an altogether different proposition.

Negative thoughts cascaded through his mind until he was walking in a daze, unaware of his path or direction. The only sound was the rough cadence of his boots scratching along the dusty ground.

*Splash.*

Zac found himself standing in a small stream. He was in desperate need of water. Still, he expected the current running around his feet to once again be undrinkable. He bent down and rinsed his hands. The fast-moving water was cold, numbingly cold, but he cupped his hands together and brought it up to his face. He tested it with his tongue and it tasted clean enough. He knelt down and drank until his stomach cramped, but this time the pain was only from drinking too quickly. He smiled.

*Small victories.*

Zac stayed by the stream until he was rehydrated. It took longer than he'd expected, but the water was like a tonic, and with it came renewed strength and clarity of mind. He stripped naked and washed his filthy body and clothes in the cold water.

He looked to the east. The light of dawn was already glowing over the mountain peaks. Even with his limited survival and evasion training, he knew that he should travel under the cover of darkness, but he also knew that he needed to put more distance between himself and the shot-up Toyota that would soon become the starting point for the Iranian manhunt.

The sun rose above the distant mountains, warming him as he dressed. He reached down into the stream bed and smeared the thick clay over his face and hands. It would camouflage his exposed skin and serve as a primitive sunscreen.

He headed south, along the side of the mountain to avoid being silhouetted against the sky. It took almost two hours of steady hiking to reach the trees he'd seen the night before. The tallest ones, twenty-five to thirty-five feet high, turned out to be pistachio trees. He shook them like an angry bear and nuts fell everywhere. He filled his stomach and then the pockets of his parka. It was the first food he'd had in over four days. Zac emptied most of his canteen to wash down his food and set off with renewed vigor and confidence.

The topography changed during the next several hours of hiking. The land became less arid and the sagebrush shared the ground with low grasses and more frequent stands of trees. Down in the valley, the colors were more vibrant. There was less gray and more green.

Only the relentless pounding of the sun remained constant. By the afternoon Zac was again stumbling across the ground. He'd slept little more than an hour in the past day. Each unsteady step risked a dangerous fall in the unforgiving wilderness. It was time to rest.

He found a patch of shade under a saxaul tree and

lowered himself to the ground. His body was shutting down in stages, demanding more water, more sleep, and more food. He set the rifle against a rock and stripped off his boots and the parka. Exhaustion overwhelmed him as he closed his eyes.

A light breeze blew in from the west, providing a moment of relief for his overheated body. The tiny leaves on the saxaul tree rustled softly. It was the first peaceful moment he'd had since landing in Iran.

He was sure he was dreaming when he heard a voice.

*"Salam!"*

It called out again. *"Khosh, amadid."*

Zac turned to see a wiry man clad in dusty clothes walking toward him. He was a few inches taller than Zac, and probably fifteen or twenty years older. His tone was neutral, but the language was completely foreign.

*"Shoma ahleh koja hastid?"*

The man's ruddy face and scruffy beard were framed by a white *chafiye* wrapped around his head to protect against the sun and sand. He swung a walking stick in one hand as he approached.

*"Mitoonam ke komaketoon konam?"*

The man stopped twenty feet away. He'd been smiling at first, but his expression changed to one of concern. Concern for whom, Zac could not be sure. The stranger was staring at Zac's torn and bloodied shirt.

*"Zakhmee shodee?"*

The man was perplexed by Zac's silence, as if a foreigner in such a remote and hostile place was inconceivable.

Zac made the "OK" sign with his thumb and index

finger, slowly stood up, and walked toward the man, his palms up to show he meant no harm. The man stiffened and moved back. Zac halted, anxious to avoid a confrontation.

*"Man bayad beravam. Mo'afagh bashed."*

The man turned and began to walk away. He looked over his shoulder and the two men locked eyes. Zac tried to appear conciliatory, but he was bloodied, battered, and the rifle lay near him on the ground. The man burst into a run and Zac instinctively gave chase.

# EIGHTEEN

CHRISTINE KIRBY WALKED into the gym at CIA's London station and spotted Ted Graves across the floor, dripping sweat and doing sit-ups with a ten-kilogram plate held to his chest. She stood at his feet until Graves finished and slid the weight to the floor.

"Thirty-seven reps, not bad for an old guy," she said.

"I guess you missed the first sixty-three," said Graves. "How did you find this place? I didn't know you knew where it was."

"I'm free anytime you'd like to test your stamina."

Graves looked at Kirby and smirked. Though he was in peak condition, she was ten years younger and had been a nationally ranked distance swimmer at West Point. Now she won half-Ironman races in her spare time, which was almost nonexistent. They both knew she'd kick his ass in anything that didn't involve pure strength.

"I'm guessing you didn't come down here to support your boss's physical fitness. What's up?" He extended his arm for a hand up off the floor.

She threw a gym towel in his face and motioned to an

empty bench along the wall. They sat down and Graves took a long drink of water.

"It's about SNAPSHOT," she said.

"Have you found Miller?"

"No, and we're not the only ones looking for him. There was a murder in Paris and INTERPOL has matched the prints at the scene with Miller's."

"Wonderful . . . Who's the victim?"

"Female, late twenties, maybe early thirties. No ID so far. Multiple stab wounds and evidence of sexual activity, but the French police haven't determined if it was consensual or not. It wasn't pretty."

"How the hell did they match Miller's prints?"

"He's in the FBI's IAFIS database. He has a pistol permit back in the States."

"What a disaster. This is the kind of thing that Clements doesn't understand. You can't just send someone out into the field without a full psychological workup. Giving an analyst a polygraph and vetting someone for clandestine ops are totally different exercises."

They sat in silence until Graves took out his secure cell phone and Kirby stood to leave.

"Stay here," Graves said as he dialed. Peter Clements answered after a few rings.

"Hey, Peter. Do you remember when we called Miller in Paris just before he left? What was he doing there?"

"I don't know exactly. He mentioned something about staying at a friend's apartment. What's up?"

"Nothing really, just building a timeline. You don't have a name by any chance, do you?"

"No. He was only planning to be gone for a day or two until we got the take from Sirjan."

"OK, thanks."

Graves hung up the phone. "Where did the murder happen?"

"Upscale apartment building. Don't know if it was the victim's place or not."

"Clements said Miller may have been staying at a friend's apartment while he was there. Maybe that's where he killed her."

"Ted, I don't know Miller well, but I just don't see him as a 'crime of passion' type of guy."

"Neither do I. And if cold-blooded murder is cover for whatever is really going on, we may have a much bigger problem on our hands. Find out everything about Miller's trip to Paris, ASAP."

## NINETEEN

Z AC DOUBTED HIS decision almost immediately, but he kept up the pursuit. The older man was surprisingly quick over the rocky ground, using his walking stick for balance. But youth was on Zac's side. Ignoring the pain in his bare feet, he sprinted over the ground and tackled the stranger. The man tried to get up, but Zac grabbed one of his legs and threw him to the ground. The man lay back on his elbows, looking hateful and defiant. Zac stared back, and realized he had no idea what to do next.

A dozen goats dotted the rocks below, foraging for vegetation. The man was probably a herder, maybe even a nomad, who had stumbled upon a sleeping stranger. Zac realized that he would either have to let the herder go on his way, or kill him. With no common language there could be no middle ground, no negotiating, no apology for a simple misunderstanding.

Zac decided to leave. He was not going to murder an innocent man. He turned and began to walk back uphill. He made it two steps when his right leg erupted in pain. He cried out and fell to the ground.

The herder had swung the heavy end of his walking stick into Zac's knee. Writhing on his back, Zac looked up and saw the stick coming again, its thick end cutting a wide arc through the air. He rolled to his side and the hard wood thudded against his back. A third blow struck the side of his head and his world turned blurry. He saw the silhouette of the herder above him.

Zac watched in slow motion as the herder flipped the walking stick in his hands and grasped it by the thick end. He raised it above his head and thrust it down like a spear toward Zac's chest. He rolled out of the way and the stick plowed several inches into the hard ground. When his attacker bent to retrieve it, Zac grasped the narrow end and swept the man's legs. The herder fell and the stick broke free from the hard earth.

The two men fought on the ground, each trying to wrest the weapon from the other. The herder kicked Zac in the face, and Zac jammed the stick into the herder's gut, but neither man yielded. The herder landed a second kick to Zac's face, then a third. Zac couldn't get out of the way. He began to feel faint. The herder connected with another kick to the head and Zac realized that he was in a fight for his life, and he was losing. He rolled onto his side and twisted the stick, forcing the herder to roll with it or lose the weapon. When the herder turned onto his stomach, Zac let go of the stick and rose to his feet. He jumped onto the herder's back and drove his knee into the man's spine, pinning him to the ground. The herder screamed.

Zac punched him in the back of the head, trying to knock him unconscious, but the herder thrashed about, trying to free himself. The man was strong. Twice he rolled onto his side and nearly broke loose. Zac was desperate. He hooked his arm under the man's neck and pulled. The herder gasped for air. Zac pulled and twisted, wrestling with his stubborn enemy. The exertion was too much for Zac's weary body. Stars formed before his eyes. His balance began to slip away. In a last, desperate move, he reached down with his free hand and wrenched the man's neck until it snapped.

Zac rolled off the dead man's back and lay on the ground, staring up at the sky and struggling to catch his breath. He looked at the herder's body, just inches away. His head lay unnaturally to one side, his eyes open. Zac was overcome with despair. The man didn't deserve to die. He was just in the wrong place at the wrong time. Zac exhaled deeply and stared into the distance. This was not how he'd imagined his life unfolding. He'd joined CIA to protect people, not kill them.

After a while he dusted himself off and got back into survival mode. He switched clothes with the dead man, donning his faded green pants and blue windbreaker. He tied the *chafiye* clumsily around his own head and neck. There were cigarettes and a lighter in the man's jacket, but nothing else. Zac kept the lighter and dragged the body a few yards before setting it down at the edge of the rocky slope. He left and returned with his boots and rifle.

He crept to the top of the rockslide and lowered himself to the ground. He leveled the AK-47, exhaled, and dropped the nearest goat with a clean shot just behind the shoulder. The rest of the herd scattered as the report of the rifle echoed through the valley. Zac scrambled down the rocks and slit the wounded animal's throat with his knife. When the goat had bled out, he butchered one of its meaty legs and tossed the carcass off a nearby cliff.

He looked at the dead herder. The sound and feel of his spine as it snapped would haunt Zac for the rest of his life, but there was nothing he could do about it now. He lifted the dead man onto his shoulder and heaved him onto the rocks below. The lifeless figure tumbled down the steep slope, scattering the goats that had just begun to return. Anyone finding the corpse would be hard pressed to tell that it wasn't the fall that had killed him.

Zac walked until sunset. He found a secluded spot on the side of a hill and made a fire ring out of nearby stones. He built the sides high, to hide the flames and concentrate the heat. Soon the smell of roasting goat meat permeated the night air.

He climbed to a nearby peak while the meat cooked. It was a clear night, and he could see for miles in every direction. He lay down with his head on a rock and stared up at the heavens. The stars shone brilliantly, like diamonds scattered across black velvet. Out in the wilderness, with no cities or highways, Zac savored the solitude and the silence. The aroma of the cooking meat and the natural beauty around him helped him relax. He took several slow, deep breaths and went to check on dinner.

He devoured the goat leg and decided to put some miles behind him in case anyone had spotted the smoke from his fire. He hiked for two hours before exhaustion forced him to stop.

\* \* \*

IT WAS MID-MORNING when he awoke, splayed out upon a hot and uneven slab of rock. His nostrils burned as he inhaled the dry desert air. The *chafiye* shielded his face from the sun, but the heat broiled his body where it lay. His training told him to find some shade and wait until night to move again, but he set out in search of water.

Zac's head pounded as he stumbled through dry stream beds and thickets of scrub. He looked under rocks and in the shade, but there was no water. He searched for hours until he tripped over an exposed root and fell. Sprawled on the ground, unable to move, his cheek lay flat against the dusty desert floor. Out of the corner of his eye he could see the hazy blue sky. Wisps of white cirrus clouds blew gently through the upper atmosphere. His body was shutting down.

*It's time to stop fighting, time to quit running. I give up.*

## TWENTY

"THERE ARE THOSE in my government who see a resurgence of the Muslim Brotherhood as a desirable outcome, Mr. Graves. They think that by supporting the organization, regardless of how destabilizing it might be, they can gain control over it," said the representative from Egypt.

"We learned with bin Laden in Afghanistan that that strategy doesn't always work." Appearing as a mid-level program officer with USAID, Ted Graves was attending a cocktail party at the Polish embassy as part of his official cover.

"I have used the bin Laden example many times," said the Egyptian. "And the Saudis have learned the same painful lesson with the Wahhabis. Yet our leadership believes that once the Brotherhood is on the payroll they will be able to turn the insurgency on and off like a switch. However, I fear the Brotherhood will not be so easily controlled."

"And no one in your government will listen?" Graves's carefully constructed facade was a critical part of his job. More than half of CIA's foreign assets were "walk-ins," individuals who approached American officials at events such as this one. Graves thought the Egyptian might be taking the first step, but it was a dangerous dance, and no one wanted to have their toes stepped on.

The envoy was about to respond when Graves's secure cell phone rang. He excused himself and walked to the middle of the room. Any listening devices in the embassy would be useless among the dozens of conversations.

"Ted, it's Christine. I need you. We have some developments on SNAPSHOT. Miller was exchanging suspicious text messages with someone in Paris just before he left London. He was setting up a rendezvous."

Graves subtly changed the grip on his phone to obscure his mouth.

"Was it the victim?"

"I don't think so. The French police believe the vic was a streetwalker, and the phone bill is tied to a fancy address in the sixth arrondissement."

"Who owns the phone?"

"It's registered to a G. Marchand."

"What do we know about Marchand?"

"Nothing. I didn't want to beat the bushes in case he was somehow connected to the Agency, but it sounds as if you've never heard of him. Do you want me to call a contact over there and do a little digging?"

"Definitely not. Marchand might be involved in the murder or Miller's disappearance in Iran. The Iranians and the French have a long history of intelligence sharing and commercial ties, and if they don't know that Miller is CIA, then I don't want to alert them. I don't trust them any more than they trust us." A few partygoers drifted within earshot and Graves moved casually across the room. "What did Miller's text messages say?"

"Aside from setting up the rendezvous, not much. They took place over a couple of weeks and they're cryptic. Stuff like, 'Is this finally going to happen?' 'That's up to you.' 'I'm not sure I'll recognize you.' 'I'll reserve a table under my name.' Stuff like that. No useful details."

"I want surveillance on Marchand and get NSA into his e-mail and phone to see if he's made contact with Miller since he left Paris. Dig up everything you can on this guy, but keep it in-house. I don't want to draw any more attention to Miller."

Kirby hesitated for a moment. "Ted, there is one more thing . . ."

"Go ahead."

"Miller killed someone in Singapore too."

# TWENTY-ONE

THE THREE OFF-ROAD trucks were painted in the tan desert camouflage of the Islamic Revolutionary Guards. A dozen soldiers sat on the ground, resting in the shade of the parked vehicles while their officer conferred with two of his sergeants at a nearby map table. The temporary command post had been up and running for less than four hours when the men heard the distinctive sound of an approaching two-bladed helicopter. They turned to watch the Iranian Huey fly swiftly through the valley, the pilot skillfully banking and turning as he negotiated the rocky hills and mountains. A massive cloud of dust enveloped the brown-and-tan helicopter as it landed.

Most men crouched as they exited a helicopter, knowing that contact with the rotor spinning above their heads would be instantly fatal. Colonel Arzaman walked tall as he emerged from the Huey.

"Captain Jafari!" he bellowed. "Where is Captain Jafari?"

The captain waited at attention just outside the radius of the dust cloud. He knew Arzaman's little game from experience. The colonel, with the helicopter's dust cloud at his back, would summon others to him, forcing them to cover their eyes and mouths so they would appear weak and defensive as they approached him.

"Right here, sir."

"What's happening with the search, Captain?" he shouted over the noise of the helo.

Captain Jafari of the Revolutionary Guards Special Forces held the map with both hands while the helicopter rotor wound down. He gestured awkwardly to a notation on the map.

"The two soldiers were found there, along the road. The dogs followed the target's scent east from Bar Aftab but lost it up in the mountains. Yesterday we searched a twenty-kilometer radius around the site. We found nothing. Today we're tearing up every town and village inside this red perimeter . . ." He pointed at the map.

Arzaman scowled. "He may have a support network in-country. He could have preplanned rendezvous points around the area to coordinate his escape. We moved him out of Sirjan for just this reason, but with every hour that passes, it becomes more likely that he will figure out where he is and make contact with his network. Why are you not checking the countryside?"

"No Westerner could survive out there on his own. He'll need to steal food and water. My men are interviewing the locals to see if anything has gone missing. We'll have the whole area cordoned off soon, then we'll tighten the perimeter as we get closer to his last known position. He couldn't have moved far."

"Search the countryside and the outlying areas. I will get you another helicopter from Shiraz," Arzaman said.

He stared at the map. "What do we think happened to the two soldiers?"

"They were both found dead at their vehicle; looks as if they were ambushed."

"I heard shell casings were found on the east side of the road, along the valley wall."

"I heard the same thing, Colonel. There was probably a firefight beforehand, but we don't know for sure. They never radioed in."

"Be careful you do not underestimate this man, Captain. I would like him captured alive, for there is still much questioning to do, but if there is any chance of him escaping again, your men are to shoot to kill. Do you understand?"

"Yes, Colonel."

A senior sergeant interrupted them. "Five of the eight squads are in position, sir. The others should be ready to go within the hour."

Arzaman looked expectantly at the captain.

"I'll keep you posted, Colonel. Where will I be able to find you?"

"I am heading to Bandar Abbas to supervise the search there. Find this American, Captain, or you will find yourself in the grave meant for him."

---

## TWENTY-TWO

THE IRG SPECIAL Forces soldiers lamented the bum mission they'd been assigned as their small convoy rolled through the valley. The area around the Khabr National Park was vast and rugged terrain, and they'd been driving for almost seven hours, scrambling their insides as their two heavy vehicles bounced over the rough desert floor. It was almost impossible for an experienced native to survive alone in this land, much less a foreigner. It was even crazier to think that they could find a single man among the never-ending wilderness.

But orders were orders. One soldier on each side of the trucks had been tasked with binoculars, but the rough ride rendered them useless. Amid the dust, discomfort, and boredom, the conversation devolved into one about cars, weapons, and women. But the country was officially the Islamic Republic of Iran, and the IRG was ostensibly the guardian of the faith, so the conversation was slightly less animated than it would have been in any other army.

The first sergeant rode shotgun in the lead vehicle. Unlike the mostly conscripted regular army, the men in the special operations teams were volunteers, highly trained and heavily dependent upon one another. With interdependence came trust and familiarity, and so rank failed to protect the sergeant from good-natured ribbing from his men about why their unit had been selected for such a long and tedious patrol. The laughter helped pass the time as the scenery blended together and the men's senses dulled. The sun was at their two o'clock as they wound their way south through the valley. In another hour it would drop below the mountaintops, but for now it was low in the sky, casting long shadows on the hillsides.

ZAC LAY FACEDOWN on the ground, close to death. The sun's relentless rays had split his lips and burned his skin. Now the hot, dry air scorched his throat with every feeble breath. He wanted to give in, to simply close his eyes and die.

He thought of his aunt and how she must have felt like giving in when she was sick, wishing that the cancer would simply take her and end the agonizing struggle. His aching head lay on the hard ground as he looked out over the rocky, mountainous land in front of him. Shimmering waves of heat rose from the earth.

Zac knew that he wasn't thinking clearly, but in a lucid moment he decided that he wasn't ready to die. He'd accepted the mission and the responsibility that came with it. He had to fight the urge to sleep. If he closed his eyes now, they might never open again. He stood, slowly and unsteadily. Though battered and bruised, he had to find water or he might not last through the day. He trudged toward the top of a ridge to get a better view of his surroundings. Maybe he could find a village, or even a house. He had to try.

Half a mile away, a trail of dust snaked up from the valley floor. Exhaustion and heat addled his thoughts, but he knew something was moving. He stumbled behind a sagebrush and knelt down. Two military trucks were headed his way, but the steep terrain would keep them down on the valley floor. They would pass below and well to the side of him. He watched them bounce over the rough earth, their knobby tires spewing wakes of dust into the air. Zac lowered himself to the ground behind the sagebrush. The sound of the trucks' engines echoed through the mountains.

The rifle and pistol would do little against a dozen soldiers except hasten his death. If he were to turn and run, they might see him and give chase, or simply shoot him. There was also a chance that he could remain motionless and blend into the background. With the first two choices guaranteeing a speedy death, it was an unappetizing menu. He decided to sit tight and hope for the best.

"POSSIBLE CONTACT, RIGHT side," said a soldier in the lead vehicle.

The driver began to slow the truck.

"Keep driving," snapped the first sergeant. "There's

no reason to warn him. I don't see anything. Hadi, don't point, but tell me where you are looking."

"Two o'clock, about a hundred meters up the hill, on that ridge. You can't see anyone directly, but look at the ground. All the shadows from the brush are soft and blurry, except one; it's dark and long, and I'm sure it just moved."

It was quiet for a few moments as they all strained to see.

"I see it now, Hadi. You have the eyes of a falcon. Can you see him with the binoculars?"

"Not with the truck bouncing around like this, but I'm sure it's a man."

Everyone was silent for a few more seconds as the trucks continued along the valley floor.

"I agree. Raise the rest of the team on the radio. Here's the plan . . ."

ZAC COULD BARELY breathe. Twice he had to shift his body to stay hidden behind the sagebrush while the trucks wound their way through the valley. Eventually they drove around a bend and out of sight, but he remained frozen behind the shrub. His heart was pounding. The sun was dropping quickly toward the mountain peaks and it would soon be dark. Like never before, he craved the cover of the night. He rose unsteadily to his feet. He was certain that the men in the trucks were hunting him. He retraced his steps along the ridge to make sure they were gone for good, but the trucks were not gone. They were stopped on the valley floor.

\* \* \*

THE SOLDIERS CLIMBED out of their vehicles and gathered around the sergeant.

"We're going up the side of this hill. You four take the second truck and circle around to cut off his escape. The captain said to take him alive if we can, dead if we have to. He's already killed six of our men, so use your best judgment . . ." The sergeant racked the charging handle on his rifle for emphasis. "Who are we to stop him if he wants to be martyred for his cause?" A few chuckles broke out. "Be safe and stay on the radios. Let's go."

The second team sped to their insertion point while the first team made ready. One of the soldiers unloaded a sniper rifle. Another opened the rear doors of their truck. A huge German shepherd jumped down and started barking as he strained against his long, black leash.

ZAC LOWERED HIMSELF onto his stomach and crawled out of view. The area they were in was so remote, so far from anything man-made, that the trucks couldn't have stopped there by coincidence. They'd spotted him for sure. He moved far enough to stand without being seen and ran like hell.

He stopped when he saw the second truck moving to encircle him. Zac had a head start, but that was all it would be. The soldiers would have to hike up from the valley floor, but they were rested and well trained. They would close the gap in thirty or forty minutes. He couldn't outdistance them, so he would have to hide, but the rough landscape left few options. Once again, his only choice was up.

He started climbing, his body fighting every step. His throat burned from thirst and his head ached as if it were in a vise, but he pressed on. He crested a ridge and cursed when he found several scree-lined chutes dominating the face of the mountain. The sharp, loose stones were the remnants of prior rock slides, physical testaments to the dangerous ground underfoot. In an instant he could twist an ankle, break a leg, or be crushed in a rockslide; but the soldiers had cut off the other escape routes. Every moment he hesitated brought his pursuers closer to him, and him closer to death.

Zac walked tentatively onto the scree, shifting his weight carefully, but the loose footing gave way and he slid several feet down the steep mountain face. He tried again, and the footing held. Carrying only the rifle and the pistol, Zac was light enough to endure the small rock slides without causing an avalanche, but the soldiers would be laden with rucksacks, ammunition, and maybe even body armor. They would be too heavy to cross the field without triggering a major rock slide. If Zac could get high enough on the scree to reach the next ridge, the soldiers would be unable to follow.

He scrambled slowly up the chute, using his hands and feet to distribute his weight. Several times he put too much pressure on a single hand or foot and the rock gave way, sending him sliding down the mountain. Each step was different, every handhold a new risk. The pace was agonizingly slow as the soldiers closed in.

Zac climbed for twenty minutes before he reached the

top of the chute and stepped onto solid ground. His head pounded and his muscles burned, but he'd reached the mountain summit where the soldiers and their dog would be unable to find him. He stumbled along the peak, dizzy and exhausted, stopping just short of a cliff. With a five-hundred-foot drop-off on one side, and the scree fields on the other, there was nowhere to go. Zac's knees buckled and he fell to the ground. The last thing he heard before he passed out was the sound of the soldiers below him talking among themselves.

# TWENTY-THREE

ZAC OPENED HIS eyes but saw nothing. He was either dreaming or dead. Soon he tasted the dust and felt the pain that proved that he was still somewhat alive. Night had fallen and there was no sign of the soldiers, but something had roused him from a very deep sleep.

A loud noise filled the air. He looked over the cliff and across the moonlit valley for the source of the strange sound. He closed his eyes and concentrated. The noise was deep and steady, but the pitch and volume varied with the wind. It was something man-made, and it was big. Reverberation in the valley obscured its precise nature, but it was definitely mechanical. Perhaps there were railroad tracks nearby. The sound suddenly became much louder, and Zac opened his eyes.

A fast-moving attack helicopter climbed swiftly out of the valley and thundered past one hundred feet overhead. The Iranian Cobra gunship had been ascending the side of the cliff, the muted "whump-whump" of its rotor echoing off the rock walls. Zac dove onto his stomach. The helo was flying so fast that there was a chance the pilots hadn't seen him.

The chopper began a tight turn back toward his position. He looked up at the Cobra with its 20mm cannon jutting out from under its nose. In a few more seconds the pilots would be headed directly toward him, and they wouldn't miss him a second time. His options were the scree field or the cliff. Jumping off the cliff meant certain death, the scree field only likely death.

Zac put his feet together and jumped into the scree. He slid down, his heels driving through the loose stones. With the rifle slung across his back, he used his arms for balance. Zac stared at the attack helicopter as it leveled out and flew toward him. He didn't see the boulder underfoot until it was too late. His feet jammed into the big rock, buckling his knees and sending a shock wave through his body. He fell headfirst, stones hammering his body as he tumbled down the steep incline. He glimpsed the rifle cartwheeling through the air, the broken sling streaming behind it.

The mechanical roar of the attack helicopter was deafening as it drew closer. If the noise or the rotor wash triggered a rock slide while he was still in the chute, he would be pulverized. He grabbed at the stones. The sharp rocks sliced open the skin on his palms, but he was able to spin his feet downhill. He dug in his heels and stopped the slide.

The Cobra was almost overhead, its three-barreled cannon probing the air like the tongue of its namesake. Zac lay still and watched the helo close in. A half-moon and clear skies made for a brightly lit night, but the steep sides of the chute sheathed him in darkness. Zac prayed that the pilots were not wearing night-vision goggles.

The helicopter flew on, oblivious to its quarry. Zac crawled down the loose rocks to the bottom of the chute and collapsed onto a sagebrush. Bruised, bleeding, and nearly unconscious, he was barely clinging to life.

## TWENTY-FOUR

ZAC AWOKE IN the middle of the night, his body damaged and stiff. He'd been badly hurt escaping from the attack helicopter, but he knew that death's imminent touch would come from dehydration, not his injuries. There would be no tomorrow without water today. He stumbled along for hours before he found a small stream, really no more than a trickle of water, where he was able to drink, rinse his face, and refill his canteen. He lay down between two bushes to conceal himself and in less than a minute he was fast asleep.

By late afternoon he had rested for close to twelve hours. His body began to function again. He was not healthy enough to venture far, but it was more dangerous for him to stay too long in one place. The soldiers may have given up their search last night, but they would be back. He moved slowly at first, his body protesting every step.

Eventually he reached the rim of a wide valley. He sat down and took out the knife he'd found in the truck. He drew it from its scabbard and inspected its seven-inch blade, catching his reflection in the polished steel. His face was deeply tanned, his features obscured by several days' growth of facial hair. With the clothes he was wearing, he barely recognized himself. To anyone else, he would look like just another goat herder.

Zac put the knife away and surveyed the expanse below. He'd stuck to higher elevations since escaping from the warehouse, but avoiding the valley would mean an enormous detour, and an expenditure of energy he simply didn't have. More than once he'd taken such detours only to find his path blocked by a cliff or an impassable crevasse. Now he needed the path of least resistance.

He found a well-worn game trail and began to wind his way down into the valley. The gentle grade and easy hiking were a blessing for his weary body and allowed him to relax after his escape from the attack helicopter. When he saw something move on the trail up ahead, it took a few seconds for his mind to register that it might be a source of danger. He looked more carefully. Someone was lurking in the shadows.

Zac took the pistol from his pocket and moved closer. He squinted to see if it was a soldier, or maybe another herder, but the light played tricks on his eyes. He raised the pistol with both hands and approached. Zac closed the distance until he realized that it was only a boy of seven or eight years of age. Clad in sneakers and sun-bleached clothes, he sat alone on the ground, clutching his ankle. Zac put the pistol in his pocket and walked over. The boy looked up, his eyes wet with tears, and said something. Zac didn't understand the words, but he recognized the fear in the boy's eyes; the fear of utter, abject loneliness. Zac himself had felt it as a child. The boy pulled up the leg of his pants to reveal a swollen and badly bruised joint.

Zac helped the child up. The boy stood tentatively on one leg, struggling to maintain his balance. He tried to walk, but the slightest weight on his injured ankle caused him to cry out and grab Zac's arm for help.

*What on earth is this kid doing out here alone?*

He couldn't have wandered far without someone noticing. Zac scanned the area again but there was no one in sight. He knew firsthand how cold and inhospitable these mountains would be in just a few hours. If he left the boy in this condition, he would die.

This was not part of the plan. Zac needed to avoid local contact and get to the Persian Gulf before the soldiers found him again. He looked down at the child. The boy had stopped crying and was pointing down the mountain. Zac's arrival had given the child hope. Naturally, the boy expected Zac to take him home and, to his own amazement, Zac was considering it.

Graves had warned him to avoid people. Zac didn't speak the language or know the customs. He was guaranteed to attract attention. The authorities would have undoubtedly told the residents that he was an enemy of the state or a dangerous, escaped killer.

But Zac had to decide whether or not he was still a member of civilized society. He'd killed the herder because the chance encounter had quickly spiraled out of control. Zac had done what he needed to do to survive, but leaving the boy to die was unconscionable. He decided to save the boy's life to compensate for the one he'd unjustly taken. He knew the math of morality was not so simple, but it was the best he could do. He scooped the child up in his arms.

The boy guided them onto a path in the shade of the mountain where it quickly became cold. Zac wrapped his jacket around the shivering child and carried him piggyback style. The boy even managed to laugh a few times when they bounced along the rough trail. Zac smiled. The child's innocent happiness made him feel human again. It was amazing how quickly life could throw you a curve. Zac had planned to be out of Iran and on his way to Singapore six hours after he'd landed, yet he'd been arrested in less than an hour. But chance worked both ways. If not for his predicament, the little boy on his back surely would have died.

They followed a gently sloping trail as they neared the floor of the valley. Zac had seen most of the area from the higher elevations, but he hadn't noticed any villages or even roads. They hiked for another half hour yet were no closer to civilization. He began to worry that the boy was lost. Zac was barely surviving on his own. He could not afford a traveling companion, especially a small and injured one.

The pair walked up a small hill and Zac's concern deepened. He should have seen the boy's village by now. Or maybe the boy had thought it funny, in the way small children do, to lead an adult on a wild-goose chase. Thoughts of leaving the boy alone in the wilderness crept back into Zac's mind, but he fought them down.

The unlikely duo crested the small hill and Zac's eyes came upon a sight from biblical times. In the twilight he could see a dozen people, several large tents, a few donkeys, and dozens of goats scattered around the hills. They were nomads, probably herders, encamped in the valley. One of the men called to Zac. He waved tentatively and began to walk into the camp. When the nomad was close enough to see their faces, he began shouting into one of the nearby tents. A chill shot down Zac's back. What if the herder he'd killed was one of their clan? Zac was wearing his clothes.

## TWENTY-FIVE

ZAC INSTINCTIVELY REACHED for the pistol, but it was in the pocket of his jacket, draped over the boy who was still riding piggyback. He felt behind him, fumbling blindly with the zippered pocket. He couldn't reach the gun. A woman came running out of one of the tents and the two nomads ran up the hill together. Zac had found their son.

The woman put her hand to her chest and bowed her head. The father embraced Zac and kissed him on both cheeks before taking his son into his arms. A flood of questions followed from the grateful parents, which Zac deflected to the boy. The happy child handed the windbreaker back to Zac.

He watched the emotional reunion play out in front of him, appreciating the parents' obvious love for their child. A few other nomads gathered around and one of them spoke to Zac. Assuming the authorities were looking for an English-speaker, Zac responded in French, the only other language he spoke. He explained that he was a hiker who had gotten lost and had been wandering for days when he happened upon the boy. The herder interrupted in his native Gulf Arabic. He said something to one of the women, who ran off and returned a few seconds later with another boy who was dressed in the same faded, hardscrabble clothing worn by the others. He was fourteen or fifteen, with short hair and the scruffy beginnings of a moustache on his upper lip.

He asked, "English?"

Zac again responded in rapid-fire French, but the boy persisted.

"I am Hani. I speak English," he said in a high-pitched voice and a thick accent.

"Ah, *oui*. I speak a little English too. I am . . . lost?" Zac spoke slowly, pretending to search for the right words.

"Where you from?" asked the boy.

"France. I was hiking and I am lost."

Hani spoke to the group of men. Several responded at once, gesturing with their hands and shouting instructions. The boy was unsure of what to do until an older man spoke up. He was of average height, with rounded shoulders and a wispy salt-and-pepper beard. His tone was gentle and quiet and his eyes moved to each member of the group as he spoke. The men listened in silence. When he was finished, he took his young translator by the arm and walked over to Zac. The old man looked him over carefully before asking him to tell his story. Several of the other men gathered around to listen to the translated conversation, but the old man's eyes never left Zac.

Zac explained that he had been hiking by himself for a week when he fell down a mountainside, losing his backpack, his camera, and all of his supplies. The pack had fallen into a gorge and he'd been unable to retrieve it. His map and compass had been in the backpack and, since the fall, he had been navigating by the sun. He had been wandering around the wilderness for five days. More than once, Zac's feigned lack of fluency in English was used to mask important details, but much of the story was true. His ragged appearance and lack of supplies supported the fiction.

After several minutes of questioning, Zac turned the tables and began to ask where he was and how far it was to the closest city. A lost hiker would be overjoyed at having been found, and Zac needed to play the part. The elder told him that Bandar Abbas, a large city on the Persian Gulf, was about one hundred kilometers to the south.

Zac and the group continued their fragmented conversation while more men arrived intermittently from outside the camp. He could tell by their obvious relief that they'd been searching for the boy. The herders spoke among themselves. Again several men spoke at once. One man in his early twenties was particularly animated. He had close-cropped hair and a bushy beard. He gestured toward Zac, raising his voice and shaking his head while he spoke to the others. He wore a well-used windbreaker and carried a dagger in his belt. Despite his youth, he had the hard look of one who worked the land. He was not happy with their newfound guest and shot Zac a look of contempt. The father of the rescued boy jumped into the fray and shouted back at the younger man.

Zac considered leaving camp to resume his trek alone before the scene turned violent. He'd walked fifty or sixty miles already, although he doubted it was in a straight line or even in the right direction. To get to Bandar Abbas, he would have to cover that distance again, and the first time had nearly cost him his life. Unless the nomads were going to kill him or turn him over to the authorities, leaving in such a depleted state would be foolhardy. There was a chance that these people would welcome him as a fellow traveler of the land and give him food, water, and shelter. If he could stay here for even a day or two to regain his strength before setting out again, he would do it.

The quarrel among the herders had reached a crescendo when the old man again raised his hands. The others fell silent as he spoke, softly and patiently, to the angry young man. His name was Husam, and he scowled and shifted on his feet as he listened to the elder, clearly displeased with what was being said. But he paid attention, as did the others, and in the end the old man and the rest of the group approached Zac and spoke through the teenage boy.

Hani explained that a trader with a truck met the nomads every few weeks to bring them supplies and take their goods to the market in Bandar Abbas. It would be three days until his next visit. Until then, Zac would be allowed to stay as their guest. He could avail himself of water, food, and a place to sleep. The trader would take him to the city. Zac shook the old man's hand and thanked him profusely.

Zac was led to a large, wood-framed canvas tent that he would share with several others. He was given a bed roll, water, and a few pieces of stale pita bread, which he quickly devoured. Conditions that would have seemed primitive and uncomfortable just one week ago now seemed luxurious. He kicked off his boots and fell asleep on an empty cot.

One of the nomads awakened Zac for dinner. A clear and starry night greeted him as he stepped outside the tent. The air was full of delicious smells. He smiled while he walked, not knowing what lay ahead, only that tonight he would not be hiking through treacherous terrain and evading capture.

Fifteen or sixteen men were seated on the ground around a campfire. Many were talking, some were listening, and a few just stared into the flames. Everyone seemed relaxed. Zac was directed to a spot next to the old man. The air was cool, but the ground was still warm from the heat of the day. The sound and smell of the crackling fire reminded Zac of the many camping trips he'd taken back in the States.

Several women approached to serve the dinner and plates were handed to each of the men. Zac looked at the plates, which were filled with rice, flatbread, and chunks of roasted meat. He was ravenous, but when his own plate came, he saw that he hadn't been given any meat, only a small serving of rice and a single piece of bread. He tried to mask his disappointment. He knew that food did not come easily to these people. It would not do to be an ungrateful guest.

The men ate with their hands while the conversations continued. Zac finished his small serving and placed his plate on the ground in front of him. The discussions around the fire abruptly stopped. Every pair of eyes focused on Zac.

The expressions of the other men turned sour. Only the night wind and the snapping of the fire broke the silence of the camp. Had Zac offended them somehow? The Persian and Arab peoples were proud, with long histories and long memories. Zac glanced at the group elder for guidance, but the old man turned away and stared into the fire. The stern expression on his face did nothing to calm Zac's nerves. He looked for Hani but the boy was nowhere in sight. Husam was even more displeased than before. Zac looked back at the village elder.

The fire glinted in the old man's eyes as he fixed his gaze on Zac. Slowly his face broke into a wide grin and the circle of men erupted in laughter. As Zac looked around, a second plate, stacked high with meat, bread, and rice, was handed to him by the mother of the boy he'd carried into camp. Zac too began to laugh, having fallen for the prank. He devoured the delicious food while the other men smiled and returned to their own meals and conversations.

Zac retired to the tent exhausted and feeling better than he had in a week, but despite the friendly hazing at dinner, it was clear from the body language of some of the men that he was not unanimously welcome in camp. The elder's decision had ruled the day, but Zac would tread carefully until the truck came. Perhaps the army had warned these people about a dangerous foreigner or maybe they were wary of outsiders. Tonight he would sleep with the pistol close at hand.

B Y THE TIME Zac awoke it was daylight and his bunkmates were already outside. He leaned against the wooden frame of the tent and gazed out over the camp. Some of the men stood with the goats near a small stream. Zac guessed these people knew the location of every stream, river, and watering hole within hundreds of miles. The women of the tribe wore *hijabs* that covered their heads, but without the veils required by some of the stricter Muslim sects. Several women were gathering sticks for the fire. Others carried baskets on their heads and shoulders as they performed chores. He walked outside, subconsciously touching his jacket to confirm the presence of the pistol, much like he used to check for his wallet before leaving his flat in London.

Zac decided to pitch in with the work. He looked for Hani to translate, but he didn't see the boy. A lone woman was tending the fire. She was young and pretty, with classic Arab features and an elegant profile. Zac walked over and waited a moment for her to notice him. When she looked up and met his eyes, she let out a short scream that sounded more surprised than fearful, but it was loud enough to attract the attention of everyone in camp. Husam and two other men ran up from the stream. Two older women who were close by also headed toward the fire. They each kept a wary eye on Zac as they spoke with the girl.

When Husam was twenty feet away he drew his dagger. The nomad would be upon Zac before he could get the pistol from his pocket. With his eyes locked on the blade, he flexed his hands and prepared for the attack.

One of the older women turned and yelled. Husam stopped just out of arm's reach. He kept the dagger up and shouted back at the woman, who was now hurrying toward Zac and Husam. Soon several people were gathered around. The older woman explained to the group what had happened, but Husam stood his ground, glaring. The woman barked at him again. Reluctantly, he broke eye contact and sheathed his knife. One of his friends led him away by the arm.

When Hani finally appeared, he explained to Zac that unmarried men and women were never to be alone in their culture, even in the middle of camp. Most of the nomads simply returned to their work, unfazed by the incident, but a few threw suspicious looks at Zac and spoke among themselves.

That afternoon, Hani took Zac to the village elder. The old man had heard about the incident by the fire. He said that the girl was Husam's sister, and her brother was furious about her unsupervised contact with a man, but she would not be punished. The elder looked Zac in the eye for what seemed like an eternity before he spoke again.

He explained that the nomads' ancestors had been the first settlers of this region. Indeed they had been one of the original peoples who'd emigrated south from the Fertile Crescent. For thousands of years their tribe had lived off the land as hunters and gatherers, following the food and water throughout the seasons. Now they raised domesticated animals and made carpets. They were traders and storytellers. They had survived without, and often despite, outside influences.

Zac was rapt. He stared intently at the elder as he spoke, forgetting even that Hani was translating. It was like being a participant in history, stepping back in time to when this man's ancestors had lived as he did now; a hundred generations of nomads surviving off the difficult and forbidding land. The elder paused in thought before he spoke again. He said that the government did not value the nomads. It saw them as backward, an embarrassment to the aspirations of the state. The ayatollahs and their soldiers saw the rich oral history of the nomadic peoples as an obstacle to the future of Iran.

The nomads were Sunni Muslims of Arab descent, not Persian like the mostly Shi'a Iranians. The soldiers and police would occasionally harass the wandering peoples, often kicking them out of lands that they had traveled for centuries. The elder paused again. His eyes were dark and penetrating, and they never left Zac. With his chipped and crooked teeth, the old man smiled. He said that he did not believe that Zac was a lost hiker, but neither did he care. Their culture dictated that travelers and guests were to be treated graciously, and Zac had saved the little boy. Actions were the true measure of a man, said the elder. They would get Zac to the trader's truck where he could make his way down to Bandar Abbas.

The elder turned away and stared into the distance. Almost as an afterthought, he spoke again. He said that soldiers had visited the nomads, looking for a man fitting Zac's description. He said that Zac would be safe in camp, but he should be careful in the city. It could be a dangerous place.

# TWENTY-SEVEN

THE SOLDIERS AT the temporary command post turned when they heard the sound of an approaching helicopter. The big Huey orbited their position and touched down fifty meters away. The rotors were still turning when Colonel Arzaman jumped out of the open door. He emerged from a cloud of dust to find Captain Jafari waiting for him.

"How is it possible that you have not captured the American yet?" Arzaman asked.

"We've had a couple of false alarms; wildlife and nomads mostly, but no luck so far. We've been running a grid search and canvassing the locals with sixteen squads of our best men. Captain Rajavi has taken the southern half and my men are up here. We have two helicopters running expanding box searches from north of Gozm where Squad Five may have spotted something in the mountains, but the birds were late getting here and we had to suspend air operations for lack of daylight. We could really use some air support with infrared search gear, sir."

"Two more helicopters are on their way from Isfahan,

but they couldn't leave the Nuclear Technology Center without coverage in case this American's incursion was the start of something more. Show me your maps."

Captain Jafari led the colonel to the table with the large-scale topographical map pinned to its top. Dozens of new markings in different colors denoted search areas, times, and any contact made along the way. Arzaman was angry, but Jafari was doing a thorough and professional job, and they were looking for a single man within a thousand square miles of rugged wilderness.

"We're pursuing a lead that came in about two hours ago." Jafari pointed to the map. "One of the helos spotted a man dressed like our target sprawled out on a rock slide. Animals were picking at the corpse but they hadn't finished it off, so he's probably been dead for less than twenty-four hours. Squad Four has already dismounted and are on their way in on foot. ETA is about an hour. If it's our guy, it means the other sighting was probably just an animal."

"Let's hope that it's him, but in the meantime I'm ordering roadblocks on all the highways and deploying smaller units to patrol the back roads. General Behzadi is taking his orders directly from the supreme leader on this. There will be repercussions all the way down the chain of command if we fail."

"We won't fail, sir. We'll get him."

"You had better, Captain."

# TWENTY-EIGHT

"I HAVE SOMETHING YOU want," said Kirby as she stepped into Graves's office.

Ted continued to scowl at his computer. "I'm in the middle of something . . ."

"Do you want the good news first or the bad news?" she asked.

He looked up and pushed back from his desk. "Do you know who Philippides was?"

"Of course. Did you forget that I'm a triathlete? He was the messenger from the Battle of Marathon, the inspiration for the modern race."

"Do you know what happened to him after he delivered *his* important message?"

"Legend has it that he died on the spot."

"Well then . . . maybe I'll get lucky and history will repeat itself," Graves said without the slightest hint of a smile.

Kirby took a chair across from his desk and sat down slowly, keeping a wary eye on her boss.

"So . . . do you remember how Miller set up a rendezvous in Paris with G. Marchand just before he left for Iran?" she asked. "It turns out Marchand is DGSE."

"How sure are you?"

"At first we just had an Agency contact report filed a couple of years ago that listed Marchand as a 'probable,' but the surveillance team I set up followed Marchand's car right into the Administration Center."

"Any chance it's a professional contact?"

"I checked Miller's Agency records, plus his phone and e-mail account. No hits on Marchand."

"Please tell me that wasn't the good news."

"No. That's definitely the bad news. We were operating under the assumption that Miller was meeting a man, but it turns out Marchand is a woman, and she's beautiful."

Graves raised an eyebrow as Kirby continued.

"I'm serious. She's probably five-ten, long dark hair, athletic body, just gorgeous. The surveillance team leader actually thanked me for putting him on the job. He asked me if I wanted to set up some surveillance inside her apartment, but I think the creep just wants the footage for . . ."

"I get the idea, Christine. Do we have any idea what she does at DGSE?"

"No, but I'm guessing she's not field operations if she's driving her car right in the front gate to work every morning. It's certainly no way to build a legend."

Graves let out a mirthless laugh at the irony of the statement.

"Mention that to Clements the next time you see him . . . What about SIGINT? Anything worthwhile?"

"Nothing. Her phone calls and e-mails are all with friends and family. She probably has secure comms for work. We're tracking those down right now."

"See if there is any tie-in between the murder victim and Marchand. We need to expand the surveillance too. I want her vehicle tailed twenty-four-seven."

"We could just put a GPS tag on her car."

"I wouldn't. There's a chance DGSE security walks the parking lot scanning for emissions. We do it back at Langley. If they find the tag, Marchand will change everything she does and be useless to us. I want to see who she makes contact with, especially Middle Easterners. Be cautious and assume she's a pro. You know the drill: penetrate the apartment indirectly, use a floating-box for the vehicle surveillance, passive electronic intercepts . . . the whole package."

Kirby sat back in her seat and stretched her legs. "You know, she could just be his girlfriend. Miller *is* pretty cute."

Graves looked askance at Kirby. "Or he got himself caught in a honey trap and now she's blackmailing him. Don't let your guard down on this one, Christine. There's more at stake here than just Miller's whereabouts."

## *TWENTY-NINE*

THE NEXT MORNING Zac volunteered to help with the chores around camp. He joined a group of men shepherding the goats into the nearby hills. There was scarcely any vegetation in sight, but the animals put their heads down and managed to find something to eat. Despite the heat, their ragged, short fleeces were already beginning to grow out for winter. Zac spent most of the day watching the goats, but he couldn't stop thinking about what he'd discovered in Sirjan. The responsibility weighed heavily upon him. He knew that there was more than just his life riding on his survival. Much more.

Hani had news for the men upon their return to camp. The trader's truck would be coming the next day. Hani explained that they would load the containers of goat milk onto the donkey carts tonight and Zac would accompany three other men to meet the truck in the morning. Hani saw the enthusiasm in Zac's face and quietly led him away from the group. There was one more thing he needed to know—Husam would be leading the group to Bandar Abbas.

\* \* \*

BY THE LIGHT of dawn, the three carts were hooked to the donkeys. Most of the camp was up to help or simply wish the travelers well. Goat milk was the only commercial asset the herders had until the spring, when the animals would be shorn and their wool made into the carpets that had made the region famous.

Husam moved purposefully about the camp, checking the carts and the animals, taking inventory of the sealed milk containers, and consulting with the village elder. As the one who would take the milk into Bandar Abbas, negotiate the sale price, and buy supplies, Husam held a position of great responsibility. Zac realized that he must have the confidence of many in the tribe.

Zac brought Hani with him to speak with Husam, but Husam seemed focused on the business of the day.

Hani translated for Zac, "I understand this is an important time. I will help if I can, or stay out of the way if I cannot. I will do whatever you need from me."

Husam stared at Zac for a few seconds and walked away. Hani looked at Zac with a worried expression and did the same.

*Great . . .*

The small traveling party left camp with Husam leading the way. Zac and the two other men each led one of the donkey carts. The air was still quite cool, and the plan was to be off the trail before the worst of the midday sun. The group moved steadily through the mountainous terrain. With the carts in tow, they stuck to a well-worn trail through the valley where the going was easy and only the soft creaking of the wheels broke the silence.

The temperature rose quickly as the sun climbed over the eastern peaks. The deep blue sky contrasted vividly with the grays and golds of the mountains. Husam held up a hand and signaled for the group to stop. He took a jug of water and some food from one of the carts, which he shared with the other two nomads, but not with Zac. Eager to avoid another confrontation, Zac pulled out his own canteen and sipped from it. The other two men chuckled at Husam's pettiness, but he snapped at them and trudged off, leaving an uneasy feeling over the group.

The small caravan resumed its journey. As they made their way up a rocky incline, one of the milk containers broke free from the back of Zac's cart and tumbled to the ground. It was dented but intact. He stopped and lifted the large container back into the rear of the cart.

Zac felt a sharp blow to the side of his head. It stunned him and knocked him back against the cart. He turned and saw Husam with a rock in his hand. The herder was naturally strong, and a life of manual labor had turned him into a mass of muscle. With Zac off balance and pinned against the cart, Husam dropped the rock and threw a punch to Zac's stomach. Husam cocked his arm for a third strike when Zac pushed off the cart and stepped forward, swinging his elbow into Husam's jaw. The nomad fell back to shake off the blow while Zac moved sideways, away from the cart. The other men shouted and gestured for the fighting to stop, but Husam ignored them. He drew his dagger and lunged.

Zac had practiced defending himself against an armed

attacker dozens of times in martial arts classes, but he'd never actually faced one until now. He pushed Husam's arm away to block the blade, then landed another elbow strike to the head before driving his knee between the nomad's legs. Husam dropped the knife and doubled over in pain. Zac struck with his knee again, this time to the face. The herder dropped to the ground, clutching his groin and bleeding from his mouth and nose.

Zac stepped back and watched. The other men were stunned by the sudden violence. It had taken just a few seconds and, in the end, it was Husam who lay beaten and bleeding on the ground. The two herders were only spectators, but the swift beating that Zac had unleashed upon their fellow nomad had clearly put them on edge.

Zac could kill the three of them with the pistol if he had to, but he still needed a ride to Bandar Abbas. One of the things he'd learned while working for the government was that there was a time for force and a time for diplomacy. Sensing a pivotal moment, he offered a hand to Husam to help him up. The herder lay on the ground, clutching his knees to his chest. He looked up at the outstretched hand and wiped his bloody nose on his sleeve. One of the other nomads said something but Husam turned away and wiped more blood from his face. With obvious difficulty he stood up on his own. Zac withdrew his hand and stepped back, mindful that wounded predators were often the most dangerous. Husam took a swig from the water jug and spit out a mouthful of pink water. He started walking, slowly and with difficulty, on the trail in front of the carts.

The next hour and a half passed in quiet tension.

Nothing was said and no breaks were taken. The sun blazed down upon them, but the nomads were unfazed by the heat, and even Zac had built up a tolerance for it.

Husam eventually resumed a normal pace and the blood on his clothes dried in the hot sun. By the time they reached the road he appeared almost normal. He spoke with the other nomads and the three of them tied a small tarp between the carts to create some shade. The four men crawled under the tarp and sat quietly in restless rapprochement as they awaited the arrival of the trader. The nomads mostly dozed, waking to the occasional sound of a passing car or truck, but Zac remained alert. An army jeep drove by without incident. With his deeply tanned skin, worn clothes, and scruffy beard, Zac was hiding in plain sight. But it was the thinnest of disguises. His camouflage would not survive even a single question.

One of the nomads roused the others when he spotted a medium-sized truck coming from the north. The men crawled out from under the tarp as the truck pulled off the road in front of them, the diesel engine groaning loudly as the driver downshifted. The old truck looked like the bastard child of a city bus and a dump truck, its indeterminate color buried under layers of dust and dirt. With a four-passenger cab, four wheels in the back, and a fenced-in bed, it was built for hard use.

The driver jumped down from the cab and walked to the back, which was filled nearly to capacity with a tower of hay. He was a fireplug of a man, with a barrel chest, thinning hair, and a clean-shaven face. Husam and the others greeted him warmly and exchanged hugs. One of the other nomads explained Zac's presence and the driver gave him a bear hug as well. To Zac's immense relief, the trader spoke some English. He introduced himself as Ahmet and told Zac that he would gladly take him to the market in Bandar Abbas. Husam remained silent.

With the four men working together, it took less than ten minutes to shoehorn the milk containers into the truck's bed. Husam spoke with one of the herders who would be returning the carts to camp while the other herder spoke with Ahmet. Zac could tell by the body language, and the expression on the trader's face, that the conversation was likely about the history between Husam and Zac. The driver nodded solemnly as the men parted.

With an encouraging shout, Ahmet climbed into the cab. Husam entered on the passenger side. He pointed at Zac then gestured to the bed of the truck. Zac hesitated for a moment until Ahmet looked over and yelled for him to get in the cab. Zac climbed up slowly and slid onto the wide bench seat, leaving plenty of room between Husam and himself.

Despite its heavy load, the truck performed well on the road. Ahmet occasionally made small talk with Husam or Zac but the ride passed mostly in silence. As they drove south, the rocky mountains and scrub-covered hills gave way to windswept dunes. They could see the heat rising off of the land. Even with the windows lowered, the temperature was stifling. Zac was grateful that he wasn't sleeping in a cave or staggering over the hot ground.

When they passed a sign indicating that Bandar Abbas was twenty kilometers away, Ahmet spoke to Zac.

"Where you want to go? Police? They help you?"

Zac hesitated then said, "No police. I lost my passport."

Ahmet looked over at Zac, then back out the windshield as he continued driving. The trader led a simple life, but he was not a simpleton. Like the elder in the nomads' camp, he likely doubted Zac's story about being a lost hiker. He spoke quietly to Husam, who nodded almost imperceptibly.

Ahmet stared straight ahead and said flatly, "You come to market with us. Find your way from there."

The remaining miles passed quietly until they rounded a corner at the outskirts of the city. Ahmet slowed the truck and merged into a long line of traffic. There was an army checkpoint on the road ahead. Ahmet scowled, Husam smiled, and Zac took a deep breath and reached for his gun.

## THIRTY

TWO ARMORED PERSONNEL carriers flanked the road ahead. Half a dozen heavily armed soldiers were deployed around the checkpoint, while two more crewed a 12.7mm machine gun mounted atop one of the APCs. The troops were alert and focused despite the heat and humidity. Ahmet muttered something while the three of them waited in the truck. Zac watched the cars ahead of them stop at the checkpoint. Four soldiers formed a box around each vehicle while two others interviewed the passengers.

Zac's heart was pounding. He could feel each bead of sweat as it dripped down his face. When their truck was next in line, he poked Husam in the ribs. The nomad shot back a contemptuous look until he saw that it was a semi-automatic pistol that was pressed against his side. The arrogance drained from his face and he immediately sat up straight, swallowed hard, and looked out the windshield. Zac draped his parka over the pistol and gazed out the window.

The soldiers waved the old truck up to the checkpoint. Zac slouched in his seat and tried to look bored. The mounted machine gun was barely twenty-five feet away and he could see the ammunition belt hanging down from the weapon, the sun glinting off the copper-jacketed bullets. Two soldiers approached the truck and the one on the driver's side began to question Ahmet. He shook his head while he talked with the soldier. The soldier on the passenger side spoke up a moment later. In his hand was a full-page photocopy of Zac's passport photo. The picture had been taken several years ago and enlarged so many times that the reproduction was a poor likeness. Still, Zac could barely breathe as he looked at the image of his own face. The soldier said something Zac didn't understand. His hand tightened on the grip of the pistol. The soldier looked directly at Zac and spoke again. This time he held up the paper and made an exaggerated display of the photo. Zac glanced at the picture of himself taken just before he'd joined CIA. He was young, pale, and clean shaven. He shook his head, his profile to the soldier.

Husam looked at the picture and hesitated. His eyes widened as he recognized the man in the photo. Husam looked at the soldier. The two men made eye contact. Zac pressed the muzzle of the pistol deeper into Husam's ribs. If bullets started flying, Zac wouldn't make it out of there alive, but he'd decided days ago that dying quickly in a shootout would be better than being tortured for the rest of his life by Colonel Arzaman. Husam mumbled a couple of words and shook his head. The soldier yelled to his squad mates and the truck was waved through.

Everyone was quiet in the cab of the truck as Ahmet drove down a wide boulevard into the eastern part of the city. Zac pulled the pistol off Husam's ribs but continued to grip it tightly. Staring out the window, Zac quickly realized that Bandar Abbas was not the beautiful seaside metropolis he'd expected. Except for an ornate mosque, everything that wasn't dust or sand seemed to be concrete. The buildings, the open space, and even the trees seemed to have been poured into dull, geometric forms. As they drove deeper into the heart of the city the buildings grew in height but not in character. The entire city looked like a prison.

The waterfront market came into view a few blocks to the south. Despite the overpowering heat and humidity, the streets were crowded with pedestrians. Most of the men were dressed comfortably in long pants and short-sleeve shirts, but many of the women were clad from head to toe in black *chadors*, their faces covered with red veils. Stalls and carts lined both sides of the road with purveyors of everything from spices to livestock. Ahmet slowed the truck as they threaded their way through the crowds and past an enormous fish market.

He spoke quietly with Husam for a moment, then parked on a side street and stepped down from the truck, beckoning the others to follow. Husam quickly slid off the seat and walked into a shop. Zac tucked the pistol in his pants and covered it with his loose-fitting shirt before jumping down.

Ahmet took Zac gently by the arm and spoke. "We unload milk here. It best if you go now."

Zac wanted to trust Ahmet, but he and Husam had spoken several times in the truck and Zac hadn't understood a word. There was also a chance that Ahmet recognized Zac as the man in the picture at the checkpoint. Husam and Ahmet had cultural, business, and maybe even family ties that bound them together. They would look out for each other.

And they'd left Zac no choice but to use it against them.

"I'll help."

He climbed into the bed of the truck and started handing down milk containers. Ahmet smiled and nodded in appreciation, not realizing that he'd just become a hostage.

He told Zac that it would take a few hours for Husam to locate what he needed and negotiate prices with the various merchants. The two Iranians would sleep in the truck tonight and drive back early in the morning. Zac smiled and lowered another container down. When they'd finished unloading the milk, he jumped down and leaned against the truck. Husam emerged from the shop with a fat man in a filthy shirt. The two men reviewed a bundle of papers on a clipboard. Ahmet gestured toward the man carrying the clipboard.

"Husam will be haggling with that one forever. He's so tight even water doesn't run out of his hand."

The fat man and Husam walked back to the shop. Husam looked over his shoulder and motioned for Ahmet to join them, but the trader just smiled and waved for Husam to go on alone. Husam shook his head crossly and beckoned Ahmet again. Zac put his arm around Ahmet's shoulders and gave him a comradely squeeze.

"Tell Husam we'll be fine. You can help me find the French consulate."

Husam was persistent. He started walking toward the truck. Zac kept his left arm around Ahmet's shoulders and slid his right hand under his shirt to the pistol tucked in his waistband. Husam saw the gun and understood immediately.

*Rat me out and Ahmet dies.*

Torn between his desire to exact revenge and his need to ensure Ahmet's safety, Husam rejoined the man with the clipboard and disappeared into the store.

"Let's see what we can find," Zac said as he headed toward the waterfront.

Keeping Ahmet close would allow Zac to do his reconnaissance in greater safety. There were a few tourists about, but he wanted to blend in as much as possible. Crossing the street in the wrong place, failing to observe proper Islamic customs, or being unable to read a simple sign could cause an alert policeman to stop and question him. With no language skills, no identification, and a loaded pistol, Zac would be as good as dead.

A steady breeze helped offset the stifling heat as they neared the water. Zac looked out to sea while they walked along the coastal promenade. Brightly painted container ships, dilapidated ferries, and armed military vessels all plied the waters just offshore.

Zac was well aware that the United States didn't maintain diplomatic relations with Iran, but he hoped that he could find the consulate of a friendly Western nation where he could make a call to Langley or London. He occasionally wondered aloud if the French consulate might be around this block or maybe the next, but for the most part the two men wandered in companionable silence. Ahmet knew nothing of any foreign presence in the city beyond the many Pakistani and Indian immigrants who worked there.

The pair walked past a massive artificial harbor that was protected by breakwaters on three sides. A narrow channel provided the only access to the Persian Gulf. Inside the harbor were passenger ferries, commercial fishing boats, and a number of smaller vessels in a variety of sizes. There were plenty of boats he could take if he decided to leave Iran by sea; but the larger ones, forty to fifty feet long, would require a crew to operate while the smaller ones, simple skiffs with outboard engines, would never make it across the Strait of Hormuz. Zac kept searching until a white sailboat on the eastern side of the breakwater caught his eye. He wanted to run onto the docks at that very moment, but he didn't want to give Ahmet any clues about his method of escape. Zac would return alone.

The end of the promenade dovetailed with a dark, sandy beach. Ahmet suggested they turn around, assuring Zac that there was nothing of interest to him down there. Zac nodded, still thinking about the white sailboat. Off in the distance, past the beach, was the seaport. It was massive. Even from two miles away, Zac could see warships and commercial vessels in the harbor. Security there would be tight. It would be a place to avoid.

Zac glanced out to sea as they walked back to the center of town. He'd spent half his career studying maps of the region and he knew where he wanted to go, south across the Strait of Hormuz to the United Arab Emirates. Oman was a few miles closer, but he knew nothing about it. Saudi Arabia was too far, and probably had hundreds of miles of undeveloped coastline. He could make land there and be worse off than he was now. The UAE was a modern and Western-friendly country and Dubai was a cosmopolitan and sophisticated Middle Eastern city. Zac had been there once before, and could easily find the U.S. consulate once he made land.

He was deep in thought when he noticed Ahmet approaching a man in uniform, a policeman. Zac's heart almost stopped, but the officer mostly ignored the two nomads and pointed in another direction.

"He say it over here," said Ahmet with a grin as he motioned for Zac to follow.

The officer had directed them to what turned out to be the Indian consulate. As they stood out front, the Great Mosque began to broadcast the *azan*, calling the faithful to sunset prayers. Ahmet said he needed to leave to find a place to pray, so Zac thanked his new friend one last time and dashed up the steps.

The encounter with the policeman confirmed for Zac that he needed to get out of Iran as soon as possible. Even if he could reach someone at CIA, it would take them hours, if not days, to mount a rescue mission, and Zac's presence on the streets was a disaster waiting to happen. He figured he had maybe two hours before Ahmet made it back to the truck and Husam went to the police.

Zac stepped into the consulate and took a seat by a window, pretending to read a brochure and visa application. When most of the people on the street had risen from their prayers, he stepped outside and headed for the waterfront promenade, dumping the papers in a garbage can along the way.

The area was brightly lit and brimming with people. Even from a distance he could smell the harsh aroma of the local cigarettes. Crowds of men stood about, chatting in groups and strolling through the flea market. Those walking along the waterfront were of the city's middle class. The men wore collared shirts and kept their heads uncovered. Zac's ratty clothes and *chafiye* were fine around the farmers' market, but out here they invited stares and an occasional chuckle. Eager to avoid attracting attention, he walked onto one of the docks and ducked out of sight behind a storage shed. He stuffed the *chafiye* in his jacket and rinsed his face and hair with brackish water from a nearby hose.

Only a few mariners remained on the docks, unloading the day's catch from their fishing boats and making ready for the next day. Zac walked around the bottom of the U-shaped harbor and started up the eastern side, heading toward the white sailboat he'd spotted while walking with Ahmet. He walked out along the dock until the light from the promenade faded away and only the moon lit his way. Twice he stopped and pretended to look at the boats tied up along the pier, checking for anyone behind him, but he was completely alone. The sailboat was halfway out, tied up among a few other pleasure craft in various states of disrepair.

It was white fiberglass, twenty or thirty years old, with a small forward cabin and a fixed compass. He paced it off as he walked. It was twenty-two feet long. The sails were aboard and it looked as if it had been reasonably maintained. It wasn't perfect, but it was the best he'd seen, and with Ahmet on his way to meet Husam, it would have to do.

Zac had stuffed his pockets with food before he left the nomads' camp, but his canteen held only enough water for half a day at sea. The water he'd used earlier to wash up had been brackish, but it wasn't seawater. If he could find a bucket to store some, it might mean the difference between life and death if his journey took longer than expected. He found another maintenance shed farther out, near the mouth of the harbor. The door was locked, but Zac threw his shoulder against it and it broke easily. He used his lighter to look around and smiled at his good fortune. Stacked against the wall were cases of bottled water and half a dozen fishing rods. In ten minutes he'd loaded the boat and raised the sails.

Zac pushed off on his way to freedom, vowing to never again set foot in Iran.

---

## THIRTY-ONE

CELIA HAD BEEN back in London less than twenty-four hours. Still feeling the effects of jet lag, she was resting in her bedroom when the telephone rang in her South Kensington home. She was grateful when her housekeeper answered the call.

A soft knock on the door made Celia sit up in bed. The housekeeper had been with her for over ten years and had excellent intuition. If she was knocking now, then either someone had died or one of Celia's grandchildren was calling. The housekeeper was very good about collecting messages from everyone else.

"Yes, Fiona?"

"It's Sir James from Singapore, my lady. He said it was important."

"Of course. Thank you. I'll pick it up in here."

Celia stood and rubbed her eyes. James was the de facto leader of their merry band of expats and more than once he had been the bearer of bad news.

"Hello, James. Fiona said it was important. Is everyone all right?"

"Yes, yes, Celia. I suspect Geoffrey is probably still

recovering from the Irish flu but it's nothing he hasn't had a thousand times before. Sorry to interrupt your rest, but I have a piece of news I thought you'd want to hear. What was the name of that young American chap you befriended on your flight from London? The one you mentioned to us at the Raffles Grill?"

"Zachary Miller. Why?"

"I'm afraid that's what I thought. Honestly, I was hoping I'd misremembered."

"Slim chance of that. What's happened?"

"Well, it seems as if he's in quite a spot of trouble. I just saw on the telly that he's wanted for offing a street-walker over here. It's getting quite a bit of press."

"Impossible."

"Unfortunately there's a pile of evidence. Forensics, you know."

"Has he confessed?"

"No. They're searching for him now. That's why it was on the news. They're asking for assistance from the public."

"James, you've known me a long time. I'm an excellent judge of character. I know when someone is spinning me, and that young man was not the sort. I told you something was wrong with that fellow at the immigration counter and now I'm utterly convinced that there's foul play afoot."

"I do remember what you said and frankly I'm surprised this murder is getting so much media attention over here. It's the kind of thing the government usually downplays."

"You see? That's something else that's not quite right. James, I need you to do me a favor."

"Oh, I hadn't seen this coming."

"Of course you did. Could you make a call? I know you still know people over at MI6, or SIS, or whatever it's called now."

"What makes you think that?"

"James, you worked for the Foreign Office for forty years and you're one of the sharpest people I know, yet you never seemed to get a decent promotion. You bounced from country to country as a commercial attaché, diplomatic liaison, or half a dozen other vague occupations, the duties of which no one ever seemed to know. You disappeared for weeks at a time . . ."

"OK. I'll make the bloody call. Just stop talking before we both end up on the wrong side of the Official Secrets Act."

# THIRTY-TWO

A GENTLE NIGHT BREEZE carried the little sailboat south toward the Strait of Hormuz. Gone were the fishy, tidal smells of shore and the sounds and lights of Bandar Abbas. Zac tied off the tiller and soon fell asleep on the cockpit seat, waking only occasionally to the passing wake of a distant ship.

He was wide awake by sunrise. He reckoned he'd covered twenty or thirty miles, yet there was still no land in sight. The Strait was supposed to be a strategic bottleneck for the world's oil, a chokepoint where ships and even whole economies could be held hostage, yet it appeared to be massive. He began to think that he might be lost. He knew that he was navigating imprecisely, with only memories of maps to guide him, but he'd been disciplined about heading south. Still, between detours for ship traffic and the unknown effects of the current, there was a real chance that he'd been pushed miles off course. If he was wrong by twenty degrees in either direction, he could end up lost in the Gulf of Oman or deep in the Persian Gulf.

The sunset that night seemed to happen in slow motion. The cloudless blue sky lingered overhead until the falling light struck the dust-filled air of far-off deserts. In seconds, orange and red streaks erupted from the horizon and shot high into the atmosphere. Zac had been at sea almost twenty-four hours, and panic was setting in. A few times during the day he had seen faint images of distant land but each time the sightings had proved fleeting and ultimately false. By this time he'd expected to be across the Strait and to the northern tip of the UAE, if not all the way to Dubai.

Within an hour it was dark and the sky and sea blended together into a single, interminable blackness. Ships were visible only by their lights. Depth perception and navigation became nerve-racking and imprecise. He could easily be run down by a ship or miss his destination altogether.

Constantly distracted by hunger, he thought of the steaks his mother used to grill when he was a boy, and of the duck dumplings at Park Chinois, his favorite restaurant in London. He recalled the melted raclette he'd been eating in Paris just before his ill-fated trip, but the memory of the food quickly gave way to thoughts of the woman he'd been sharing it with. His mind was ensconced in pleasant memories when a powerful wave crashed into the side of the sailboat and nearly rolled it over.

Zac tumbled across the cockpit and his face slammed into the hard fiberglass. A second wave crashed over the side, flooding the cockpit and pushing him toward the open sea. The boat rolled to its side again and he was swept overboard. He made a desperate lunge for the rail with both hands. He caught it with one. He held on with all his strength, fighting the onslaught of water that was trying to separate him from the boat.

The water kept coming, forcing its way into his nose and mouth before pushing him under. Zac began to gag, inhaling more seawater. His grip on the wet rail weakened. Only the tips of his fingers kept him from being cast adrift.

But he held on and raised his head above the sea. The black hull of a supertanker blocked out the sky. The huge ship pushed a hundred million gallons of water out of its path every thousand feet. The displaced water formed the ship's wake, meaning fifty million gallons of water would have to pass under, over, or through Zac and the little fiberglass boat before the ship would be gone.

Zac looked up at the tanker and came to the horrific realization that it was only the lesser bow wake that had so violently upended his own small craft. He hauled himself back into the sailboat and watched, awestruck, as the tanker passed alongside. The sailboat was nearly swamped. If he didn't turn her toward the upcoming stern wake, the giant waves might send her to the bottom. Zac spat out a mouthful of blood and followed it with a curse as he pushed the tiller over hard. With hundreds of gallons of seawater aboard, and the tanker fouling the wind, the little boat wouldn't turn. He pumped the tiller back and forth, trying to generate enough speed to turn into the oncoming walls of water. The tanker's engines grew louder as the stern approached.

Zac leaned over and pulled the tiller to his chest. Slowly the bow began to swing around. When the wake hit, the sailboat rolled to her side, but Zac was able to steer again as she crested the wave. He pointed her into the next wake and the seawater inside the sailboat acted like ballast, steadying her as she rode out the remaining waves and sailed into calmer water.

After a few minutes the little sailboat finally stopped pitching and rolling. Zac stood in the knee-deep water, spat out another mouthful of blood, and swore at the tanker's stern as it steamed off into the night.

## THIRTY-THREE

T HE SUPERTANKER HAD been gone for several hours by the time Zac finished bailing out the sailboat. He was weary and sore, yet his spirits were high. He'd spotted a faint aura of light in the distance. It soon turned into a steady stream of civilization. Clusters of buildings illuminated the coastline and the lights of distant planes were visible as they flew between unseen airports.

Finding Dubai would not be hard if Zac had in fact located the Emirati coast. The United Arab Emirates was a union of seven wealthy monarchies, and Dubai was the most open and flamboyant of the group. Zac was especially interested in its often outlandish buildings, not out of any keen appreciation for architecture, but because it made the city-state nearly impossible to miss from the sea.

Dubai was home to not only the tallest building in the world but one of its finest hotels too. The sail-shaped Burj Al Arab was located on a small island attached to the mainland. Zac hadn't stayed there on his government expense account, but the hotel's distinctive shape would be easy to spot, and the staff would know how to contact the American embassy. If he could get to the Burj, he would be safe.

After a thorough check for ship traffic, Zac tied off the tiller and settled in for a quick nap. He awoke to the light of dawn and sailed closer to shore. From ten miles out he could easily distinguish major buildings and prominent features on land. He was pleased that his escape plan was working. It had been rough, and it had been dangerous, but everything he saw led him to believe that he was on his way to Dubai.

The marine traffic picked up and Zac trimmed the sails and headed toward a seaport that lay dead ahead. Cargo ships and private boats plied the waters just off-shore. A hundred-foot motor yacht raced past at thirty knots, its white hull and gold fittings gleaming in the bright sunshine. Zac felt for a moment as if he were back in the West. It wasn't Monaco or Newport, but it sure as hell wasn't Bandar Abbas either.

A freighter laden with stacks of containers sounded its horn and put to sea from the port, putting Zac directly in its path. He tried to turn the little sailboat but the breeze had died. The freighter sounded its horn again, but Zac was dead in the water.

Hemmed in by several small islands, the six-hundred-foot ship closed in on the sailboat. Finally, with its rudder over hard and engine reversed, the ship was able to navigate around the much smaller boat and avert a collision. Zac waved sheepishly before turning around to resume his search for the Burj. Only then did he notice the power boat slowing to a halt a hundred feet off his bow.

He didn't recognize the sleek craft from its white and red exterior, but the flashing blue lights atop the bridge meant the same thing everywhere.

*Busted.*

The police boat was nearly fifty feet long, with a raked bow and three inboard engines. It hailed Zac over its loudspeaker in a language he didn't understand. He pointed at his empty sails and turned up his hands in an attempt to convey his predicament. The motor boat coasted past. The four officers aboard appeared relaxed, though one of them had a rifle slung over his shoulder. The police boat circled around behind the sailboat and stopped twenty feet off its side.

"Do you speak English?" Zac shouted.

"You are *American*?" one of the officers responded with surprise.

"Yes. The wind just died on me. I'm sorry."

"That ship had right of way, you know."

"I tried to get out of her way but I couldn't turn." Zac again gestured at the slack and unmoving sails. "I'm making my way to the Burj Al Arab."

The officer said something to the other policemen, and they both looked at Zac.

"Is this your boat?"

"I rented it at the hotel."

The English-speaking officer conferred with another man aboard. Neither took his eyes off Zac while they spoke.

Over the loudspeaker this time: "We are coming aboard to inspect your vessel."

The police boat maneuvered deftly alongside and two

officers stepped down into the sailboat. The one with the rifle watched from the police boat.

The English-speaking officer asked, "May I see your passport, please?"

"It's back in my hotel room. I was afraid I might lose it out here. I'm an American citizen."

While Zac was speaking, the other officer searched the boat. He was short and stocky, with a stern expression and eyes that darted about.

"I see. And you are a guest at the Burj Al Arab? You rented this boat from there?"

"Yes. Well, nearby. If you call the American embassy, they can verify my citizenship."

"The American embassy is down in Abu Dhabi. We have a consulate here in Dubai, but first I think I will call the Burj Al Arab. There is no need to involve the consulate at this point." The officer pulled out a cell phone but didn't dial. "What is your name?"

Out of the corner of his eye Zac saw the stocky officer pick something up. It was Zac's windbreaker.

"Please call the consulate. They'll straighten this out right away."

Zac saw the stocky one heft the rolled-up windbreaker in his hand, as if he was wondering what made it so heavy.

*The pistol.*

"Your name, please?" asked the English-speaking officer again.

"Zachary Miller, but please call the consulate first."

The stocky officer lifted the windbreaker by its collar.

"Is there a problem? You do not want me to call the Burj?"

The right side of the jacket was sagging. The stocky officer began to unzip the pocket.

"I am an American citizen. Please call the consulate immediately," Zac shouted.

The officers stopped what they were doing and looked at him. Apparently, they all spoke English.

"Very well. I will call the consulate."

He began to type into his cell phone when the stocky officer shouted, "Gun!"

The officer with the rifle pointed it squarely at Zac's chest. Zac slowly raised his hands above his head. His last chance for talking his way out of his predicament had just disappeared. Within minutes he was handcuffed and in a life preserver, riding in the police boat as they towed the sailboat to shore. He was furious with himself for keeping the gun aboard the sailboat.

He stared out the window of the BMW police car as it drove along the coast and past the seaport. Massive gantry cranes moved on rails over colorful stacks of shipping containers, swiftly loading and unloading the ships berthed along the pier. When they arrived at the police station, Zac took solace in the modern brushed steel and glass building. With rows of neatly parked police cars, the polished, professional appearance contrasted starkly with the dusty warehouse in Iran.

He was promptly booked by a desk officer and told the U.S. consulate would be notified, as it would be anytime an American citizen had been arrested. Zac smiled. Before he'd left London, Peter Clements had told him that his name would be on a secret watch list at all U.S. embassies and consulates. CIA would be notified if there was a hit anywhere in the world. Possession of the gun would complicate the situation, but he had committed no violence in the UAE and governments had long histories of handling these sorts of things discreetly among themselves.

A plainclothes officer escorted Zac from the holding cell a few hours later. He was in his mid-forties, with a muscular physique and streaks of gray peppering the edges of his thick black hair and trim beard. A guard let the two men into an interview room and the plainclothes officer motioned with one of his meaty hands for Zac to sit. He looked thoughtfully at Zac as he stroked his beard.

"So, Mr. Miller," he began in very good English, "I am Colonel Assad of the Dubai police. Please tell me why you are here."

Zac looked up at the imposing figure.

"I'm an American citizen and I lost my passport. If you let me speak with someone at the U.S. consulate, I can straighten everything out."

"The desk officer called the U.S. consulate. Apparently it is closed today for the American holiday of Thanksgiving. He also tried the embassy in Abu Dhabi. It too was closed." He folded his arms across his chest. "Which brings us back to my question, which you did not answer: Why are you here?"

The officer obviously knew why Zac had been arrested, but he was fishing for something else. If Zac told him the whole story, Assad would dismiss it as the ramblings of a madman. But how could Zac explain being in Dubai with no identification, no money, and a gun? He'd assumed that once the consulate was involved he could tell the truth, but that wasn't going to happen today. He said nothing.

"Perhaps we should work our way backward," Assad continued, a touch of irritation in his voice. "Why are you in Dubai?"

Zac stared blankly at the floor.

"Let's keep it factual, then. Where did you get the boat?"

The officer frowned as Zac remained mute.

"I'll answer all your questions," he said eventually. "But I'd like someone from the consulate here."

"Mr. Miller, I hope you are not under the illusion that the laws of the United States apply here. We notify your consulate merely as a courtesy." His voice remained calm as he spoke. "We are here to protect the interests of the Emirate of Dubai. For your own sake, I suggest you start giving me some answers."

The truth was out of the question. Zac was an American agent who had killed six soldiers and a civilian inside Iran. He needed to avoid tying himself to Iran at all costs. If the Iranian government became involved, it would have legitimate grounds for extraditing him. He was fighting a sovereign nation, a government that relished conflict with the Western world. Any alibi he might invent would be useless without the support of his own government. He had to contact the U.S. authorities.

Zac looked up, but said nothing.

Assad went on. "Maybe I should start. The marine officers approached you because you failed to yield to a ship leaving port. Hardly a capital offense." He shrugged. "Their intent was only to remind you of the rules of the sea. However, upon nearing your vessel, several inconsistencies quickly became apparent." A contemptuous edge crept into his voice. "You claimed to be staying at the Burj Al Arab, the finest hotel in Dubai. It is quite expensive, yet you are an American dressed like an Arab peasant. Your clothes are tattered and filthy." Assad raised an eyebrow as he looked at Zac. "The boat you claimed to rent from the hotel was old, dirty, and unlikely to be rented from anywhere in Dubai, much less the Burj."

There was no disputing what Assad had said.

"Fine. Any police officer in the world would notice these inconsistencies, but then . . ." He scowled as he spoke the next words. "There was Perso-Arabic script on the back of the boat, and you were carrying a gun."

Zac's breathing quickened. He'd noticed the writing on the stern of the boat when he'd stolen it, but given his lack of other options he hadn't given it a second thought. Now it had tied him back to Iran.

"Do you know that pistol is made in Iran? It's a PC-9, made only for their army officers. It's quite unique, really."

Zac could feel his heart pounding.

"We don't get many Iranian pleasure boaters down here and no one ever takes a small boat like that across the Strait," Assad said with almost a touch of admiration in his voice.

Zac's survival instincts were kicking in. The two men were about the same height, but the cop was thicker everywhere, and he probably knew how to handle himself. With his adrenaline pumping Zac could give him a fight, but they'd still be locked inside the interview room.

Assad sensed the change in Zac's demeanor and rapped on the door. A guard entered immediately.

The police officer looked back over his shoulder before he left. "Let us not make this more difficult than it needs to be."

ASSAD RETURNED A few hours later with a different guard. The new man stepped into the room and roughly handcuffed Zac before leading him into the hallway. The trio passed through an unmarked door and down three flights of stairs before exiting into a long and dimly lit passageway. The concrete walls and floor were dirty, and appeared to predate the main building by several decades. The men walked for a few minutes until the guard stopped and unlocked a door. Assad motioned Zac inside. The room was lit by a single lightbulb inside a wire cage. The pale green paint on the cinder blocks was peeling from years of neglect. The guard removed the handcuffs and shoved Zac against the wall.

"I will be back. Think about your situation, Mr. Miller. Think carefully," said Assad.

The guard closed the heavy steel door and the locking bolts slid into place. It was utterly silent inside the cell. It had no ventilation, no furniture, and no toilet. The optimism Zac had felt upon entering the Dubai police station was a distant memory. He slumped to the ground and stared at the door, with his back up against the wall.

## THIRTY-FOUR

T HE HOT AND stagnant air inside the cell drained
what little energy Zac had, yet he slept only in fits
and starts, curled up on the concrete floor. The
single overhead light robbed him of any sense of time.
Eventually he relieved himself in a corner of the room,
only to be further tormented by the acrid odor.

The cell was nothing like the rest of the Dubai police
station. The room was more like a dungeon; isolated, silent, and far removed from the main building. It was a
place where things were done off-the-record and out of
the public eye. Hour after hour, Zac sat and stared at the
light, alone with his destructive thoughts. When the deadbolts finally slid back, he didn't know whether to be relieved or terrified.

Assad entered the cell in a fresh suit and smelling of
strong cologne. A guard closed the door from the outside.

"Good news," Assad said with a grin. "We have spoken with your consulate and they are going to send
someone to meet with you."

"When?"

"Soon. Perhaps in the next few hours. Diplomats work on their own schedules."

"Did they say anything else?"

"Only that they would send someone over. We need to get you ready for your meeting." Assad rapped on the heavy steel door and shouted something to the guard outside.

The bolts slid back and the guard opened the door with one hand resting on his holstered pistol.

"Come, we will prepare you."

The guard handcuffed Zac and they walked in silence to another room, which was furnished with a heavy wooden table and four sturdy chairs. It had the same pale green cinderblock walls and stale air as the rest of the dungeon. Assad motioned Zac to a chair. The guard left and locked the door behind him.

"We need you to sign a few documents before the representative from your consulate gets here." Assad laid two sheets of paper on the table in front of Zac. They were full of Arabic script with a place for his signature at the bottom. Assad handed him a cheap ballpoint pen.

"I can't read this," Zac said.

"Not to worry. The first page says only that you entered the country illegally. The second page acknowledges that you were in possession of a gun. We left out the origin of the gun and the boat. There is no point in complicating matters by involving the Iranians."

"I'll sign these when I've had the chance to speak with someone from the consulate."

"There is nothing to be afraid of. These are mere formalities."

"Then I'll wait until the rep from the consulate is here before I sign them."

"Life here will be easier for you if you cooperate."

"I'm not going to sign something I don't fucking understand."

Assad cleared his throat. "What you don't seem to *understand* is that you have no rights here."

"I have the right not to sign these. All I want is for someone from the U.S. government to be here."

Assad paced around the room. He spoke softly. "Perhaps I will call the consulate and tell them that the man we picked up turned out not to be American after all. The man we caught trying to enter the country illegally, in a stolen vessel, with a foreign military weapon, was only pretending to be American. It would be one less headache for them, and we have a very cordial relationship with the United States. They wouldn't give it a second thought."

Zac stared at the forms.

Assad glared at Zac. "Sign the papers."

"Not happening."

Assad shouted to the guard, *"Iftah il-baab!"* and the door opened a moment later. Assad stormed out of the room.

AFTER SEVERAL HOURS the door opened again and a new man entered the room. Tall and nearly emaciated, with an expressionless face and a mat of greasy hair, he pushed a wooden cart into the center of the room. Zac pushed back against his chair.

Assad entered a moment later. "This is Sabir. He does not work for the police department. In fact, right now, I am not working for the police department." Assad carefully folded his suit coat and placed it on the table, revealing a semi-automatic pistol on his hip.

"So why was an American sneaking out of Iran? I know the two countries have very strained relations, but it is most unusual. Of course, Iran is no great friend to the Emirates either. The Iranian government has what you call an 'inferiority complex.' Did I say that right?" He smiled. "They are bullies. However, the Persian people are some of the finest in the world; educated, artistic, philosophical. My wife was from Iran, from Bandar Abbas, in fact." He smiled again, acknowledging Zac's connection to the city.

"Many years ago, she took a trip home with our son to visit her parents. On the day they were to return, their flight turned out over the Gulf and began to climb. It was toward the end of the Iran-Iraq War and American warships were in the Gulf, keeping the Strait 'safe' for your shipments of oil. One of the American ships fired two missiles at the plane carrying my family, and a minute later my wife and son crashed into the sea, dead. I have seen it in my mind ten thousand times."

Assad's tone changed. The emotion left his voice. "The families of those killed gathered for a memorial service in Tehran. In the following days and months, I learned much about what happened over the Strait that day."

He resumed pacing, looking only at the floor.

"I learned that the American ship, the *Vincennes*, had

the most sophisticated radar system in the world, able to track over one hundred targets at once. I learned that planes attacking ships do not climb slowly as they approach their targets, but descend rapidly, to pick up speed and hide from radar. I also learned that the captain of the ship was given a medal for his actions . . . But the most important thing I learned was from an Iranian army officer whom I met at the memorial. His brother had been the copilot of the flight. This officer learned through his own contacts that the attack was not the mistake of a frightened ship captain, but a calculated act of murder, ordered at the highest levels of your government as a 'lesson' to Iran for defending itself from America's steadfast and trustworthy ally, Iraq."

Assad stopped in front of Zac and shook his head in disgust.

"You." He jabbed a thick finger into Zac's chest. "You Americans supported Saddam Hussein in the war with Iran. And for what? You have invaded Iraq *twice* since then. What kind of ally does that? An 'ally' of convenience, an 'ally' whose only concern is its own supply of oil. Nearly a million Muslim boys died from Western weapons in those three wars. They were the future of our culture. They were the bearers of our hope and prosperity, the husbands and fathers of generations to come. They were my son."

Zac stared down at the floor. He had felt the same pain and loss, the anger and hatred. He too had wanted retribution for the reckless actions of the person who had shattered his own family, but Assad was wrong about America.

Zac looked up and shook his head.

"You don't know what you're talking about."

Assad slapped him across the face. "You don't think so? You still want to see someone from your government? Fine. But you will answer my questions first."

He muttered something in Arabic to Sabir. The man nodded and removed a set of thick jumper cables from the cart. He clamped one of the leads to Zac's right hand and another to his left foot. Slowly and methodically, Sabir attached a rheostat and a heavy-duty car battery to the other end of the jumper cables. He glanced up at Assad and received a simple nod in return.

The first shock was mild, just enough to confirm that the system was working. Zac's body tensed. The voltage shot from his hand to his foot, stimulating every nerve and muscle in between. Satisfied with the reaction, Sabir looked at Assad and smiled.

"Those many years ago when I was in Iran mourning my lost wife and son," Assad began, "I spent much time with that young army officer. He had been gravely wounded in battle, but he held his head high and his back straight. We befriended another police officer who was also grieving. The three of us were kindred spirits. We spoke as if we'd known each other our whole lives. The army officer taught us about using adversity to grow one's character. So often in life disasters become debilitating. People lose heart, lose the will to continue the daily struggle that life can be. He taught us that we must steel ourselves to do what must be done, however difficult or unpleasant it may seem. He taught us about true courage. He taught us about suffering and pain."

Assad looked Zac over. "And now, I am going to teach you about suffering and pain."

Sabir smiled again.

"I am going to ask many questions. I suggest you answer them quickly and truthfully. I already know the answers to some of the questions; to others, I do not. If I think you are lying, or taking too long to answer, then what you just felt will not even be a taste of what is in store for you."

Assad launched into a rapid-fire interrogation.

"What is your name?"

"Zachary Miller."

"Where are you from?"

"The U.S., but I live in England."

"Who do you work for?"

"E.A.D."

Assad shook his head and held up one finger.

Sabir twisted the dial briefly. Zac's eyes widened as the shock ran through his body. He felt fine as soon as it stopped, but his heart was racing.

"Consider that a warning. Why were you in Iran?"

"My plane had some sort of mechanical trouble. We made an emergency landing."

"What was the problem with the plane?"

"I'm not sure. We had an engine failure, I think."

"What flight was it?"

"British Airways. I don't remember the number, London to Singapore."

"Who do you work for?"

"E.A.D. Electronic Architecture Development."

Assad held up three fingers. Sabir turned the dial and

Zac felt like a dozen knives stabbed him at once. He strained against the handcuffs and his breathing became shallow and rapid. The questions came more quickly.

"Where did your plane land?"

"I don't . . . Wait, I think it was Sirjan."

"That's a long way from Bandar Abbas. Why did you not stay with the other passengers?"

"They grabbed me when I went to the bathroom."

"The other passengers grabbed you?"

"Soldiers."

"Why you?"

"I took a picture, a couple of pictures, of the sunset. It was all a mistake."

"What was in the pictures?"

"Nothing. Mountains. Maybe some houses. I don't know. I never left the airport."

"Are you with the CIA?"

"No."

"SIS?"

"No! I was on a business trip. The plane . . ."

Assad held up five fingers and Sabir sent another jolt of electricity blasting through Zac's body. He screamed and his body convulsed until the cable fell from his foot.

Sabir bent down and tied Zac's ankles to the chair as Assad watched, his elbow resting on his holstered pistol. The electrician reattached the jumper cable to Zac's foot.

"Tell me, spy, who do you really work for?" Assad whispered.

This time he did not wait for an answer. He held up five fingers and kept them up. Zac let out a long, guttural scream. When Sabir finally cut the voltage, Zac's body went limp but Assad resumed the questioning immediately.

"Where did you get the gun?"

Zac hesitated for a second and Sabir didn't wait to be told. He shocked Zac again.

"Where did you get the gun?"

"I found it."

Assad grabbed the controller and twisted the knob to full power. Zac thrashed about in pain, screaming. He feared his heart might explode inside his chest. Assad cut the power and threw the controller back in Sabir's lap.

"How about some water?" Assad asked. He lifted a jug from the cart and dumped it over Zac's head, soaking his clothing and leaving his bare feet resting in a puddle.

Assad flashed one finger at Sabir and the shock hit Zac like a city bus. His limbs exploded against their restraints as if repelled from his body by force. He screamed; a long, agonizing plea, but Assad was relentless.

"Where did you get the gun?"

"I . . . I got it from a soldier," Zac answered breathlessly.

"He gave it to you?"

Zac hesitated and was shocked again. His limbs felt as if they were on fire. Even in his worst nightmares he had never dreamed that such pain existed.

"I killed him."

"Where was this?"

"I don't know."

Assad jolted him again, this time on setting number three. Zac was numb.

". . . A building in the mountains. I don't know."

"Tell me who you work for!"

"E.A.D! I told you . . . E.A.D."

Assad held up five fingers. Sabir turned the dial to full power but this time Zac went limp. His eyes rolled back in his head and his body twitched.

"Stop!" Assad cried. "He's of no use to us dead."

Sabir cut the power and cowered like a scolded dog.

Zac lapsed in and out of consciousness, his chin now resting on his chest.

Assad felt a pulse in one of Zac's arteries and concluded that the prisoner would live. The police officer stood in contemplation for a few moments before he called for the guard. As he walked out of the room he looked over his shoulder and said, "OK, Mr. Miller. You will have your visit with the U.S. government."

## THIRTY-FIVE

ZAC REGAINED CONSCIOUSNESS in the interrogation room. He was seated behind the table and facing the door. His legs had been untied and his left wrist handcuffed to the chair's arm. The room had been cleaned too. The electrical cart was gone and the water had been mopped up.

Zac stared at the door for what seemed like hours until Assad entered carrying a small cardboard box. He sat on the edge of the table and scratched his beard before he spoke.

"I am sorry about the vigorous interrogation, but we had to be sure you were telling the truth. You can appreciate that everything becomes more complicated when foreign nations are involved in police matters."

Assad opened the box and passed a sandwich and a bottle of water across the table. Zac drank the entire bottle of water before tearing into the curried chicken wrap.

"The representative from your consulate is upstairs. She is taking care of some formalities and will be ready soon."

Zac looked up from his first real meal in days. Gone

from Assad's face was the creased brow and the tight jaw. He looked relaxed, almost relieved.

"Finish your meal. I will fetch her now."

He yelled to the guard through the thick steel door before leaving the room. Zac contemplated the puzzling sequence of events he'd experienced since entering Dubai. His treatment seemed to vary from cordial to cruel at the whim of his jailer. Assad could be playing a one-man good cop/bad cop routine, but once Zac had a face-to-face meeting with a U.S. government official, he would gain a measure of protection that had eluded him so far. No country wanted a foreign national to die in police custody.

When the door opened again Zac saw that Assad had remained true to his word. A woman entered the room, staring down at the floor. Tall and lithe, she wore a simple red pencil dress with long sleeves. Assad gestured to the chair across from Zac and she tried to slide it closer to the table before she noticed the carriage bolts holding it to the floor. She sat and crossed her legs at the knee.

Assad sat at the end of the small table and took the lead. "This is Emma Rogers from the U.S. consulate."

The woman glanced at Zac before turning away. Her dark blond hair cascaded across her forehead, highlighting her pale blue eyes.

But Zac barely noticed.

"May I see your credentials?" he asked.

Miss Rogers reached into her briefcase and practically thrust her State Department ID into Zac's free hand until Assad intervened.

"I am sorry. No contact is permitted with prisoners. Mr. Miller, you may look, but do not touch."

Zac and Rogers made eye contact.

"Miss Rogers, you may begin your interview."

The representative from the consulate asked Zac some basic questions about his identity and health. She glanced at Assad, who nodded in return.

Rogers stared down at her notebook as she spoke.

"Mr. Miller, Colonel Assad has told me of the charges against you and I'd like to hear your side of the story. So before we discuss what happened here in Dubai, I need you to tell me about Iran. You can appreciate that this is a sensitive time given the state of their nuclear program."

Zac regarded the woman. She was the first American he'd seen in weeks.

"Where are you from?" he asked.

"What?"

"Where are you from in the States?"

"How is that relevant?"

"I'm just curious."

Rogers looked at Assad. He waved his hand dismissively.

"Boston," she answered.

"Really? You don't have much of an accent."

"Not everyone does."

"I love Boston. You must be a big Giants fan."

For the first time, Emma Rogers smiled. "No. I root for the Pats, the Sox, and the Bruins. I can tell you the history of the Battle of Bunker Hill and which T line to take to Faneuil Hall too . . . Satisfied?"

Zac smiled back. "Thank you."

Assad watched the exchange like the finals of a tennis

tournament. His eyes darted back and forth, careful not to miss a single word or look.

"Continue with the interview," he instructed.

The smile left Rogers's face and she looked down at her notebook. "You were about to tell us what happened in Iran . . ."

Zac contemplated the body language of Assad and Rogers. She was an American diplomat, working to assist a fellow countryman, yet Assad seemed to be in charge. It was his country and his police station, but something didn't feel right.

"What made you decide to join the State Department?" Zac asked.

Rogers shifted in her chair.

"I wanted to see the world."

"Did you always want to be a political officer?"

"Yes." She put her pen down. "Now, my questions first."

Zac looked at Assad. The police officer was leaning forward in his chair, his elbows resting on the table, his eyes fixed on Miss Rogers.

"OK. I was flying from London to Singapore on a British Airways flight when the plane developed engine trouble. It was a last-minute business trip . . . Did you take the State Department exam in college or after?"

Before Rogers could speak, Assad stood and pounded his fist on the table.

"Enough! You have been asking to see someone from the U.S. government from the moment you were stopped in that wreck of a sailboat and now you waste our time with these idiotic questions? This interview is over!"

Assad glared at Rogers. Zac knew enough State Department employees at the embassy in London to know that she was faking it. The two Americans locked eyes and Zac knew in that instant that she was terrified. Though he was the one in jail, handcuffed to a chair, he saw the pleading in her eyes, the desperation and the fear. Zac nodded once before Assad grabbed her arm and pushed her toward the door.

She looked back at Zac in one last, desperate appeal, and he steered her gaze toward Assad's gun.

"Wait!" Zac shouted. "I'll answer your questions. I'm sorry." His tone was defeated, his posture sunken.

Assad turned and cocked his head at Zac. "I am warning you. Do not waste any more of my time."

"I'll cooperate. I just wanted to make sure she was who she said she was. I'm satisfied now. I'm sorry."

As the two men spoke, Assad's years of training as a police officer kept his eyes focused on Zac's hands, even though the real threat was behind him.

Emma lunged for his gun and pulled it from the open holster, backing away as she held it in her hand. Assad spun around, but she was already out of reach. She raised the 9mm Caracal in her quivering hand, her finger on the trigger.

The policeman slowly raised his hands and stepped toward Rogers. She took another step back and bumped into the wall behind her.

"Stop! Stop, you son of a bitch or I'll pull the trigger. Don't think for a second I won't do it."

Assad stopped.

"Slide your handcuff key over, on the floor, slowly,"

Zac said. He looked at Rogers. Her hand was shaking so violently he thought she might pull the trigger by accident. "If he gets cute, just shoot him."

Assad glared at Zac but did as he was told, sliding the key across the floor. Zac reached down with his free hand to retrieve it. When he had removed the cuff from his wrist he took the pistol from Rogers and directed the policeman into a corner of the room.

"Take your clothes off," Zac said. He looked Assad in the eyes.

The policeman stared back but did not move. Zac pistol-whipped him across the face. A trickle of blood ran down Assad's forehead.

"Get undressed," Zac said.

The police officer complied, but he never took his eyes off Zac. When Assad had stripped down to his underwear Zac motioned with the gun for him to sit in the chair farthest from the door.

"Cuff him to the chair," he said to Rogers. She did as she was told, looping the chain around the thick, wooden armrest.

Assad sneered. "You will both pay for this in unimaginable ways. You are making a terrible mistake."

Zac aimed the pistol at Assad's chest. "I've had your worst and I'm the one who's in control now, so shut up before I decide I don't need you at all."

"You think this will end with me?" Assad shook his head. "I think you know better, much better. There are forces at work here that are far more powerful than any man. So go ahead, kill me. I will be the lucky one. You will be begging for death long before it comes."

Zac stared at the corrupt cop for a moment, then lowered the pistol until it was pointed at Assad's crotch. Zac wrapped his finger around the trigger and took up the slack.

"Now," he said, "I'm going to knock on the door and you're going to call the guard."

Assad nodded slowly but Zac shook his head.

"I know what you're thinking, that I don't speak Arabic, and you're right. But I heard you say it a dozen times when you left me down in this sewer. If anything but *'Iftah il-baab'* comes out of your mouth, you'll be singing soprano for the Dubai Boys' Choir."

Zac moved to the door, positioning himself against the wall. He would be able to cover the guard the instant the door opened. He motioned Rogers to the corner behind the thick steel door in case lead started flying.

"Ready?" Zac said. He knocked twice on the door.

*"Iftah il-baab,"* Assad called out.

Nothing.

Zac swung the gun toward Assad. With his left hand he rapped twice on the door.

"Louder," Zac said.

*"IFTAH IL-BAAB,"* Assad yelled.

Zac shifted his aim back to the doorway, but the door did not open. Zac wondered if Assad had somehow tipped off the guard, if there was a code Zac hadn't picked up on. With fury in his eyes he turned the gun on Assad, but the deadbolts inside the old door began to creak, and Zac returned his aim to the door just as it opened.

The heavy door was open just a few inches when the

guard looked up from the key and saw Zac. The guard's other hand went to his holstered pistol.

"Don't do it," Zac said. The muzzle of his own pistol was aimed at the guard's chest.

The guard released his grip on his weapon but used his other hand to try to yank the door closed. Zac stuck his foot into the gap and the heavy steel door slammed into it.

Zac cried out in pain, but his gun never moved. He pushed the door open with his foot.

"Inside," he ordered the guard through gritted teeth.

The guard walked into the room and spotted Assad. Zac told the guard to drop his duty belt and watched as the man's weapon, handcuffs, and other gear slid to the floor. Rogers cuffed the guard to a chair and the two Americans began to plot their escape.

# THIRTY-SIX

ZAC'S PEASANT GARB had helped him hide inside Iran, but in cosmopolitan Dubai, it had the opposite effect. The camouflage had to match its surroundings. He put on Assad's gray sharkskin suit. The jacket and pants were loose, but not awkwardly so, and with Assad's gold bracelet and sunglasses, Zac looked like just another Middle Eastern businessman. He took the rest of Assad's personal effects as well, including his weapon, wallet, and police credentials. The two men didn't look much alike, but Zac hoped no one would scrutinize the photo.

Rogers was sitting in a corner, shaking. Zac walked over and squatted down. "You did great," he whispered. "We'd probably be dead if it weren't for you."

Tears ran down her cheeks.

"Who are you?" she asked.

"I'm sure he told you horrible things about me," Zac said, gesturing toward Assad, "but you have to trust me. I'm one of the good guys." Zac lowered his voice. "We're going to get out of here and make our way to the U.S.

consulate, or maybe the embassy down in Abu Dhabi. They can protect us there."

Zac helped her up and steadied her as she regained her composure. After a minute she picked up her phony State Department credentials and headed for the door.

"Let's get the hell out of here," she said.

"You're going to leave us here to die?" Assad challenged.

Zac turned and drew the pistol, shifting his aim between Assad and the guard.

"You have two choices. You can take your chances that someone finds you down here, or I can kill you now and take the guesswork out of it."

"I'll take the first one," said the guard. "The wait-and-see choice."

Assad shot a look of disgust at his coworker.

Emma turned back to Assad and the guard. "I'm finished with listening to these two," she said. The Emiratis stiffened in their chairs as she walked over to them, but all she did was gag each man with a sock tied around his head.

Zac led Rogers into the hall and locked the door behind them. He figured his stay in the dungeon probably wasn't sanctioned by the Dubai police, so there had to be an exit that bypassed the police station. Along the hallway were several identical doors and one without a lock. He opened it slowly and peered through the crack. It was a stairway, poorly lit and lightly used, judging by the layer of dust on everything. They walked up two flights, Zac's right hand resting on the holstered pistol. On the landing was a sturdy door, locked with a deadbolt. The next flight of stairs led to the top floor. If they couldn't get out there, they'd have to go back into the dungeon and make their way out through the police station.

The exit door on the top floor was secured by a powerful magnetic lock. An electronic access panel and a glowing red LED told them they weren't getting out that way. Zac turned to walk back down the steps, but Rogers tugged at his arm.

"Try his wallet. He used it to get down here."

Zac pressed Assad's wallet against the panel and the LED turned green. Zac nodded at Rogers and opened the door. It was another empty stairwell, but this one was clean and well lit. They moved silently up the steps and found a door with a push bar and no lock. Zac opened the door half an inch, his hand now wrapped firmly around the grip of the holstered pistol.

Cool air rushed in as he looked into the lobby of a modern Emirati office building. There was a man in uniform behind a desk, but he looked more like a receptionist than a police officer. Another man in an elegant white *dishdasha* was exiting the building, but otherwise it was deserted.

Zac looked at Emma and she nodded. She was ready. He adjusted his sunglasses, buttoned his suit coat, and stepped into the lobby. The two of them spoke casually in hushed tones as they walked through the glass entryway and out onto the darkened street. Zac was pleased that their bluff had worked but it wouldn't do to linger. Rogers's good looks and Western dress would draw stares from every man they encountered and Zac's disguise was razor thin: a suit and a pair of sunglasses.

He looked to his left. The police station was five hundred feet away.

"We need to get out of here."

Rogers motioned to a brightly lit hotel a few blocks down the road and the two set off on foot.

Assad's mobile phone vibrated in Zac's pocket. He glanced at it. It was an international number. It was the country code for Iran, and Zac would bet his life's savings that it was Arzaman wondering what had become of his prize.

"Can we go to the consulate?" Rogers asked as they walked.

Zac glanced at the phone again. "It's almost eleven p.m. It'll be closed for the night."

They walked in silence for a few minutes. Rogers hesitated as they approached the hotel. "We're still too close to the police station. We could go to my hotel."

"They'll check there too." Zac rummaged through Assad's wallet. "There's a decent wad of cash and a few credit cards in here. We need to get off the streets and I need to make a phone call."

"Can't you use the cell phone?"

"It's locked."

The phone started to vibrate again and Zac looked at Emma.

"Ask the doorman to call us a cab to the Burj Al Arab."

"I don't think we should go somewhere so obvious," she said.

"Just ask him."

Emma spoke with the doorman, who dutifully walked out to the curb to summon a taxi. Zac circled around behind the valet stand and planted Assad's cell phone in an unlocked suitcase. He rejoined Emma out of earshot from the doorman.

"That'll keep anyone trying to track Assad's phone off our tail."

The two Americans walked to the approaching taxi and climbed in.

Zac spoke to the cabbie as it pulled away from the curb. "Forget the Burj. Take us somewhere out of the way."

The Pakistani driver regarded his passengers in the rearview mirror. "I know just the spot," he said with a salacious grin.

Zac looked over at Rogers as the car wound its way through the city streets. She was staring out the window, crying softly.

# THIRTY-SEVEN

NSIDE THE TAXI, Zac reached for Emma's hand to comfort her, then stopped. She was scared. Scared of the trouble she was in, scared of the unknown, and probably scared of him. And, Zac reflected, neither of them knew even a single important detail about the other. They rode on in silence, two involuntary partners in crime.

The driver took them to a part of Dubai that Zac had never seen before. The poorly maintained low-rise buildings and the throngs of pedestrians on the streets contrasted starkly with the hyper-affluence and the auto-centric culture of the rest of the city. There wasn't a Westerner in sight.

The taxi stopped in front of a run-down motel and Rogers wiped her eyes before getting out. Zac waited for the taxi to leave and the two of them walked to the next block, choosing another hotel in case the cabbie spoke with the police. Zac checked in, giving the clerk a fictitious name and address in France. Since the charging of interest was forbidden by Sharia law, many Muslims did not own credit cards and the clerk accepted a token amount of cash for the room deposit. After buying a few items from behind the counter, Zac and Rogers stepped into the elevator.

The small room was clean and furnished with a double bed, a dresser, and a single chair. Beige paint covered the walls. There was a television but no telephone. Zac turned back the heavy window curtain to see if they'd been followed. He spoke rapidly as he scrutinized the street for signs of unusual activity. "I need to go out and find a phone; a cheap prepaid one or a pay phone, some way to contact my boss back in London."

He turned from the window and saw Rogers sitting on the bed, fighting back tears.

"What did they tell you about me?" Zac asked.

She put her face in her hands and started sobbing.

Zac continued, "You probably think that I'm some sort of monster, that I've done terrible things to innocent people, but it's not true. I promise that I won't hurt you. We're in this together now."

She looked up and met his gaze. "That's supposed to make me feel better? We're in *what* together? What the hell have I gotten myself into?"

Zac regarded the woman who had shown such courage in the police station. She'd disarmed a man almost twice her size and saved Zac's life. She was angry and scared, and she had a right to know the truth. Well, most of it anyway. He surveyed the street again before speaking.

"I work in London. Two weeks ago I was headed to Singapore on a business trip. We were halfway there when the plane had to make an emergency landing in Iran. I took some pictures of the area outside the airport and a group of soldiers separated me from the other passengers. They asked me a lot of questions but didn't listen to anything I said. They drugged me and moved me to a warehouse in the mountains where an army colonel tortured me for days. I would've been executed if I hadn't escaped."

Rogers had stopped crying. She looked up at Zac as if searching for something solid in the world that was crumbling around her.

"The police said . . . they said you did some bad things over there. They wanted you to confide in me so I could find out the details."

"I did what I had to do to get away from some very dangerous people. I made my way to the coast and stole a boat, which is how I came to Dubai. The marine police stopped me and one thing led to another."

"How did they know what happened in Iran?"

"I guess they gave the case to Assad when they figured out that I had come from Iran. He has contacts there, including the Iranian colonel I mentioned. They both lost family when the U.S. Navy shot down an Iranian passenger jet back in 1988. But they're after me for more than just the pictures I took. This is a vendetta, revenge for an accident that happened decades ago. They were going to push me until I told them what they wanted to hear, or I was dead."

"Are you some kind of secret agent?"

A rueful smile crossed Zac's mouth. "Far from it, apparently. I stare at computer screens all day."

Emma exhaled deeply before speaking. "Obviously, I don't work at the consulate, but that policeman threatened to kill me if I didn't cooperate. I work in private banking in New York. I was early for a client dinner so I stopped in the hotel bar. After about twenty minutes I stepped outside to use my cell phone and one of the locals followed me out. I didn't think much of it until he pushed me into an alcove. I drove my heel into his foot and ran back into the bar before he could do anything. The bastard had the nerve to walk—well, limp—back to his table and rejoin his friends, so I called the police." Emma shook her head in disbelief. "And then they arrested me, for *'zina.'* I think it's like making a false report. They said I needed four male witnesses to prove that the creep tried to assault me. On top of that they said I was being 'morally corrupt and subversive.'"

"Maybe your attacker was somebody important. They usually give tourists a pass on minor Sharia violations."

"They were blaming *me* for being attacked." Anger replaced her disbelief. "They took me to that police station and locked me in a cell by myself. They told me the American consulate was closed for the night and I'd have to wait until the morning to contact them."

"Couldn't you call your client or your office in New York?"

"I know this sounds stupid but I was too embarrassed. My client is a good man. He'd probably help me, and I'm sure he's wondering why I didn't show up for dinner, but I was afraid that it would get back to my colleagues and I'd be fired. I figured I'd just wait until morning and call the consulate myself. I didn't think what I did was really a crime. I thought they were just going to give me a hard time and let me go."

"But they didn't."

"Assad came into my cell about an hour before I met you. He told me they would release me if I helped them with an investigation. When he told me I had to impersonate someone from the consulate, I refused."

"And?"

"And he threatened me. He told me women don't have the right to refuse *anything* in Dubai." Emma rubbed her face with both of her hands as tears welled in her eyes. "I agreed to do the impersonation. I know I shouldn't have, but I was scared. He brought me this dress, had me redo my makeup, and spent twenty minutes writing a list of questions they wanted me to ask you. He even used my mug shot photo for this." She threw her phony Department of State credentials on the bed. "I think he just used a color printer and laminated it. I'm sure that's why he wouldn't let you touch it." She wiped the tears from her cheeks. "While we walked downstairs he spent another ten minutes telling me the horrible things that he would do to me if I blew the impersonation. Five hours ago I was getting ready for dinner with a client whom I've known and liked for almost two years and now I'm here. I swear I hate this country."

"It's not the country. He's a corrupt cop, and I don't blame you one bit for going along. But Assad was right about one thing; this is much bigger than you or me."

"I really don't care. I just want to get out of here and never come back."

Zac understood. He'd felt the same way the night he'd pushed off from the dock in Bandar Abbas. Emma sat in silence while he peeled back the curtains once more. The streets were deserted.

"I need to go out and make a phone call."

"Can't you use the phone in the lobby?"

"Definitely not. There are probably five other places in the hotel where someone could listen in on that line. I might as well call the police directly."

"Who are you calling? It's three in the morning in London. Zac, please don't go."

"I promise I'll be back in twenty minutes." He moved toward the door.

Emma grabbed his jacket and pulled him back.

"Zac! Please, I'm begging you. Don't go. Please, I can't be alone right now. Stay with me."

Emma looked terrified, but it wasn't her pleading that caused him to stay. Zac didn't have Clements's mobile number. He knew the main number for CIA/London, but like all field ops, SNAPSHOT technically belonged to Ted Graves, and the watch officer would route the call to him. Zac's intuition told him to wait a few hours until Clements was in the office and speak with him first.

"The call can wait until the morning."

Emma let out a nervous laugh. "You must think I'm such a disaster. I swear I'm not normally like this."

Zac dragged the hardwood chair to the far corner of the room. From it he'd have a clean line of fire at anyone coming through the doorway. "Don't worry about it. You did great today."

Emma sighed and stepped into the bathroom.

Zac turned on the television. BBC World News was

on. Current events hadn't changed much since he'd left London. Tensions were high in the Middle East as the United States and Iran continued to debate the scope of its nuclear program. The Iranians were threatening to close the Strait of Hormuz to shipping traffic if the U.S. didn't make further concessions. The local spin was that the seaport at Jebel Ali in Dubai was the largest one in the region and the UAE stood to lose hundreds of millions of dollars in trade revenues if Iran managed to close the Strait. Zac's eyes glazed over and he shut off the TV.

Emma stepped out of the bathroom wearing a robe and shrouded in a cloud of steam. "Zac." She hesitated. "What are we going to do tomorrow?"

"I'll know after I make my phone call. You should get some sleep now. It's going to be a big day."

He turned away and opened the curtain to check the street again.

Emma slid into bed.

"Good night, Zac."

He nodded to her and sat in the chair. When she'd fallen asleep he drew his pistol and rested it on his lap. Despite his exhaustion, sleep would not come. He could only stare at the door and think about Arzaman. The Iranian was close. Zac could feel it.

WHEN MORNING FINALLY came Zac rose stiffly from the chair and peeled back the edge of the thick curtain. The streets were still dark and deserted. He assumed that Arzaman had been looking for Assad and eventually found him locked in the basement cell. Every police car in town probably had Zac's and Emma's pictures in it.

He closed the curtain and stepped into the bathroom. He used the razor and the scissors he'd bought in the lobby to trim his beard. He stared in the mirror as he worked, fascinated by his dark skin, chiseled body, and shaggy hair; but mostly by his eyes. Something about them was different. There was a look, a predatory alertness, that hadn't been there before. He'd noticed a change inside as well, and a small part of him relished it. He liked the constant flow of adrenaline pumping through his veins.

Zac showered and once again put on Assad's sharkskin suit. When he emerged from the bathroom Emma was already dressed and brushing her hair. He debated what to do with the pistol. It would be incriminating if he were caught with it, damning evidence that would likely cost him his life. But going back to Iran, or to the depths of the Dubai police station, would mean months if not years of pain and torture. They would ask the same questions, he would give the same answers, and so it would go until he was all used up. Zac slid the weapon into the holster.

"I need to buy a prepaid cell phone," he said.

"Zac, why can't we just call someone local to help us? I could call the client I came to visit. He thinks of me as a daughter. I'm sure he would come."

"Too risky. My boss is very plugged in. He can work the situation from London and get someone to pick us up."

Emma simply nodded and they rode the elevator

down to the lobby. There was a new clerk behind the counter. When they reached the front door Emma stopped short.

"I should wait here," she announced.

"Are you sure you don't mind being alone?"

She looked out the window as the streets began to fill with cars and pedestrians. "I'm sure. Besides, I'd need to get a headscarf."

"I can't believe you're thinking about shopping at a time like this. So like a woman," Zac teased gently in an attempt to lighten the mood.

"There are no Westerners in this neighborhood. I'd stand out here without a headscarf," she said.

"Look, I'm sorry about the shopping comment . . ."

But there was no humor in Emma's expression. "I'm serious."

"What's wrong?"

"Nothing's wrong. It's just that they're looking for a man with a Western woman. Together we'll attract too much attention, especially in this neighborhood."

Zac didn't like the idea of leaving her alone, but she had a point. It was a blue-collar area of the city and most of the people on the streets were laborers or in the service industries. Her fair hair and red pencil dress were like optical magnets.

"You're sure about this?" he asked.

"One hundred percent."

"OK. I'll meet you back in the room in half an hour. Don't open the door for anyone."

She nodded. "I'll see you in thirty minutes."

She watched Zac reach for the door handle and step into the street. He didn't look back. If he had, he would have seen Emma approach the front desk.

"May I use your phone? It's a local call."

# THIRTY-EIGHT

ZAC WALKED SLOWLY down the street, checking reflections in shop windows for anyone who might be following him. Though he was being cautious, he wasn't worried. With his beard, and Assad's suit and sunglasses, he looked like a typical Emirati businessman.

He found what he was looking for almost immediately, but the wireless store required identification to buy even a prepaid mobile phone. He wasn't going to risk using Assad's credentials. The two men looked nothing alike.

Zac walked down a side street and soon found a bank of pay phones. He dialed his office number and asked for his boss. Peter Clements had been with CIA for nearly twenty years and developed a reputation as an aggressive leader with keen instincts for people and details. In the three years Zac had worked for him, they had forged a strong relationship based on excellence in their work and mutual respect. Clements would go to the wall for his people and that was exactly what Zac needed now.

"Hello," answered the London chief of station.

"Peter, it's Zac. I'm calling from a pay phone on the street in Dubai."

"What the hell are you doing in Dubai? Did you decide to go to the camel races instead of Singapore?"

"I'll fill you in on everything once I'm safe. I need a ride out of here."

"Who's after you?"

"The guys across the Strait and now the locals."

"How was your layover?"

"It was a disaster. I never made it to Singapore."

Clements was quiet on the other end of the line.

"I'm sorry things didn't go as planned during the layover," Zac said. "But it was everything I'd feared. I'll fill you in once I'm back in London."

"Give me your address and I'll send someone to pick you up."

Zac gave his boss the address of the hotel.

"Sit tight. I'll have a car there in an hour or two, tops."

"Thank you. Listen, one more thing. Someone is with me, another American citizen who helped me out and is in trouble with the local cops. It's nothing, but tell whoever is coming that there will be a woman too."

"OK. We'll talk more when you're off the street. Go back to the hotel now and let me work this."

"Thanks, Peter."

The streets had become more crowded in the few minutes he'd been on the phone. When he was one block from the hotel he saw Emma step onto the sidewalk, her dark-blond hair and her red dress contrasting sharply with the gray cityscape, and he wasn't the only one who'd noticed. Everyone on the sidewalk was looking at her, and she was supposed to be hiding in the room.

Zac crossed the street and walked faster, fighting the

urge to run. Emma was facing the opposite direction, looking for something. When he was a hundred feet away, a white Bentley sedan pulled around the corner and stopped in front of the hotel. A heavyset man in an immaculate *dishdasha* stepped out of the rear seat and called to Emma. She said something back but didn't move. She looked down the sidewalk and saw Zac.

"Hurry!" she shouted to him.

Zac ran to the car.

"Emma. Who is this?"

"This is the client I was telling you about. He's going to help us." Emma moved to enter the car. "We can trust him."

Zac grabbed her arm. "How did he know you're here? Please tell me you didn't call him from the hotel."

No sooner had the words left Zac's mouth than a blacked-out SUV stopped on the other side of the road. Two thick-set men stepped out and waited for a gap in the four lanes of traffic. One of the men stepped in front of a car, causing the driver to slam on his brakes and lay on his horn. Everyone turned to see the cause of the noise, including Emma and Zac.

Zac saw the two men watching him as they started to cross the street.

"Get in the car!" Zac yelled. He pushed Emma into the backseat. The Bentley's owner waited for Zac to get in, but Zac stepped back and drew his weapon.

Emma screamed as she looked through the window at the men crossing the street. Zac yelled at the car's owner, "Go! Go!"

Emma yelled again, "Zac! Come with us."

"It's me they want. Just get yourself to the consulate."

The Bentley's owner saw the gun and the two men crossing the street. He climbed into the backseat and shut the heavy door. The big sedan accelerated away from the curb and melted into the heavy traffic.

The SUV's driver pulled into the intersection and began to make an aggressive U-turn while the two men on foot watched the Bentley drive away. Zac yelled to draw their attention away from Emma, but the horns of angry drivers drowned him out. He raised the pistol and fired once into the air. Pedestrians on the sidewalk screamed and scattered, and the two men realized that their prize was not in the white car after all.

Zac ran to the corner and down a side street. A red light on the main road pinned the SUV in traffic, but the men on foot were not lost so easily. One of them shoved a pedestrian out of the way and drew a pistol. There were more screams and the crowd scattered. The man fired twice down the busy sidewalk, narrowly missing Zac but striking a bystander.

Zac kept running through the crowd. The SUV had found a gap in the traffic and came around the corner with tires screeching. Zac looked over his shoulder and saw the two men and the SUV closing in. He ran around another corner and ducked behind a Dumpster for cover. A siren began to wail in the distance.

The two men slowed as they approached the corner, unsure of Zac's whereabouts. The SUV pulled up behind them, stuck behind a car at a red light. From behind the Dumpster, Zac could see the driver yelling something through the open passenger window. The two men turned in Zac's direction, weapons drawn. When they were twenty feet from the Dumpster, Zac leaned out and fired, striking one of them. The other one fired back, but the bullet ricocheted off the metal garbage bin. The three men exchanged a dozen shots while more sirens closed in. The blacked-out SUV cleared the light and roared around the corner. A submachine gun erupted from inside. Bullets slammed into the Dumpster and the concrete building behind it while the two passengers climbed into the backseat. The SUV's tires screeched as it sped off.

Zac came out from behind the Dumpster and fired, emptying the magazine into the rapidly departing truck, peppering its rear with bullet holes and shattering the back window. He reached for Assad's spare magazine and reloaded, but the SUV was gone.

By now the streets were in a full-fledged panic. Pedestrians had scattered in every direction and the remaining vehicle traffic had stopped or turned away. Zac holstered the pistol and walked around another corner. Except for the din of the rapidly approaching sirens, the scene was strangely silent.

He kept walking and turning corners until he found an empty taxi. He climbed into the orange-and-white van and met the driver's eyes in the rearview mirror.

"U.S. consulate."

"OK, boss."

The cab pulled away as Zac thought about the men in the black SUV. The response had been swift, almost guaranteeing that they were tied to the police. It meant that Assad had been found. But the men hadn't acted like police officers; they'd fled from the approaching sirens, just like Zac. They'd probably been Arzaman's men who'd come from Iran. It would explain why they'd fired into the crowd without worrying about innocent bystanders. The Iranians had even beat the police to the scene, which meant Assad was probably working behind the scenes to get the goons there first.

It also meant that whoever Peter Clements sent to the hotel would find no sign of Zac and no indication that anything was amiss. All of the police activity would be around the corner, blocks away from the hotel where the shooting had taken place.

It was a lot for Zac to process, but any way he looked at it, it meant that Assad was on the loose, and he was a dangerous foe. He knew all about Zac and his intent to get to the consulate. With Arzaman and Assad working together, Zac would have to be very careful.

After several minutes the cab turned into a cluster of high-rise office buildings and approached a busy turn-around in front of the consulate building. A security guard was directing traffic away from the large no-stand-ing zone outside the entrance. Most of the cars idled for no more than a few seconds to drop off passengers before pulling away, yet there were two black sedans with tinted windows parked in the driveway that the guard com-pletely ignored. They were the same 5-series BMWs that the police drove, but that type of car was common in Dubai, and almost everyone had tinted windows to stave off the heat. Zac scowled. Maybe he was being paranoid.

But was he paranoid enough?

Something didn't feel right. The security guard was shooing away every car except the two black sedans. As the cab entered the turnaround, the low angle of the morning sun revealed four men in each car. No one was getting out and no one was getting in. They were waiting. They might be diplomatic security or bodyguards for a rich sheik, or they might be local cops and Iranian goons. It didn't matter who they were. Eight men was a lot of muscle, and Zac had to assume the worst. There would be no second chance if he was wrong. He told the driver to keep going.

The cabbie drove smoothly around the traffic circle and back onto the main road. He looked back at Zac in the rearview mirror.

"Where to now, boss?"

"Take me to the American embassy."

"Embassy in Abu Dhabi, boss. Maybe two hours from here. Very expensive ride, boss."

Zac held up the wad of cash from Assad's wallet.

"OK, boss."

Zac stared out of the window as the cab pulled onto the highway and entered an industrial section of town. Like his incursion into Iran, his carefully crafted plan to escape Dubai with Emma had gone to hell almost immediately. Whether he'd been spotted leaving the hotel, or someone had overheard Emma's call to her client, her fate was out of his hands now.

Most of the morning rush-hour traffic on the highway was headed in the other direction, north into the city. The southbound lanes were nearly empty, yet Zac noticed the cabdriver repeatedly checking his side mirrors, then glancing at Zac in the rearview mirror. After he'd done it a few times, Zac spoke up.

"Is everything OK?"

The driver glanced in the rearview mirror again.

"Don't know, boss. One of those black cars from the consulate may be following us."

Zac realized that the driver knew exactly why Zac didn't get out at the consulate. The man's intuition should not be dismissed out of hand.

"That's a pretty popular kind of car around here. What makes you think he's following us?"

"Cars like that usually pass me very fast, but this one's just staying back there. I move left, he moves left. I move right, he moves right."

"Do you think you can lose him?" Zac asked.

The cabdriver scowled as he quickly looked over his shoulder. "Lose him? Do you think you're in the movies? 'Follow that car,' 'lose him,' 'shoot first, ask questions later.' What is it with you Americans? I am an honest man trying to make a living. I don't want any trouble. Do you know what they do to Sri Lankans who violate the law here? No way, boss, no way."

The cabdriver was pulling over to the side of the freeway.

"What the hell are you doing?" Zac shouted. "Don't slow down!"

# THIRTY-NINE

Z AC TURNED AROUND in the backseat of the van. The cabbie was slowing down and the black BMW was barely a quarter mile behind them. He couldn't tell for sure if it was one of the cars from the consulate, but there was no room for error.

"Drive, dammit! I'll pay you double," said Zac.

"Get out. Get out of my cab!" the driver yelled.

Zac pulled the gun and put it to the driver's head. "Keep driving!"

The van nearly rolled over as the cabbie slammed on the brakes and swerved onto the sandy shoulder.

"Son of a bitch," Zac muttered as he put the gun away. He jumped out of the car and onto the shoulder. The BMW was closing in fast. Zac sprinted toward an industrial park that was a hundred feet from the highway. A chain-link fence blocked his way but he leapt halfway up the side and pulled himself over the top. He glanced over his shoulder. The cab had already pulled away and the BMW was coming to a halt.

Zac darted randomly between the buildings inside the industrial park. There were scrap yards, transportation companies, and dozens of warehouses. After a few minutes he came to a road and watched a long line of tanker trucks drive past. He stopped short as he began to cross the street. He suddenly realized that he wasn't in an industrial park at all. He was in a seaport.

To the north was a gated exit. It looked like a border crossing with eight lanes, heavy security, and a sign that read "Port Jebel Ali." It was the massive port that he'd seen last night on television. There were offices and pedestrians nearby. Zac set off toward the buildings in search of a phone.

He'd taken no more than a few steps when a voice called out in thickly accented English.

"Hey, you there. Come here."

Zac turned and saw an armed security guard with a radio and a hard hat walk from the shade of a nearby building. The man didn't look Arab and Zac quickly decided to take an enormous gamble. He slowly reached into his jacket and removed Assad's police credentials. Zac flashed the badge long enough for the guard to see the shield but not the photo. As Zac put the badge away, he brushed his jacket open so the guard could see the gun holstered on his hip.

"Police business," Zac said in English with a fake Arabic accent.

No sooner had the words left his mouth than two white-and-green Dubai police cars approached the gate from the highway.

"I was not informed," said the guard, reaching for the radio on his belt. "We are always informed when there is police activity in the port."

With one eye on the police cars, Zac improvised. "We are looking for a suspect, but must keep it quiet. He is armed and dangerous. He is dark-skinned with black hair, wearing blue jeans and a work shirt." Like a newspaper horoscope, the generic description applied to nearly everyone in Dubai.

"I must check with my command post."

The guard brought the radio up to his mouth and depressed the talk button. The two police cars entered through the gate.

"You see," Zac said, "reinforcements are here already. They are bringing pictures of the suspect. You will probably have a briefing on it soon."

He motioned to the gate with his left hand as he flexed his right hand.

The guard looked over his shoulder as the two police cars pulled into the port and stopped in front of the administration building. He released the talk button on the radio.

"OK. Good luck," the guard said as he turned and walked toward the gate.

Zac turned and headed toward a storage area stacked with containers. The narrow passageways between them looked like a hedge maze, and would be the perfect place to hide, but he'd walked barely ten feet before the guard called out again.

"Wait!"

Zac heard footsteps behind him. He turned around slowly and slid his right hand inside his jacket.

The guard held out his hard hat.

"You'll need this . . . I'll get another one inside." He nodded to Zac and walked back toward the office.

Zac walked quickly to the container storage area and threaded his way through the fifty-foot-high stacks of metal boxes. He emerged from the stillness of the container maze into a hive of activity unlike any he'd ever seen. A line of cargo ships was in front of him, their multicolored containers rising up from the horizon. Arrayed across the quay were dozens of trucks and hundred-foot-high cranes on rails, all working in a carefully choreographed effort to load and unload the container ships. Zac took in the scene for a few more seconds before resuming his search for a telephone. He saw one of the police cars pull around a corner and block the road. To his front and left was the sea, to his right were the police, and behind him was the security guard who would soon realize that he'd been talking to the wanted man just a few minutes earlier. Zac's world suddenly became very small.

He approached a short man in a neon vest who was checking containers as trucks brought them around.

"Where are these ships headed?" Zac asked as he flashed Assad's badge.

The man glanced over at Zac and his badge but kept walking as he spoke.

"All over the world, my friend." He grinned, clearly enjoying the hectic pace of his work. "Inside these containers come electronics from Japan, wine and clothes from France, and once in a while a Ferrari or a Lamborghini from Italy."

"Where, specifically, is this ship headed?" Zac asked with an edge to his voice.

"That I don't know. I just scan this barcode and the crane takes it from there." Within seconds a mammoth yellow gantry crane was overhead, lowering its giant claws toward the forty-foot-long metal box. "There's a monitor over there if you want to know where it's going." The man pointed to a hut a few hundred feet away.

Zac found the monitor. It listed the destinations and the arrival and departure times at Jebel Ali. He scanned the list quickly. There were several vessels destined for ports in China, Africa, and Western Europe, but two in particular caught his eye: the *Simmons Acadia* was leaving for Southampton, England, in fifty minutes and the M/V *Castor* would sail for Marseille, France, in two hours. Either one would suit his needs, but steaming straight to England would be far better. Zac consulted a map next to the monitor and started walking.

Zac soon found the *Simmons Acadia*. She was preparing to leave with a pair of tugboats off her bow. With roughly thirty minutes until departure, he had to find a way aboard. He spotted a group of men huddled at the foot of the gangway. Two uniformed agents were reviewing a sheaf of documents with a pair of sailors. Zac scrutinized the ship for another entrance, but the sloping aluminum stairs were the only way aboard. He leaned against an idle crane for several minutes and watched the discussion.

The sailors ascended the gangway. Zac took a few steps toward the ship but stopped short. The uniformed men weren't leaving. He looked desperately for anything that might grab their attention, but they stood quietly and watched the sailors step onto the ship's deck. The foot of the gangway lifted off the dock and rose up onto the ship.

A few minutes here, a random chance there, and the course of his life had again been dramatically altered. There would be no landing on British soil where there were proper laws and human rights, no quick phone call to the U.S. authorities to extract him from his predicament. The *Acadia* sounded a loud blast from its horn, punctuating his defeat.

Getting aboard ship had been harder than he'd expected. He needed a plan if he was going to stow away to Marseille. He was deep in thought as he walked quickly toward the next berth.

The smaller M/V *Castor* was a hive of activity. Five gantry cranes were picking containers from waiting trucks and hoisting them aboard ship, where an army of riggers was lashing them into place. Zac stepped over a pair of thick hoses as a forklift sped by.

A lone sailor in a khaki uniform stood watch atop the gangway. Zac made a conspicuous show of pulling a piece of paper from Assad's wallet and looking up at the ship before starting up the gangway. The uniformed deckhand watched carefully. Men in suits were rare in a seaport. They were either management or cops, and neither was good news when you were due to cast off in an hour.

Zac adopted a stern expression and gave a cursory nod to the sailor, a swarthy, hirsute man with broad shoulders and Mediterranean features.

*Just pray he doesn't speak Arabic,* thought Zac.

Zac used his accented English again. "This is the M/V *Castor*?"

"Yes. Can I help you?" responded the sailor in competent English. He eyed Zac warily.

"I need to speak with your captain."

Zac again held out his badge in a way that revealed the weapon holstered on his hip. The sailor reached for the radio strapped to his belt.

"No radio." Zac shook his head. "This is a criminal matter. Please fetch the captain for me."

"I cannot leave this station unattended."

"It will not be unattended. I will be here."

"It has to be a ship security officer."

"A police officer should suffice."

"I am sorry. I cannot."

Zac scowled. "Let me see your identification."

The crewman pulled a lanyard from inside his shirt and held up a photo ID. Zac pretended to scrutinize the information. He made eye contact and held it while he spoke slowly for effect.

"Mr. Roselli, get the captain down here, now."

The sailor hesitated. Zac could see the uncertainty in his face.

"Either you fetch the captain right now," Zac said, "or this ship is not leaving port and you are coming into custody for interfering with a police investigation."

Additional days in port would cost the shipping company tens, or possibly hundreds of thousands of dollars and likely cost the seaman his job . . . once he was out of jail.

"I'll take you to see the captain."

"So the fugitive can escape? No, thank you. I will be right here when you return with the captain."

The crewman nodded and walked aft toward the superstructure. Zac looked around, waiting for the sailor to disappear. The container racks above deck were almost filled to capacity. Three of the five gantry cranes were already idle and the last two had just a few containers left to load. He didn't have much time. The ship would be ready to leave on schedule.

Zac bolted for the interior of the ship the instant the sailor stepped out of view. It was his first time on a cargo ship and he soon found that, aside from the walkways, the containers on deck were packed wall-to-wall with only thin steel racks between them. There was nowhere to hide and no room to open any of the container doors.

He walked toward the monolithic superstructure. He had no intention of following the crewman inside but, towering almost one hundred feet above the deck, it was the hub of the ship. At its base was a metal staircase that descended into the cargo hold. Zac frowned at the tightly packed containers, but at the bottom of the stairs was a steel-grated walkway that ringed the ship's interior. He dashed down the steps. The air was stuffy and hot. He went aft, stepping over the thick wire lashings that held the containers in place. Far above him on deck, workers were securing the last of the load. If he couldn't find a place to hide, he would never survive the trip to France. He ran farther into the stern.

For most of its length, the ship's sides were perfectly straight, allowing the containers to be fitted atop and against one another. But as the hull faired to the narrower stern section, the curve in her sides left dead space where Zac could reach some of the container doors. Most were fitted with thick padlocks, but a few had been left unsecured. He spied a newer container along the port side and went to investigate.

In the distance he heard a siren wail briefly, followed by an enormous engine rumbling to life. Zac hauled the container door open and the screech of ungreased metal hinges echoed throughout the hull. The interior was dark and smelled of chemicals, but there was just enough light for him to see that it was empty.

Zac pulled the door closed and immersed himself in blackness. As he felt his way to the middle of the container and sat down on the steel floor, he wondered aloud what the hell he'd just gotten himself into.

# FORTY

CHRISTINE KIRBY WALKED into Ted Graves's office. "I have something important on SNAPSHOT."

"Good. So do I," said Graves.

"Me first," said Kirby.

Graves looked sideways at her. "What are you, six years old?"

"I walked over to see you. I should go first."

"Fine." Graves shook his head. "What's so important?"

Kirby sat down and leaned toward Graves's desk.

"We just received a call from SIS. Apparently an elderly Englishwoman contacted them and said that Miller didn't commit the Singapore murder. She said . . ."

"Who is this woman?"

"She met Miller on the flight from London to Singapore. She . . ."

"Wait a second. So some old lady calls in saying that Miller seemed like such a nice young man and he couldn't possibly have killed someone?"

"That's not exactly . . ."

"You're kidding me, right?" Graves was angry. "This is like the neighbor of some goddamned serial killer who goes on television after the killing spree and says, 'I never would have guessed.'"

"Ted, there's more to it than that."

"Not as far as I'm concerned, there isn't. Besides, Miller called from Dubai."

"Dubai?!" Kirby slammed her hands down on Graves's desk. "That wasn't even on our radar. What's he doing there?"

"He called Peter and asked to be brought in."

"That's great! Do we have him yet?"

"No. It's not great. It's not great at all. I sent a security team from the embassy immediately, but Miller was a no-show and he hasn't checked in again."

"So what do you think?"

"The strikes are piling up, Christine. So far it looks as if he's completely disregarded his mission, murdered two women in cold blood, and is working with a foreign intelligence agency. The guy has lost it. He has no training, no concept of covert action, and he even told Clements that he wanted to bring a woman with him out of Dubai. I'm telling you, he's a massive liability to the Agency and the country. Zac Miller seems to think he's James Bond."

Kirby nodded slowly as she processed the facts. "What can I do for you?"

"Get him off the street. I've got the original team in Dubai searching the city, but I'm not a hundred percent sure he was even there. He might be playing us to buy more time for whatever he's up to with DGSE or the Iranians. I need you to assemble more resources. I want feelers out in Iran, Saudi, Oman . . . Cover the entire Middle East. I want as much focus on this as we can muster without drawing attention to it. For whatever reason, Clements has a blind spot as far as this guy is concerned. He's only seeing what he wants to see. For his own sake, we need to keep him out of it until we have Miller."

"What languages does Miller speak?"

"Just English and French as far as we know. Aside from London, he's never lived abroad. I don't see him melting into the countryside anywhere. He has a little family money, but we're watching it. Tighten up the surveillance on Marchand too. It's possible the whole Dubai story was a red herring and she's planning on leaving the country to meet with him again."

"I'll whistle up the troops," Kirby said.

"Christine, I just spoke with the deputy director. This is now officially Operation REVOCATION. You're authorized to use whatever level of force is necessary to get Miller off the street."

Kirby looked up from her notebook and made eye contact with Graves. Despite what most people thought, CIA rarely used deadly force against anyone but high-value terrorists. It was practically unheard of for the Agency to issue a capture or kill order for one of their own.

"Just to clarify, sir . . ."

"In his current state of mind, Zac Miller represents a potentially serious threat to the security of this agency and the United States of America. Make every effort to bring him in alive and intact, but bring him in."

## FORTY-ONE

ZAC OPENED HIS eyes but saw nothing. The stifling heat made him think for a moment that he might be dead, but the noise of the ship's engine reminded him that he was inside a shipping container and not a coffin. He rose to his feet and felt the floor shift underfoot. They were at sea. He made his way along the wall to the end of the container and pushed against the door. It didn't move. He leaned into it and pushed harder. Nothing. The door must have locked as the ship rolled among the swells of the open ocean. Zac's knees felt weak. He might be able to survive a few days without water, but not long enough to reach Marseille.

The container was made from heavy-gauge steel. There would be no breaking through the walls. He would have to find a way to unlock the door. He'd seen the locking levers outside, near the floor, when he'd entered. Zac dropped to his knees and searched frantically for an interior release, but there was none to be found. Curiously, there was also no doorjamb, no edge, and no seam.

He shook his head in dismay and walked to the opposite end of the container. A gentle push opened the door with a creak of the hinges. It was nighttime and only a dim, artificial light leaked in from the deck above. He followed the metal walkway around the hold. The ship's main deck was seventy-five feet straight up. Occasionally a star or a sliver of a moonlit cloud was visible between the tightly packed containers. The only noises were the rhythmic chugging of the engine and the muted sound of the ocean washing alongside the hull. The huge space was eerily still. Even at sea, nothing moved. He walked forward until he came to the multistory engine room. Zac found a spot in the shadows where he could observe the rhythm of the ship.

Two full hours passed until a lone crewman appeared. The sailor looked briefly inside the engine room before continuing up the starboard side. Zac stepped silently from the dark recess and followed him.

The watchman occasionally shined a flashlight around the hull, but he never broke stride. He was the perfect tour guide, walking through most of the hold and the upper deck before disappearing into the superstructure. Except for a dim glow from the bridge, it seemed as if the ship was asleep for the night. Zac stayed in the shadows until he was at the foot of the superstructure. There would be no explaining away his presence if he were caught. He ran his hand over the pistol and opened the door.

The gray-painted interior was lit by a single row of fluorescent lights. The only sound was the hum of the giant engine. Zac walked deeper into the superstructure. There were cabins along the second floor, like a cruise ship, and even a small lap pool. On another deck he found a work-out room and a lounge with a pair of flat-screen televisions. But it wasn't luxuries he was after. On the fourth level he found what he was looking for: the ship's galley. The small cafeteria was closed, but cereals, fruits, and microwavable foods had been left out for the night watches. He stuffed his pockets with a little bit of everything and grabbed two large bottles of water. He ascended to the uppermost level, outside the bridge, but returned to his container when he heard men talking.

IN THE FOLLOWING days, Zac left the container only at night. He stole more food and a few plastic bags for his growing pile of garbage. One night he even chanced a shower in one of the common-area heads. He longed to stay under the hot water but was dressed and back outside in under three minutes.

Though he'd learned the rhythm of the ship and worried less about being discovered, the daytime hours spent holed up in the container were brutal. With no way to tell time, he could leave only after the night watchman had made his rounds. Zac risked discovery if he left even a minute too early. To pass the time, he did push-ups and paced the length of the container in the dark. It was easy to keep his body occupied, but his mind was adrift.

He occasionally thought of Emma. He'd initially been furious with her for calling her client against his explicit instructions, but gradually he came to understand how her fear had driven her to action. She was caught up in something she couldn't comprehend. She didn't know how much was at stake. Now Zac wished only for her safety.

Other times he wondered what was happening back at CIA. Peter Clements was a smart man who understood that life didn't move in a straight line. Zac just hoped that his boss hadn't lost faith in him. Between blowing the mission in Iran, failing to reach Singapore, and screwing up the rendezvous in Dubai, Peter's patience might be running out.

About the only positive thoughts that flashed through his mind were memories of Genevieve. He recalled the first time he'd seen her, at a conference in Brussels. She'd been speaking with a group of people and Zac had just stared at her. Roughly his age, she was a study in contrasts. She'd been wearing a plain blue business suit, but it was finely tailored, and highly flattering to her tall, athletic figure. Her hair was luxurious and dark, but it was pulled back in a simple ponytail. Her eyelashes and eyebrows were sculpted and alluring, but she wore almost no makeup. He'd found her incredibly sexy.

He had desperately wanted to know more about her but they'd each been busy with their own colleagues. The two of them had exchanged a few lingering glances, but an opportunity to speak hadn't presented itself. A few months later he saw her at another conference in London. Having chastised himself many times for letting her slip away the first time, he'd immediately excused himself from his group and introduced himself in English. At first she'd pretended not to recognize him, but after torturing him for a minute, she recounted exactly what he'd been wearing when they'd first seen each other. They'd exchanged phone numbers and spoken several times before he mentioned that he'd soon be staying at his friend's apartment in Paris, and if she was around when Zac was there, they might, you know, get together for lunch, or dinner, or something . . .

ZAC'S MENTAL DIVERSIONS kept him from focusing too much on the present, but despite his best efforts, his mind would ultimately return to his compromised mission, the trials he'd endured in Iran and Dubai, and his desperate need to reveal to his CIA superiors what he'd discovered in Iran. But he was like a prisoner in solitary confinement, forced to sit alone and wrestle only with his thoughts.

## FORTY-TWO

ZAC CLIMBED DOWN from his container and fell in silently behind the night watchman. They were almost at the upper deck when Zac stopped short. The rumble of the ship's engine had stopped. Its incessant hum had been a constant distraction during his time aboard ship. Now its sudden absence was equally unsettling. The crewman continued on to the main deck, but Zac hesitated. The deck was much brighter than usual. Perhaps they'd reached France. After five days, they had to be close.

Zac stepped up onto the starboard deck and gazed out over the rail. They were close to shore, barely half a mile away, but the land was dark and uninhabited. He walked to the port side, looking for signs of France, but discovering only that the *Castor* was in a harbor with a number of other ships. None were moving faster than a few knots and several had their anchors set. In the distance, mountains rose up behind a sandy shore. It wasn't Marseille. It wasn't even a city. And the climate was hot and dry like the desert.

He felt light-headed. Maybe he'd misread the schedule

or snuck onto the wrong ship. He leaned out over the handrail and fought the urge to throw up. A smaller vessel was making its way between the big ships and Zac watched it meander through the mooring field, coming ever closer to the *Castor*. When he could read the lettering on its side, he relaxed his grip on the rail and exhaled deeply. He was quite good at geography, but even during his boredom aboard the *Castor*, he'd completely forgotten about the Suez Canal.

The sand dunes in front of him belonged to the Sinai desert. The Suez was the border between Africa to the west and Asia to the east. Without the canal, ships heading west to Europe or the Americas would have to round the notoriously rough Cape of Good Hope at the southern tip of Africa.

The spectacle was mesmerizing. The pilot boat continued its journey from ship to ship, dropping off the men who would, for a small bribe, guide the enormous vessels through the canal. More small craft were visible, mostly tugs and other pilot boats. A container ship lowered a small mooring boat over the side to secure the ship's heavy hawsers. All around, preparations were being made for the voyage through the canal.

Two warships lay at anchor up ahead. A tanker and another container ship were moored nearby and several ships, unrecognizable in the dark, were tied up far astern. All were queued up to pass through the canal. Another blue-and-orange Suez Canal Authority vessel pulled away from a container ship and motored across the bay toward the M/V *Castor*, whose gangway had been lowered against her side. In a few minutes the SCA boat drew alongside and several men stepped aboard. All were in uniform, and four were carrying rifles.

Zac bolted from his spot by the rail, moving quickly around the stern to the opposite side of the ship. With two warships in the convoy, the security team might conduct a full-scale search of the ship. He needed to hide quickly. The stairway he usually used was by the superstructure, where the team had come aboard. To go back there now would be akin to surrender. He needed to find a new way down to his container.

Zac moved cautiously until he found a ladder well that descended into the hold. The three-by-three-foot opening was scarcely large enough for a man, and completely dark except for a faint patch of light at the bottom, seventy-five feet straight down. Zac took a deep breath and stepped cautiously onto the first rung. Slowly and deliberately, he descended. Soon, every step was taken in complete darkness, every action done by touch. He tested each rung with his foot before shifting his weight. A single misstep could cost him his life.

Several times he stopped to wipe his sweaty palms on the sleeves of his suit. He continued down, patiently, carefully, and wishing he'd found another way into the hold. He stepped off the last rung into a small alcove. The dim glow he'd seen from above was from a single lightbulb on the wall behind him. He was grateful that he'd made it but wondered why anyone would use the damned ladder in the first place.

The ship had become eerily quiet. There was no mechanical noise, no water rushing past the hull, just silence. The idling engine had been shut down and the ship lay still in the calm water. He hoped the stoppage was a normal part of the crossing.

Footsteps in the distance snapped him from his thoughts. Several pairs of feet walked along the steel decking, the steps echoing off the metal containers. Two of the men spoke in an unfamiliar language. Zac pressed his body closer to the wall, but the light projected his shadow onto the main walkway. Trapped inside the ladder well, he listened as the footsteps grew louder. Repulsed by the thought, but with no better option, he hauled himself back up the ladder. He climbed up ten rungs, then another twenty, until he was draped in darkness once again.

He clung to the ladder, motionless in the dark. Two of the canal security men were in the hold thirty feet below, speaking to each other quietly. One of the men swept the area with a high-powered flashlight. Zac watched the beam find the ladder, then rotate upward. He was illuminated for an instant before the light went out and the men left. He hoped the security men were just going through the motions, oblivious to what their flashlight had discovered. Either that or they were getting reinforcements.

Zac climbed down, listening carefully, and glanced outside the ladder well. The men were gone. He hurried to his container, anxious to get out of sight, but he froze the moment he reached it. Something was different. He'd closed the door when he'd left, but hadn't secured the latches. They were secured now. He looked inside and walked to the back of the forty-foot-long box. His cache of food and water was gone. He'd been discovered.

Zac bolted from the container. Only luck had saved him from being there when the security team had searched it. He needed to find a new hiding spot, in an area the team had already cleared. During his nighttime walks he'd seen only one other place where a man could open the doors to a container, above the engine room. It was close to the superstructure and the security team had likely gone through it as soon as they'd come aboard.

Multistoried and nearly a hundred feet long, the engine room was the size of a small warehouse and contained a single, massive engine. Zac scaled a ladder to its roof. The large, flat expanse was half-filled with mechanical equipment and exhaust stacks. The uneven shapes left pockets of open space from which he could reach the half-dozen containers stacked in front of it. Most were locked or full, but he found an empty one and pulled the door closed behind him. Hot and sweaty, he lay on his back and spread his arms and legs out from his sides like the spokes of a wheel. Zac stayed there for hours, listening for the sound of approaching footsteps.

## FORTY-THREE

Z AC AWOKE THE next morning when the engine restarted. The *Castor* passed through the canal and he spent three hellish days holed up in the container atop the engine room, leaving only briefly for food and water.

His waking hours were consumed with planning how he might escape when the ship made port. His only clue that they'd reached Marseille might be the sound of the engine stopping, but by then the rest of the ship would already be a hive of activity. He wouldn't be able to improvise as he'd done when he'd boarded.

He'd already felt the fear of being locked inside a container. He had no desire to be lifted ashore and find himself stacked fifty feet in the air, or packed tightly against another container, unable to open the door. He would have to get off before the unloading started, which meant he'd have to be hidden on deck before they reached port, or find another way off the ship altogether.

Getting ashore before they made land would be ideal. The obvious choice would be to steal a lifeboat, but the *Castor* was equipped with only one, a massive orange craft mounted on a quick-launch ramp that seemed to be accessible only from inside the superstructure. It would be impossible to steal the lifeboat, but the mooring boat was a different story. Only fifteen feet long, it was lowered into the water by a small crane called a davit. He'd seen mooring boats from some of the other ships ferrying the heavy, five-inch-thick hawsers to the buoys at the entrance of the canal. If he could get the mooring boat in the water when they were within sight of land, it could get him to shore. With any luck he'd be able to do it under cover of darkness.

On his tenth day at sea Zac dared to make his way topside after one of the watches. The only welcome change aboard ship since they'd passed through the Suez was the cooler weather. They were heading north into winter in the Northern Hemisphere. As Zac snuck toward the superstructure, he felt a light rain on his face for the first time in weeks.

But by morning the rain had turned into a storm, and he was forced to sit inside his container while the ship pitched and rolled in the heavy seas. He vomited a few times but was quickly reduced to dry heaves. The smell inside the enclosed space became unbearable. He tottered on his knees for hours, praying for calmer weather, until the engine finally slowed. Zac listened carefully between his bouts of nausea. There was no question about it. The ship had definitely reduced speed. It was the sign he'd been waiting for that they were close to land.

He made a cursory check of the hold and climbed down the engine room ladder. Night had fallen. The storm howled through the containers and the ship swayed underfoot while he staggered along the metal grating. Up on deck, cold rain and sheets of spray saturated his clothes as the *Castor* thundered through the large waves. Yet Zac was pleased. The fresh air settled his stomach and the foul weather would keep the crew inside.

But the stormy weather also brought dramatically increased risk. Not only was the sea state treacherous, but Zac couldn't see the shoreline. There was a chance that the ship was reducing speed simply because of the conditions. If he lowered the mooring boat a hundred miles offshore or pointed it in the wrong direction, he was as good as dead. He had to find out if they were close to land. The cold rain blew sideways over the night sea, reducing visibility to almost zero, but he made his way to the starboard side, where a few faint lights were visible on the horizon. Zac couldn't tell if they were from a passing ship, a small town, or a distant city, but he decided to take a chance. A chance from which there would be no turning back.

He ran back to the port side and hooked a cable to the floor of the mooring boat, then used the davit to raise it from the deck. When it was suspended several feet in the air, the full force of the wind caught the fiberglass boat and spun it sideways. The outboard motor struck Zac in the head and knocked him to the ground. He lay stunned on the deck as a warm trickle of blood mixed with the cold rain.

Zac picked himself up and pushed the flailing boat over the side, but the high winds and rough seas made it swing wildly on the cable. Again he pushed it out over the water only to have it blow back before he could lower it. On his third try the mooring boat finally dropped over the side and began its descent to the sea. The boat swayed erratically on the lengthening cable. Thirty feet down, Zac could barely see the white fiberglass in the waning arc of the deck lights. After fifty feet, the heavy rain obscured it completely. He played out the cable until it went slack and the boat was finally down. It would be taking a pounding in the rough seas. He grabbed a three-quarter-inch rope coiled on deck and tied one end around the arm of the crane. He tossed the coil overboard and gave it a tug. The rough line scraped the skin from his palms. He'd tear his hands to shreds if he tried to lower himself down bare-handed.

He pulled Assad's wallet and police credentials from the suit jacket. They'd served Zac well but would serve only as devastating indictments if he were caught with them now. He hurled them over the side and into the raging storm. Zac stepped on the back of the jacket and tore off the sleeves. The material was thin but strong. He wrapped a sleeve around each of his hands and stepped to the rail, struggling to keep his balance. The weather was worsening, and the ship pitched and rolled as it plowed through the wind-driven seas. He climbed onto the railing and clutched the line. The mooring boat was down there somewhere. Staring into the blackness below, with the wind whipping his clothing and the rain stinging his face, he recalled an expression his father used to say.

*Even the longest journey starts with a single step.*

Zac leapt off the rail and slid down the side of the ship, his hands and legs wrapped tightly around the line. The roar of the churning sea was deafening. Twenty feet from the deck he lost sight of the cable that held the mooring boat. With thirty feet of line above him, he began to swing like a pendulum as the ship pounded through the swells. The bow pitched down into the trough of a particularly large wave and Zac flew forward. As the bow lifted, he shot back, slamming into the ship. The line ripped out of his hands and he flipped upside down, squeezing the line between his legs. He began to slide down quickly and crashed into the hull again. The collision knocked the pistol from its holster and sent it tumbling into the sea. Zac grabbed the line with his hands and managed to pull himself upright before he was thrown into the hull a third time.

The next time he swung forward, he was able to time the gyration and absorb most of the impact with his legs. He continued his descent until he saw the bow wake emerge from the darkness beneath him. It was enormous; a twenty-foot-high, continuously breaking wave that ground up the sea in front of it. He glimpsed the steel cable blowing slack in the wind. It had been ripped from the deck of the mooring boat. He was halfway between the sea and the deck of the ship, and his only means of getting ashore was gone.

Zac was beaten. He was tired of fighting. If he'd only worn a lifejacket, he could just drop into the sea. At least then he could pretend that there was a chance of survival. Letting go of the line would be easy. Once he fell into the bow wake the pain would be over forever.

His shoulder slammed into the hull, snapping him out of his dangerously mounting despair. His next move was forty feet in either direction, but he couldn't give up. This wasn't just about him. He had a mission to complete. For the hundredth time in the last month he picked the harder choice, the choice to survive. Using his arms and legs, Zac climbed the rope one foot at a time. The muscles in his back felt as if they were going to tear, but he hauled himself hand-over-hand toward the deck. His strength left him twenty feet from the top. He pulled himself a little higher and paused, clinging to the line, trying to muster the energy to finish the climb. The first hint of sunrise began to illuminate the clouds. Zac hauled himself up the final ten feet and swung onto the ship. Shivering uncontrollably, he lowered himself to the deck and stared blankly at the painted steel.

Streaks of light broke through the storm-addled sky as the sun continued to rise. It would soon be light. Zac raised himself off the deck and began to clean up the lines. The ship's crew would notice the missing boat, but he hoped they would blame it on the storm. More likely, it would just confirm their suspicion that they had a stowaway. Then an idea struck him. Let them think that the stowaway had escaped in the mooring boat. It might take some of the heat off Zac for the rest of the trip. Shivering and exhausted, he threw the cable over the side and stumbled back to his container.

## FORTY-FOUR

ZAC ROSE TO his feet inside his container. His body was cold and sore from being slammed against the hull the night before, but something else had roused him from sleep. The engine had slowed to idle speed and the ship was moving slowly, as it had when they'd reached the Suez Canal. The lights he'd seen last night had been on shore after all. They'd finally reached Marseille.

Zac opened the container door a few inches. Looking skyward through the tightly packed cargo hold, he saw a sliver of gray clouds. The storm had stopped. If the crew hadn't discovered that the mooring boat was missing, they would soon. And he had another problem. He had no way to get ashore.

He paced inside the container as he considered his options. Jumping over the side would leave him with broken bones if not severe internal injuries. Even if he lowered himself into the sea he'd probably die from exposure in the winter waters of the Northern Hemisphere. He'd long ago ruled out being lifted ashore inside a container.

*I am so screwed.*

Yet there was one possibility he hadn't considered. To the French, Zac would be nothing but a stowaway, and the country was a U.S. ally. If he turned himself in, he would be allowed to contact the American embassy in Paris, where he knew some of the CIA staff. They could get word back to London and Peter Clements would begin to clear up the whole mess. It would be a relatively painless way to put the nightmare of the past three weeks behind him, and when it came down to it, he had no better option. He decided to surrender to the French customs agents when the ship reached port.

While Zac waited for the ship to dock, he began to appreciate the irony that his ordeal had started in France, when he'd received that fateful phone call, and in France it would end.

A BRIEF SHUDDER confirmed that the ship had reached its berth. Each breath of fresh air invigorated Zac's weary body as he climbed the stairs. By the time he reached the upper deck, his aches and pains were fading into memories. Low clouds and a light rain filled the sky, softening the shock to eyes that hadn't seen daylight in almost two weeks. A pack of shore-based gantry cranes was already overhead, picking away at the mass of containers like scavengers on a carcass.

Zac walked along the *Castor*'s deck, grateful that for the first time in a long time his future held some clarity. He looked for the French agents who would meet the ship. There was no one atop the gangway yet, but the steep sides of the container ship blocked his view of the wharf.

He continued to the top of the gangway and watched the action on the docks below. Three columns of trucks were idling on the quay, waiting to receive the discharged containers. Far up by the bow, two men wearing hard hats and fluorescent yellow jackets looked at a clipboard while a third spoke into a handheld radio. No one paid any attention to Zac as he descended the long aluminum stairway. There were no police or customs agents at the bottom, no immigration officers or other officials. There was no one at all.

Zac stepped off the gangway and kept walking. He'd be home free if he could get out of the port without being arrested. A small convoy of trucks drove toward a cluster of warehouses on the western edge of the port. He followed on foot, hoping to find a telephone or an exit. The rain fell harder, but it masked his stained and rumpled clothing. He found a hard hat and a fluorescent jacket hanging at the base of an idle crane and put them on.

Past the warehouses and stacks of containers was a large Exit sign with a pedestrian gate behind it. A single guard bade him an inquisitive *"Monsieur?"* as he passed through, but Zac walked on, muttering in French about the weather.

He passed a group of workmen at a bus stop and set off on foot toward town, visible just a half mile distant. His fluorescent yellow jacket was easy to spot, but it was common enough. It was the same type of jacket worn by highway crews, police officers, and, in Marseille, port workers. He dumped the hard hat in a garbage can once he crossed the street.

Low-rise apartment buildings, shops, and restaurants lined the narrow streets of the sixteenth arrondissement. Zac attracted little attention as he walked. His clothing blended in passably and for the first time in weeks he could speak the local language. After having been on the run for so long, the relief of not being a wanted man was invigorating.

Zac found a *bureau de change* where he exchanged his few remaining Emirati dirhams for euros. He was confident that his boss would come through for him again. There was a pay phone outside the *bureau* and Zac once again dialed his office number from memory.

"Peter Clements, please. It's an emergency."

# *FORTY-FIVE*

THE PHONE AT CIA's London station rang through to Peter Clements's assistant. Clements was on the line in under a minute.

"It's good to hear from you again. I'm sorry we missed each other after the last call. Where are you?"

"I'm at a pay phone in France. It's an open line. I'm sorry about the missed pickup. Things got a little hectic after we spoke and I had to leave on short notice."

"That was two weeks ago. What have you been up to?"

"I had to take a last-minute cruise. I'll fill you in on the details when I see you, but I'm in the South of France now and I need a ride home. Can you send someone to pick me up?"

The line was quiet for a moment.

"Peter?"

"Things have become more complicated since we last spoke . . . The man who arranged your travel plans was very concerned when you missed the last pickup. He spent a lot of time and resources looking for you around the old neighborhood."

Zac knew Clements was referring to Ted Graves. "Well, tell him that I appreciate it."

"It's not that simple. Your missed appointment and the media coverage started him thinking that the two were connected. I tried to calm him down, but he's seeing shadows and I'm not sure he's listening."

"He works for you, doesn't he? Can't you just shut him down?"

"He does work for me, but he also works for headquarters, and his theories are gaining some traction with the Seventh Floor no matter how hard I try to reason with them."

"So what does that mean for me?"

"It means that we can't use him to get you home. There's a good chance that your car might have an accident on the way here."

Zac stared into the distance. Ted Graves had spent nearly a decade in Afghanistan and East Africa perfecting the art of making people disappear without a trace. He was not a man to be trifled with. If Clements was warning Zac over an open line, it had to be serious.

"So what should I do?"

"Call me back in an hour. I can get an SAC team to pick you up."

Zac nodded absentmindedly. An SAC team would be a group of paramilitary officers from CIA's Special Activities Center. They were operations staff, but if Clements felt he could trust them, then Zac could too.

"And one more thing . . . Call me from another location, just in case," said Clements.

"I'll call you in one hour."

Zac was dumbfounded as he hung up the phone. Never had he expected his own agency to hang him out to dry. Through all the hell he'd endured, the one constant, the one tenet of his existence, was that the mission came first. It was that important. He'd assumed the Agency would bring him in like a conquering hero, not under a cloud of suspicion or in a body bag.

He walked down the rain-soaked streets, stunned that Graves was doubting his loyalty and circumventing Clements's authority. Zac knew that there was a long-standing rivalry between the two men from when Clements had edged out Graves for the chief of station job. But it wasn't only Graves who thought the director had picked the wrong man. Many Agency veterans didn't like the idea of the job going to someone like Clements, who'd come up through the analyst ranks. Chiefs had almost always come out of operations.

Now an analyst-chief had sent an analyst into the field, and it had gone badly. Very badly. Graves was probably gunning for the chief job again and Zac was his Exhibit A. But as much as he loathed Graves's paranoia and political maneuvering, Zac had to admit that his predicament was partially his own fault. After all, he had insisted on going to Sirjan over everyone else's objections.

Zac headed south in the light rain for twenty minutes until he found what he was looking for. The Hôtel Le Nuage, in the heart of Marseille's first arrondissement, had a baroque facade, but Zac could tell from the chic couple walking down the front steps that it targeted a younger clientele. It would be a good place for him to get off the street and collect his thoughts while he waited to call Clements back. He approached the entrance and noticed a doorman standing under the awning. Tall and blond, he was wearing black leather jackboots and a matching overcoat. He stood next to the doors with his arms folded across his chest.

*What a jackass . . .*

The doorman scowled as Zac approached. His disheveled appearance and wet and dirty clothes were clearly not the preferred look at the fashionable hotel. Zac scaled the steps but the doorman remained motionless. Zac ignored the petty slight and opened the door himself. Inside the lobby he noticed a sign for the men's restroom pointing to a back hallway. He borrowed a pair of scissors from the concierge and headed back.

The bathroom was furnished with heavy mirrors and thick wooden cabinetry. Zac glanced at the three stalls. Each of the floor-to-ceiling doors was ajar. He cupped his hand under the faucet to take a long drink and caught his image in the mirror. Once again, he marveled at his appearance. His tan had faded during his time at sea, but his hair and beard had grown shaggy and unkempt. He'd always had an athletic build, but he looked thin now, his jaw and cheekbones more pronounced.

The Emiratis had photographed him when he was arrested. They were looking for the disheveled man in the mirror, and he was still wearing what was left of Assad's suit. The Iranians probably had his old passport photo, clean-shaven and fifteen pounds heavier. Zac didn't know what Clements was planning, but it wouldn't hurt to change his appearance. He raised the scissors to his face and began to trim his beard.

His facial hair was down to little more than a few days' growth by the time he'd finished. He washed his face and was taking another drink from the tap when a man in a dark suit entered the restroom. Zac noticed the man's shoes. They were fake leather with thick rubber soles. Nobody in France wore shoes like that with a suit. Nobody except cops.

Zac took a cotton hand towel and dried his face.

"Are you a guest here?" asked the man in French.

It wasn't the question Zac had been expecting. He noticed a clear plastic earpiece in the man's ear and a coiled cable running into his suit collar. The guy wasn't a cop. He was hotel security, and the doorman had probably sent him to check on Zac.

"No. I'm sorry," Zac explained in French. "I was splashed by a passing car and just came in to clean up. I'll leave now."

"Did the car splash you with a beard too? Is that why you borrowed those?" The man gestured to the scissors next to the sink. "Let me see some identification."

Zac had thrown Assad's credentials off the ship. He had nothing to show.

"I'm sorry. I'll go now."

Zac took a step toward the door, but the man would not be appeased.

"No, you won't. I'm sick of you street people coming in here and using this place as your home. The facilities are clearly marked 'For Hotel Guests Only,' and you beggars leave this place a filthy mess. I'm calling the police."

Zac took another step toward the door, his head bowed

in supplication, but the hotel security guard grabbed his arm.

"You're not getting away this time," he said. The man reached inside his jacket for the push-to-talk switch on his radio.

Zac snapped his upper body to the left and launched his right elbow into the man's head, catching him squarely in the temple. Zac caught the man as he lost consciousness.

Zac swore quietly to himself and dragged the man into the far stall, closing the door behind them and sliding the lock into place. Zac rolled him onto his side. The guard was out cold. Zac removed the man's tie to help him breathe, and that gave him an idea.

The hotel security guard was a little heavier and a little shorter than Zac, but almost the same size. Zac stripped him naked and dressed quickly in the unconscious man's clothes. Zac kept his own shoes though. He'd seen the guard naked and knew the man's shoes would be a few sizes too small. At least.

Zac checked the guard's breathing and his pulse. Both seemed normal, so Zac stuffed the guard's necktie into his open mouth. He used Assad's belt to hog-tie the man's wrists and ankles, binding them securely behind his back. It wouldn't hold forever, but it would probably take the guard a few hours to break free, once he regained consciousness.

The guard had a hundred and fifty euros in his wallet and Zac pocketed the cash before bundling everything else into his old shirt. He listened to the radio earpiece for a minute and heard nothing but silence, so he shut it off and picked up the bundle. He stepped out of the stall and stuffed the clothes and the radio deep into a stainless steel trash bin on the wall. He had just finished when the outside door swung open and two more patrons entered the restroom. Zac calmly walked back to the far stall and locked himself inside with the unconscious guard.

Once the two patrons had left, Zac removed one of the laces from the guard's shoes. He wrapped the shoelace around the sliding lock inside the stall and stepped outside, pulling gently on both ends until the door was shut. He pulled the shoelace harder until the latch slid into place with the guard locked inside. Zac pulled the shoelace out with one hand and dumped it in the trash.

Careful to avoid the doorman, Zac left the hotel and walked to the street corner in the light rain. It was nearly time to call Clements back. As he searched for another phone, he thought about the man in the bathroom; hog-tied, naked, and locked in a stall. Zac was counting on the fact that the guard would be too proud to call for help once he regained consciousness. He'd probably stew in there for hours to avoid being humiliated. Maybe next time he'd be nicer to the homeless . . .

## FORTY-SIX

ZAC FOUND A pay phone on the street and dialed CIA's main number in London again. He asked the operator for Peter Clements, but it was Ted Graves's gravelly voice that came through the receiver.

"I'm sorry we missed you last time," Graves said.

"Where is Peter? He's expecting my call."

"Peter is indisposed. His assistant said that you need some help coming in and routed the call to me. Where are you now? I'll send some people to get you."

Zac's mind was racing. Had Clements just stepped away from his office or had something happened to him? Zac didn't know how rough the interoffice politics had become. With Clements's warning about Graves, Zac had to assume the worst.

"I'm in Antibes, by the train station," he lied. He chose another city in the South of France in case Graves had somehow learned the details of Zac's earlier call to London, and every city had a train station.

"Antibes? Living the good life, I see," Graves said.

Zac could hear him typing on the other end of the phone.

"I can have you picked up in about four hours. Don't go into the train station though; your face is probably all over the place down there."

Zac had no idea what Graves was talking about but he wanted to get off the line in case the call was being traced.

"I'll lay low. I'll call you back in four hours to coordinate the final pickup. Thanks."

Zac hung up the phone and started walking toward the waterfront. What the hell was happening? The foundation of Zac's world was crumbling underneath him. He couldn't trust Graves to bring him in and now Clements was missing. Zac didn't think Graves would physically harm Clements—he was CIA's top man in London—but perhaps the taint of Zac and the mission had become so toxic that Graves had been able to push Clements aside and make himself acting chief of station.

There was only one way for Zac to save himself and save Clements. He needed to return to London on his own. He knew that if he walked into the CIA office and told his story, it could be verified. He and Clements would be in the clear, and the mission would be accomplished. Zac increased his pace as he turned through the narrow city streets. He knew people in France; people who could help him plan his return to England.

Zac stopped at a gas station and dialed the number of his college friend in Paris. Christian should have returned from his business trip by now. He could provide Zac with clothes and money, and maybe help him figure out a way to get across the Channel. He didn't know that Zac worked for CIA but Zac was prepared to level with him. After a few rings, Zac heard his old friend's voice.

*"Allo."*

"Christian, it's Zac. Hey, I'm sorry I haven't called sooner. Did you get the note I left for you?"

The phone was quiet for several seconds.

"Christian? It's Zac Miller. Are you there?"

"I . . . I can't believe you're calling me. What the hell happened to you?"

"Something came up and I only stayed at your place for one night. Thanks again. Is everything OK? You sound upset."

"No, everything is not OK. It is so fucking far from OK that I don't even know where to start. How about with the police? They haven't let me back in my apartment for more than an hour since I got back from Shanghai."

The hairs on the back of Zac's neck stood up at the mention of the police. The apartment was in a fancy building. Even if it had been burglarized the police wouldn't have sealed it off.

"Christian, tell me what happened."

"You're a very sick person, Zac. I've known you almost ten years and I never thought you were capable of something like this. I don't think I can ever move back there. The police showed me photos. There was blood everywhere."

Zac's heart was pounding. "Christian, listen to me. I need you to tell me exactly what happened."

"Where are you? Are you in jail now?"

"No, I'm not in jail. I'm in Marseille. Christian, focus, dammit! What happened in your apartment?"

"I'm hanging up now and I'm calling the police. Zac,

what you did to that poor woman was sick. Don't ever call me again."

The line went dead.

Zac's first thought was of Genevieve. His second thought was of Arzaman. What if the psychopath had decrypted Zac's phone and discovered that he had been with her in Paris? Zac had transferred all of his personal information to the CIA phone to make it appear more authentic in case it was searched. The woman he'd barely started dating might be dead. He felt a spasm in his stomach. Clements and Graves had each made cryptic comments about Zac and the media, but he'd ignored them at the time. He was too focused on his physical safety to care about the press, but it made sense now.

He picked up the phone again. He needed to find out about Genevieve. He dialed directory assistance and hoped that she had a landline. There were four G. Marchands in Paris, and Zac dialed the first number. The call went to voice mail. The second number was answered by a man named Georges. Zac was dialing the third number when a small Citroën police car turned abruptly into the other side of the gas station. Two officers stepped out in a hurry.

Zac dropped the phone and darted around the back of the station. A siren was wailing in the distance, and then another. More police. The rain picked up as he sprinted down a side street and ducked into an alley, but it was a dead end, nothing more than a parking area for the buildings on the main road. He ran to the side and squatted behind a parked car.

The two officers stepped into the alley, weapons drawn. Walking slowly, each one methodically checked his front and side. They hadn't seen Zac yet, but they would soon. The sirens grew louder. He looked under the car, watching the cops' feet as they walked. Drops of rain burst on the pavement in front of his face. He moved around the car, keeping it between himself and the police until the cops passed by and walked farther into the alley. Zac rose slowly to his feet, crouched behind the car. When both officers searched the area in front of them at the same time, Zac darted out of the alley and back onto the side street. The rain drowned out the noise of his footsteps.

He'd walked just a few feet when two police cars with their lights and sirens on swung around the corner in front of him.

## FORTY-SEVEN

ZAC FORCED HIMSELF to walk normally as the two police cars sped closer. He lowered his head slightly and hoped the rain would obscure his features. A moment later the two cars flew past in a shroud of mist and noise. His heart was pounding. He didn't know if it was from exertion, fear, or his growing suspicion that Genevieve might be dead. He would never forgive himself if he'd led Arzaman straight to her. His imagination ran wild with the torture she'd suffered before her death.

He walked faster toward the Marseille waterfront, scanning the streets for a telephone. With his long hair and the open-necked suit he'd taken from the man at the hotel, Zac already resembled half of the men in the South of France, but he paid a street vendor ten euros for a pair of knockoff Prada sunglasses as he neared the densely populated Old Port neighborhood.

The port itself was dedicated to pleasure yachts now, and the area was filled with open-air cafés and restaurants. Even in the off-season, there were a fair number of tourists roaming around. Across the road were several upscale hotels where he could get off the street and find another phone.

The Hôtel de L'Opéra was the closest. Leaded windows and Corinthian columns adorned the five-story building, but the staid architecture was in stark contrast to the chaos unfolding out front. The harried staff was helping a long line of arriving guests unload and park their cars. The clientele looked older and well-heeled, arriving in big BMW and Mercedes sedans.

Zac spotted a telephone on the valet stand and walked over. He asked one of the valets in French if he could use the phone and the valet just shrugged, too busy to care. Zac dialed the last number he'd gotten for G. Marchand in Paris.

*"Allo."*

He recognized her voice immediately.

"Thank God you're OK," Zac blurted out in English.

The line went dead. Zac stared at the phone.

*Well, I can't say I blame her.*

A few seconds later the phone on the valet stand rang and Zac picked it up.

"Zac?" It was Genevieve.

"Yes," was all he could manage.

"I'm sorry about that," she said. "You were saying . . ."

"I just found out that something horrible happened, and I . . . I was afraid it happened to you."

"That's a strange comment," she said.

"It's been a strange few weeks. I'm sorry. I just had to call and make sure you're all right."

"I know what happened, Zac. It's been on the news. The police are looking for you."

"I thought when the line went dead just now, it was on purpose. I was surprised you called back."

"I know we've just met, but I think I know you well. I also know that you were with me for lunch right before you left Paris. The timing strikes me as implausible."

Zac hadn't expected her to be so understanding. He'd called only to hear her voice and reassure himself that he hadn't caused her death.

"Where are you now?" she asked.

"I'm in Marseille, trying to figure out how to get back to London without any identification, although I couldn't travel under my real name even if I had it."

"I can be there in seven hours."

"That's incredibly generous, but I don't want to put you in any danger. I can do this myself."

"Let me help you. Don't be such a cowboy."

Zac smirked. It was the quintessential European stereotype of an American man. He thought about her offer as he watched the mayhem in front of the hotel worsen with the approach of the dinner hour.

"Genevieve, what if I could drive halfway? Where would that be?"

"Well . . . Mâcon is just about in the middle. Why?"

"Meet me there."

Genevieve described the car she'd be driving and told him when and where to meet her before hanging up.

Zac had been watching the hotel staff and the guests while he'd been on the phone. The already busy valets were now backed up with more cars than they could handle. An older couple pulled up, unnoticed by the valets. A bellhop removed a pair of suitcases from the late-model

Peugeot and accompanied its owners inside, leaving the running car unattended. Zac casually walked over and slid into the driver's seat. As he pulled away, the scene in the rearview mirror was just as it had been a few minutes before, but he was one step closer to home.

He turned onto a main road and put some distance between himself and the hotel. After a few miles he pulled into a parking space and searched the car's navigation system for the service area north of Mâcon where Genevieve had suggested they meet. It would be a three-and-a-half-hour drive. He pulled out of the space and was on the highway in less than five minutes. Traffic on the A7 Autoroute was moving smoothly at the 130 kph speed limit.

The Peugeot was a comfortable cruiser and, despite some nighttime construction, Zac made good time as he headed north. He tensed each time he drove through a toll plaza. If the car had already been reported stolen, the electronic toll collection system might flag his license plate and earn him an unwanted police escort.

After an hour on the road his exhaustion and the monotony of the highway miles caught up with him and he began to nod off. Lighted road signs beckoned tired drivers to rest, but Zac ignored them and kept pushing forward. He was early for their rendezvous when he finally pulled into the service area.

He parked in the busiest part of the lot and rubbed his hands together for warmth as he walked to the service bridge that spanned the north- and southbound lanes. The smell overwhelmed him the moment he stepped inside, though it wasn't the odor he usually associated with weary travelers and highway food. It was the aroma of pastries, grilled meats, and freshly brewed coffee. He went to the café and treated himself to a double-serving of crêpes and a cup of strong coffee. He could get used to life in France if he wouldn't have to spend the rest of it in prison.

Though his appearance had changed dramatically, Zac decided to wait in the car on the off chance that someone recognized him from the news reports about the murder. He walked back through the half-empty rows of parked cars and was nearly to the Peugeot when two motorcycle cops atop faired BMWs turned in his direction. He hesitated for a second, then lowered his head and kept walking. The officers' eyes were invisible behind their Plexiglas face masks, but one of them spoke into his radio as they passed by.

Seconds later, Zac heard the bikes make a U-turn and begin to accelerate. He walked faster. Flashing blue lights reflected off a nearby car. The cops were fifty feet behind him when they hit their sirens.

Zac darted behind a parked car and ran to the Peugeot. The motorcycles would have to take the long way around the end of the row of cars to catch him. The mounted duo raced toward the end of the parking lot as Zac fumbled with the car key.

But instead of turning left as he'd assumed, the motorcycles turned right, toward the A7. If they blocked the entrance to the highway, he was finished. He wasn't going to run down two policemen with his car. But the lights kept flashing and the sirens kept blaring as the motorcycles crossed the median and turned onto the southbound side of the highway. Zac watched the cops disappear into the traffic, their sirens drowned out by the noise of the northbound lanes. It wasn't Zac they were after.

*At least not this time.*

He decided that waiting in the stolen Peugeot wasn't the greatest idea after all, so he wiped his fingerprints off the car and walked across the bridge to his meeting spot on the southbound side. He sat in the dark and digested his first decent meal since passing through the Suez Canal.

Ten minutes later a black Mercedes-AMG sedan downshifted and pulled to the curb. Genevieve lowered her window halfway and made eye contact with Zac. He climbed into the passenger seat and she immediately checked her mirrors.

"Are you sure you're comfortable doing this?" he asked.

She glanced at him, her expression inscrutable, and accelerated quickly onto the southbound ramp. "There's a jacket from the Paris Saint-Germain Football Club in the backseat. Put it on."

"I'll take that as a yes," he said. He gazed at her as she drove. The dim light of the highway accentuated her dark eyes and the delicate curves of her face. Her long hair fell casually over her shoulders. He even studied her slender hand and fingers as she worked the gear shift.

"Were you in prison?"

"No," Zac said as he checked the passenger-side mirror. "But that could change any second. Why?"

"You're staring at me like a man who just got out of prison. Try talking to me . . ."

She smirked and Zac relaxed again. "I'm sorry. I'm

just really happy to see you and I can barely believe that you trust me enough to help."

"Zac, if I thought there was the remotest possibility that you were a murderer, I would not have come."

"I appreciate that. Why are you so sure that I'm not a killer? We don't know each other that well yet."

"I think we know each other better than we let on. And I said I didn't think that you're a *murderer*," she said as she wove the car through traffic.

Something beeped inside the car and Genevieve slowed.

"What was that?" Zac asked.

"Radar detector. There's probably a speed camera up here."

"I thought radar detectors were illegal in France."

"So is speeding."

"I'm just thinking you might not want to get stopped with me in the car."

Genevieve looked at Zac, her full lips slightly pursed. She tilted her head to one side and her dark hair fell across her face. She spoke in a sultry voice.

"I am very sorry, Officer. The car is so powerful, I can barely control myself when I'm inside it."

Zac smiled.

"I haven't had a ticket in years," she said with a laugh as she exited the highway and reentered on the north-bound side.

"Maybe no tickets, but I'd frisk the hell out of you if I were a cop."

"Mmm . . . maybe later. So where have you been the past few weeks?"

Zac weighed things over in his mind for a few seconds

before answering. "I'm sorry. I can't say. I know that makes me sound guilty, but I'm not going to lie to you."

"I have an idea. Let's stop with the games. I know what you do and you know what I do, so can we speak to each other like adults?"

Zac sat in silence.

Genevieve continued. "You're not a technology consultant and I'm not with the Ministry of Foreign Affairs. Can you at least admit that? For heaven's sake, we met at a NATO conference in Brussels and then again at the Jane's defense and security conference in London. The only people at those meetings who are who they claim to be are the people in uniform. I work for DGSE and you work for one of the twenty U.S. intelligence agencies."

Zac smiled. "CIA," he said.

"Thank you for trusting me the way I trust you. I was almost sure before our lunch in Paris, but after it, I was convinced. You went from trying to seduce me to leaving for the Gare du Nord in ten minutes. That's not how normal men operate."

"Maybe I remembered that I had tickets for the Manchester United game that afternoon."

"Nice try. It's also the reason I didn't go to the police about the murder in Paris. It would have led to too many questions about who we are and how we know each other. I also thought it was very likely that you were on company business and the victim wasn't who they said she was."

"I don't know anything about her. I think I'm being framed to keep me underground. With this over my head I can't go to the police."

"That explains Singapore."

"What happened in Singapore?" Zac looked over at Genevieve.

"You don't know . . . I'm sorry. It was the same thing, another young prostitute and a great deal of evidence pointing to you. Whoever did this wanted you boxed in in both hemispheres."

Zac slammed his fist against the dashboard. Over the next hour he told Genevieve in broad terms how he'd been in the Middle East and made his way back on his own. He explained how some "confusion" within CIA was causing him problems and how he needed to finish the last leg of his journey back to London on his own. They discussed putting him on a flight, or the Eurostar train, but decided that public transportation would be impossible without proper identification, and going to DGSE would probably land him in jail. Zac told her how he was planning to steal a boat to cross the English Channel. They discussed his plan and she approved, suggesting that he leave from the coastal town of Dieppe, which had a large marina without the heavy security of a major port city like Calais. They were silent for barely three minutes when Zac fell asleep in the passenger seat. When he awoke, they were pulling into a quiet alley.

"Where are we?" he asked.

"My parents' town house. You need rest and a change of clothes. We'll leave in the morning."

"I need to get to the coast tonight. Please, let's keep going. I can drive if you're tired."

"It's already midnight, Zac. It's two more hours to Dieppe, and you still have to find a boat and supplies. It's a quiet city in the winter. Any activity in the middle of the night will attract attention. Come inside and get some sleep."

She backed into a parking space and unlocked the doors. In a minute they were standing in the town house's marble-tiled foyer. Zac admired the antiques and original works of art.

"Nice place, but why are we here?" he asked.

"Because my parents are traveling and I'm under surveillance."

"What?!" Zac peered at the street through the sidelights. "Why didn't you tell me . . ."

"Relax, Zac. This is the world I move in. At first I thought it was related to my work, but when I got your call it suddenly occurred to me that it might have to do with you. That's why I hung up on you earlier when you called. I called you back on my secure DGSE phone. The *police judiciare* can't break it. I'm sure your NSA can, but you'll be long gone before they do."

"What about your car?"

Genevieve gave him a patient smile.

"It's my brother's. We switched cars before I came to get you. He works in the family textile business, so he finds the intelligence world very exciting. I asked him to take the surveillance team for a little ride. Right now a white Peugeot van, a black Renault Clio, and a silver Audi A3 are following him back from Luxembourg."

Zac nodded appreciatively. "I won't underestimate you again."

"See that you don't!" She smiled, dropped her keys on a demilune table, and walked into the kitchen. "Why don't you take a shower and I'll make something to eat. My brother's room is on the third floor, the second door on the left. He usually leaves some clothes here and you're about the same size."

Zac walked up behind her and put his hands on her waist. He smelled her hair, kissed her shoulder. "Thank you."

"You're welcome. Now go take a shower. You smell like a skunk."

Zac laughed and headed upstairs. When Genevieve finished cooking, she walked into her brother's room and found Zac dressed in her brother's clothes, sound asleep on top of the covers. She lay down next to him and gently stroked his face.

## FORTY-EIGHT

GENEVIEVE VENTURED OUT in the cold morning rain to buy some fresh food. She prepared a hearty breakfast of eggs, berries, and chocolate-filled croissants. Zac devoured it all. She'd even found one of her brother's old ski jackets for Zac's trip across the Channel.

At eleven sharp they were back in her brother's Mercedes and on their way out of the eighth arrondissement. The route took them onto the Champs-Élysées and Genevieve drove slowly up the scenic boulevard. The sun broke through the rain clouds, illuminating the Arc de Triomphe as they passed by.

"I remember being here with my parents when I was very young," Zac said. "My father pointed out the Arc and told me the history behind it, but I only remember one thing he said. 'You can lose a lot of battles and still win the war.' He always said it to encourage me after a setback. It's strange. I see the Arc almost every time I come to Paris, but this is the first time I've thought about that trip . . . They died a few years later."

"I'm sorry."

Zac was surprised that he'd opened up about his per-

sonal life, but he had dropped his guard around Genevieve and the story had just slipped out. He automatically
turned the conversation back to the day ahead.

"So what do you know about Dieppe?" he asked.
"Have you ever been there?"

"A few times. It's a beach town with ferry service to
the U.K. and a large marina, although I suspect it will be
nearly empty today. Are you sure you want to go in this
weather?"

The two of them had examined the forecast on her
laptop during breakfast. Strong winds and rain had been
lashing the coast for days, generating heavy seas up the
Channel. Genevieve had tried to convince him to wait
another day before returning, but he'd been adamant
about leaving as soon as possible.

"I'll be fine. I've sailed in worse than this."

She dropped the subject and resumed her usual pace
behind the wheel once the congestion of Paris was behind them. Endless gray clouds obscured the sun as they
drove through mile after mile of farm country. They
spoke about the murders, Zac's trip back from the Middle East, and what he might be returning to at CIA/
London. Though there was little traffic, and they hadn't
seen any police, Genevieve tapped the steering wheel
nervously with her fingertips.

The wind and rain picked up as they neared the coast.
A few seabirds soared overhead, buffeted by strong gusts.
The farmland eventually gave way to commercial development and they reached the outskirts of the city at a
little past one o'clock in the afternoon. Zac looked out

the window and wiped the sweat from his palms as they drove through downtown Dieppe. If everything went according to plan, he would be in England before the next sunrise.

## FORTY-NINE

CELIA HAD JUST reached the foot of the Albert Memorial when Sir James appeared. Kensington Gardens was lovely throughout the year, but less so as winter approached. She raised the collar of her heavy wool coat and walked to meet him.

"I hope you're not playing up the whole cloak-and-dagger bit for me, James. We could speak just as privately in front of a fire at my home, you know."

"If you must know, I'm on my way to the Royal Albert Hall to listen to a Prokofiev string quartet."

"And I'm on my way to becoming an exhibit at the Natural History Museum if we don't get out of this damp cold. What the devil have you found out?"

Celia took the arm of her dear friend and the two of them walked west through the bare trees.

"You really are fond of this American, aren't you?"

"He was courteous, charming, and civilized, but beneath his gentlemanly demeanor there was an intensity, an intellect that was absorbing and processing everything around him. You could see it in his eyes, and in his speech and movement. He reminded me of you, actually."

"My goodness, he must be quite dashing."

"A half-century-younger version of you . . . Oh James, I just can't rid myself of this feeling that something's not quite right."

"Well, I'm afraid your intuition may be correct. After you and I spoke I phoned up an old chum, a rather senior fellow over at Six, and asked if they had any interest in your boy. He said, 'Possibly,' which is the intelligence community equivalent of jumping up and down and screaming 'yes' at the top of one's lungs."

"So what did he say?"

"I told him about your time together on the plane, the photographs, and then the incident at Changi with the 'other' Mr. Miller. He listened carefully, but I didn't hear from him for over a week. When he did call, he said only that he was still looking into it. He finally phoned me back this morning and asked to meet. Apparently, he ran it by the Americans and they dismissed it out of hand."

"Well, that's no good. Do you think he's telling you the truth?"

"What he did told me more than what he said. Why wait two weeks, then insist on meeting in person, to tell me that my concerns were of no concern? That's a polite way of saying that there's something there, but he can't discuss it. This fellow owes me his career, and even his life on one occasion, so he's tipping his hand to me without appearing to do so. I suspect that whatever your friend is involved in is either very hush-hush or royally cocked-up. One way or another, the Americans know who he is, and they don't want to talk about it."

"Well . . . We shall see about that."

## FIFTY

Z AC'S EYES DARTED over the wet roads as Genevieve drove through the city. Louis XIV–era buildings with white brick facades and gray-tiled roofs lined the historic streets of Dieppe, but he wasn't looking at the architecture. He was searching for anything that might help him, or hinder him, in his journey across the English Channel tonight.

Genevieve drove along the Quai Henri IV to the city's only marina. The docks were inland, surrounded on three sides by land, with a man-made channel leading to the sea. Less than half of the two hundred slips were occupied on the cold December afternoon. They drove past the marina, wanting to reconnoiter the surrounding area as well.

Genevieve pulled into a nearly deserted parking lot at the beach and shut off the engine. They stepped out of the car and Zac was in his element once again. Just as in Marseille, the smell of the salt air and the rotting detritus of the sea invigorated him like a reunion with a long-lost friend. As they walked along the beach, Zac looked out over the English Channel. The breeze blew steadily around twenty knots while leaden clouds scudded across the horizon. Pockets of rain fell in the distance.

They set out on foot toward the marina. Genevieve wrapped her arm inside Zac's while they strolled along the sidewalk. Through the fence they could see several commercial fishing boats and dozens of smaller powerboats tied up at the western end of the docks. The larger powerboats and sailboats were clustered at the eastern side, closer to the sea. Most were laid up for the winter. He'd have to steal something big enough to cross the notoriously rough Channel, but small enough for him to handle alone.

"What are you thinking?" she asked.

"About how I could get used to having you on my arm."

She looked up at him and grinned. "Seriously, what are you thinking about?"

"If I take a powerboat, I could be there in a couple of hours."

"Do you know how to steal one?"

"A lot of boat owners hide a key on board, but the wires are usually exposed underneath the dashboard if I have to hot-wire it. It's easy. The bigger issue is fuel. I'd burn a lot of it in this weather and I won't know how much is in the tanks until I get the covers off and the motors started. I'd probably have to try a few different boats."

"That will attract a lot of attention."

"Exactly. With a sailboat I could sail it off the dock if I had to." He looked up at the treetops bending in the strong wind. "It'll be a fast reach across the Channel with the breeze from the southwest."

Despite the cold and occasional rain shower, a few groups of tourists were wandering around downtown, taking photographs, looking in shop windows, and checking out the restaurants. They provided good cover for Zac and Genevieve as they loitered outside the marina, surveying the sailboats. There were easily a dozen vessels in the thirty- to forty-foot range that he could skipper single-handed, so he narrowed his pool to the boats with radar. The Channel was always packed with ferries, tankers, and cargo ships, and he had no interest in a run-in with any of them. His near-collision with the supertanker in the Strait of Hormuz had been a well-learned lesson in the importance of situational awareness.

They ambled past the marina entrance. A dozen gulls stood on the ground just inside the gate, braced against the strong winds. A sign on the fence read "Port Jehan Ango," named in honor of a local sailor and trader from the fifteenth century. The gate was locked with a digital keypad. Zac focused on it like a laser as they walked by. The 1, 3, 6, and 8 keys were worn much more than the others. The combination probably hadn't been changed in years. They kept walking. There was a harbormaster's office and two small businesses inside the fence: a ship's chandlery and a hull-cleaning service. Both were closed.

They returned to the car and drove to a parking space overlooking the marina. They studied the area for nearly an hour. There was no watchman on duty and only a single group of boaters came through the gate, looking cold and miserable. The season and the weather were keeping the marina very quiet. Dusk came early in winter and by four o'clock, Zac was ready to go. Genevieve pulled around the block and they stepped onto the sidewalk to say good-bye. Zac pulled her close and hugged her tightly. Her head was pressed against his chest as he spoke.

"I'm sorry our second date wasn't much better than the first. You must be thinking that our relationship is cursed."

"No, Zac. I think I've learned more about what kind of man you really are than I would have in a dozen dates."

"And?"

She pushed him away gently.

"And you'd better call me when you get back to London. Even if it's only for five seconds, just to let me know you're safe. We can talk about everything else after you clear your name with the Agency, and you *will* clear your name."

"I'll call, but if for whatever reason you don't hear from me by next week, I want you to call Peter Clements. He's the London chief . . ."

"I know who Peter Clements is."

"Of course you do, Mata Hari. Just call him and tell him everything we talked about; how I came to France, my plan for getting to London, and anything else you can. I don't exactly know what's going on over there but I have to trust someone."

"Office politics . . ."

"There are a lot of moving parts." Zac took a deep breath and held her again. "Genevieve, you've been so good to me. You had faith in me and trusted me when you could have just hung up the phone . . . I hope someday I can be there for you."

"Do you know what convinced me to help you?"

"You said it was the timing, that we were having lunch when the murder happened."

"It was the joy in your voice when you heard that I was alive. Only my parents sound like that when I pick up the phone."

She looked up at Zac and kissed him gently on the mouth.

"I'll call you tomorrow," he said. He turned and walked back to the marina.

He stood in front of the locked gate, facing the electronic keypad. He tried several combinations of the worn numbers he'd seen earlier until 1-6-3-8 eventually opened the electromagnetic lock. He hurried past the chandlery and the harbormaster's office to the waterfront.

A dozen large docks ran from shore into the harbor with smaller docks branching out from the larger ones. A few low-intensity lights illuminated the boats. Zac stepped onto an elegant Wauquiez forty-footer and did a quick check of the usual key-hiding places without luck. He moved on to a second boat, and then a third.

The process was taking too long. Every minute he spent walking around the docks increased the risk that he might be spotted. If he didn't find a key soon he would have to break a cabin door and take his chances with starting the engine or simply sailing off the dock.

*Serenité* was a sleek Jeanneau 45. She was larger than what he wanted, but he was encouraged by the small *"A Vendre"* sign with a name and telephone number taped to the stern. If the boat was for sale, then there was probably a key hidden somewhere for the brokers who would show the boat to prospective buyers. The companionway doors were locked, but a quick search under the cockpit seats yielded the key. Zac unlocked the doors and climbed through the companionway before descending four stairs into the cabin.

The boat was almost new, the smell of fiberglass resin still strong within her. There were a few life preservers and a small tool kit aboard but almost nothing else. He sat down inside the stone-cold boat and closed his eyes in silent prayer as he turned the key halfway in the ignition. The fuel tank was one-quarter full. It was enough. He'd only need the engine for half an hour to get out of the harbor in Dieppe and then again to dock the boat in England. The electronics came to life as well: The GPS, radar, and wind instruments were all working. It was a big boat to sail alone in heavy winds, but it was his best option.

Zac still needed some decent clothing for the trip. He shut the companionway doors and walked back to the hull-cleaning business that he'd passed on the way in. He threw his shoulder against the door and felt it budge. He hit it again, splintering the jamb and knocking the door open. The room was a mess, with lines and buoys strewn about the floor. He put on a sun-bleached foul-weather jacket that he found, but there was nothing for his legs or feet. He was about to leave when he spied a large closet built into the wall. Zac undid the catch and dragged the old plywood door across the floor. A wide grin crept across his face as his eyes danced over the shelves.

## FIFTY-ONE

**Z**AC CLIMBED DOWN into the cabin of the sailboat, hefting a large duffel bag after him. Inside it was the gear he'd taken from the hull-cleaning shop. He set it down and looked around the cabin, taking stock of any equipment he might use on his journey. His gaze came to rest on one of the life preservers. If he went overboard tonight, the flotation device would only prolong his death, not prevent it. He left it where it lay.

*Serenité*'s three-cylinder diesel motor was barely audible as she pulled away from the dock. The late hour and foul conditions were keeping most everyone indoors, but Zac knew that he would be most visible when he motored out of the harbor. He switched on the red, green, and white navigation lights, deciding to hide in plain sight as he left the marina. Heavy clouds obscured the moon and stars but the lights of the city made navigating out of the harbor relatively easy. Farther out were a pair of breakwaters. Once he was outside those, he would be in the English Channel and on his way home.

The chartplotter showed that the nearest city on the English coast was Eastbourne, almost sixty nautical miles to the northeast. He energized the radar and started scanning his instruments and his surroundings.

The wind blew from the southwest, funneled up the Channel by the coastlines of France and England. The same waves that were crashing into the western breakwater were, just a little farther out, rolling unimpeded up the Channel. The waves were high and steep. He'd once crossed from Dover to Calais on a twenty-thousand-ton ferry and seen three-quarters of the passengers succumb to seasickness.

Zac steered away from the wind before turning gently toward it, allowing him to ease the sailboat into the open sea with her bow pointed toward the swells.

The impact of the first wave was stunning in its violence. The sailboat pitched up so quickly that it buckled his knees. Zac opened the throttle and *Serenité* scaled the massive wave. The wind howled through the rigging and strong gusts blew the tops off of the waves. Salt spray and sea foam blew across the surface. A moment later, the fast-moving swell disappeared underneath the sailboat and she pitched down, accelerating into the trough between the waves. *Serenité* plowed into the face of the next wave. Frigid seawater cascaded over the front and raced aft along the deck, crashing into him and soaking his legs.

He punched the throttle to climb the next wave. He modulated his speed better and *Serenité* found her rhythm among the heavy swells. He was relieved to have his sea legs under him, but a sailboat was in its element under sail. Zac set the autopilot and raised only two-thirds of the mainsail, to make the boat more controllable in the high winds.

He turned northwest toward Eastbourne, fifty-eight nautical miles away. *Serenité* was making over eight knots with just the reefed mainsail, but that still put him over seven hours from England. Seven hours, sailing by himself in such conditions, would be exhausting and dangerous. He needed more speed and decided to use the jib as well. A second sail flying at the front of the boat would generate more power. He unrolled the jib and it instantly filled with wind. The boat accelerated to eleven knots before Zac shut off the motor.

On her new heading, the waves came from the side and rolled under *Serenité*, making standing and steering tricky. He tried engaging the autopilot but it overreacted dangerously to the boat's gyrations, and the radar was nearly useless. False contacts littered the display as radar waves bounced indiscriminately off the enormous seas.

With his hands on the wheel and his eyes darting between the instruments and the sea, Zac eventually brought the boat to a fragile equilibrium. *Serenité* was finally stable, but her captain was falling apart.

## FIFTY-TWO

ZAC HAD BEEN shivering on deck since the first wave crashed over the bow and soaked him below his foul-weather jacket. His teeth started chattering soon after. Now he'd lost all feeling in his feet and moving his legs had become nearly impossible. More than once he caught himself staring numbly at the GPS or off into space. Despite his mounting impairment, he realized that if he didn't warm up soon, he would probably die from hypothermia before he made land.

Indifferent to the risk of collision or capsize, Zac engaged the autopilot and staggered to the cabin. He made it three steps before a gust of wind and an errant wave knocked *Serenité* hard onto her side, slapping her sails against the sea. Only luck kept him from falling overboard. After a few seconds, the weight of the keel caused the boat to right herself and Zac scampered back to the wheel. He turned northeast, away from Eastbourne. With the wind at his back, he was able to engage the autopilot and furl the jib, rolling it back around itself like a cheap window shade. With only the mainsail up, the boat slowed and became more manageable.

The autopilot was able to maintain control as the boat surfed along with the waves. He monitored the situation for a few more seconds then stumbled below into the cabin, collapsing onto one of the settees. It took several minutes to strip off his wet pants. He poked his thigh with his index finger. It was cold, dense, and completely without feeling.

He'd taken a dry suit for scuba diving from the shop in Dieppe but had been so eager to put to sea that he hadn't put it on. Unlike a wetsuit, in which a thin layer of water was sandwiched between the skin and the suit, a dry suit was designed to keep all of the water on the outside. The men who scraped barnacles off of the boats in Dieppe spent hours in the cold water each day and the dry suits kept them comfortable while they worked. Zac stripped off his wet clothes and stepped awkwardly into the fleece-lined suit. With a waterproof zipper, and seals around the neck and wrists, the suit would insulate his body and prevent even a drop of water from reaching his skin. He donned his jacket, and a neoprene hood and gloves from the duffel bag, before making his way back to the wheel.

He turned back on course for Eastbourne and switched on *Serenité*'s VHF radio, turning the volume to its highest setting so he could hear it over the roar of the wind and the sea. Despite a proliferation of newer technologies, when the weather turned foul and the seas grew rough, ship captains still liked to speak to the man piloting the 250,000 tons of steel headed toward them. A few seconds after he switched it on, Zac heard a chemical tanker hail a container ship, and knew that he was on the right channel. Even if he didn't get any information out of it, the chatter alone might keep him awake.

The weather continued to worsen. A rain squall drove the wind to almost forty knots and Zac struggled to control the boat. Each gust heeled her over as it overpowered the sails, forcing them down toward the water until the wind spilled out.

Zac was wrestling with the helm when he noticed a supertanker draw alongside *Serenité*. Its massive bow smashed through the same seas that were tossing the sailboat around like a child's toy. Zac stood motionless, awed by the display of raw power. Another wave exploded in front of the ship as the two forces collided. White water shot hundreds of feet to the sides. A wall of spray soared into the air. The effect was hypnotic as the giant ship moved rhythmically and soundlessly along its course.

Despite the drama of the tanker crashing through the seas, Zac realized that he hadn't even been aware of its presence until it had been abreast *Serenité*. If it had approached directly behind the sailboat, Zac would be dead. He attempted to adjust the radar again, playing with the settings until most of the false contacts were eliminated. Its effective range was barely one mile, but it was better than nothing.

With the radar somewhat functional and visibility hovering around a thousand yards, Zac sailed in front of the tanker and ducked behind two other ships. He was making steady progress, but the weather continued to deteriorate as he sailed farther offshore. Even in the darkness, the surface of the sea was laced with veins of white, windswept water. Gusts over forty knots were common, sounding like low-flying jets as they blew past, yet he could reduce sail no further.

At one point Zac realized that he'd been neglecting the radar. He glanced down and discovered a large number of blips spread across the left-hand side of the screen. He stared at the monitor, thinking that the big waves were again wreaking havoc with the returns, but when he popped his head up and looked to the west, a kaleidoscope of faint lights dotted the horizon. For a moment he thought he'd spotted land, but he was still thirty-eight nautical miles from England. The lights were from a dozen large ships, all headed northeast, directly across his path. He realized that he'd been on the outskirts of the sea-lanes before. Now he was about to sail through the busiest shipping channel in the world.

## FIFTY-THREE

THE THIRTY-KNOT WINDS and twenty-foot seas did not deter the professional mariners from their work, and *Serenité*'s radar revealed a loose flotilla of merchant ships closing in from the southwest. But as Zac looked out over the Channel at night, he could see nothing but a smattering of flickering lights. Getting safely across the sea-lanes would be like crossing a freeway on foot.

*Serenité* soon passed in front of a commercial fishing boat. Zac watched as its bow plunged into the heavy seas and spray cascaded over its bridge. A massive container ship, much like the M/V *Castor*, appeared a few moments later. It was moving faster than the fishing boat and he decided not to risk crossing in front of it. He turned northeast, heading parallel to the bigger ship. Zac stared in awe of its size while he waited for it to outrun him.

But every minute he waited was a minute spent heading in the wrong direction; another minute that he'd have to spend beating his way back to England in the horrific weather. The container ship ultimately passed without incident and Zac once again steered for Eastbourne.

The ship traffic continued to increase until a single massive radar return edged onto the radar screen. It was the biggest one he'd seen, and it was headed right for him. When it closed to within a half mile of *Serenité*, Zac looked up to see that the single radar blip was actually two large ships running close together. There wasn't enough time to duck behind the first ship and he wouldn't make it in front of the second one. He would have to thread the needle, passing in front of the first ship then behind the second. In good weather it would require seamanship and a little bit of luck. Tonight, it would require a miracle.

The distance to the first ship closed quickly. Her lights were moving erratically, not pitching up and down like the other vessels fighting the heavy seas. Zac had been managing his fear all night, focused intently on his goal of making it to England. Only when *Serenité* was nearly in front of the first ship did he become truly terrified. It was an enormous auto carrier and it was out of control. The top-heavy, slab-sided ship was rolling precariously from side to side. It hadn't been designed for heavy winds and looked as if it might capsize each time it rolled.

Zac sailed past the auto carrier until he was halfway between the two ships. The second vessel was a heavily laden container ship like many others he'd seen. As he'd done before, he turned to the northeast, running parallel to the two mammoth vessels, while he waited for the container ship to pass him.

The slow-motion gyrations of the auto carrier became more extreme, with the ship veering slightly toward *Serenité* and the container ship each time it rolled. Zac found himself trapped between the out-of-control auto carrier on his right and the container ship on his left. If something didn't change, there was a very real chance that the two ships might collide, and Zac would be crushed between a half-million tons of steel.

The alarming condition of the auto carrier hadn't escaped the container ship either. Her captain was shouting over the radio and sounding her horns. The deep, brassy sound bellowed through the storm, but neither the radio nor the horns elicited a response from the auto carrier.

Zac's only chance was to try to stop the sailboat and let the two ships sail past. He would be dead in the water, facing into the waves and wind, but it was his only option. If he didn't act quickly, *Serenité* would be pulverized.

He turned toward the wind and was immediately knocked down. A wave crashed over the side, sending a flood of white water rushing across the deck. It lifted him off his feet and slammed him into the railing. He struggled to catch his breath as icy seawater covered his face. A second wave and a howling gust spun the sailboat back to the north, filling her sail with wind and pushing her to within a few hundred feet of the container ship.

Zac pulled his battered body off the rail and turned *Serenité* parallel to the container ship on his left. The auto carrier was less than two hundred feet to his right, and closing the gap with each gyration. The container ship had begun to slowly turn away, but it was clear that the two ships were going to collide. Zac had one last chance to avoid being crushed. He turned *Serenité* in a tight circle as he attempted to hold position while the monstrous vessels steamed past.

The auto carrier was rolling thirty degrees to each side. As long as a city block and twelve stories high, it blocked out the sky above Zac's head when it rolled.

The gap between the ships shrank to less than two hundred feet. Zac aimed for a spot just behind the container ship and punched through its enormous wake. He was less than one hundred feet behind the two vessels when the auto carrier rolled again, striking the container ship and filling the air with the screech of metal scraping against metal. Dozens of containers tumbled into the water between the two ships when the auto carrier rolled away. Several seconds later it rolled into the faster-moving container ship a second time, knocking more containers overboard and tearing a hole in the auto carrier's side. Cars plunged into the water as it rolled away, leaving a minefield of slowly sinking debris on the surface. Zac tore his gaze away from the destruction and focused on staying alive. He was still in the sea-lanes.

A few minutes later he passed behind another tanker, and a gap opened up that allowed him to turn back toward Eastbourne. Despite nearly being crushed between the two ships, *Serenité* had held up well, but the same could not be said for Zac. His shoulder and back were badly hurt from being slammed into the rail and he tasted blood in his mouth, though he couldn't remember how it got there.

Chatter on the VHF radio picked up dramatically.

From its U.K. base station, Her Majesty's Coastguard was interrogating the two ships that had collided. The auto carrier was still out of control and had sustained numerous injuries among its crew, prompting her captain to issue a Mayday call. The container ship was understandably upset but positioning itself to help if necessary. They each mentioned that a sailing yacht had been in the middle of the fracas although no one knew if it had been damaged or sunk. Darkness and the weather conditions prevented anyone from getting the sailboat's name. The coastguard station hailed the anonymous vessel over the radio but Zac did not answer.

*Serenité* hadn't been identified by the coastguard, but Zac knew that there were enough shore-, ship-, and maybe even aircraft-based radars turning to track him if they wanted to. Collisions at sea were dangerous and expensive, and there was a real risk that the authorities might intercept him for questioning. They probably wouldn't board him in such dangerous weather, but they might send a cutter or a helicopter to identify him. Worse still, if they thought he was in danger, the coastguard might launch a search-and-rescue operation.

As he'd done so often when backed into a corner, Zac went on the offensive. Affecting a thick French accent, he shouted into the radio to be heard over the wind.

"Coastguard, coastguard, *Indomptable*, over." He gave a false name in case *Serenité* had already been reported stolen.

"*Indomptable*, this is Dover coastguard. Go ahead."

"I am the yacht that saw *l'accident*, over."

"Roger, *Indomptable*. Are you all right? Can you describe what you saw during the collision? Over."

"I am fine. I do NOT require assistance. The car ship was very . . . unbalanced. It crashed into the other one."

"*Indomptable*, where were you when you first spotted the two vessels?"

"I was south of them . . . *Une minute*." Zac clicked off the radio for a minute. He wanted to appear helpful but didn't want to get tripped up by too many questions.

"Sorry, I am alone and must sail the boat in the violent winds. Can I telephone you when I make port?"

"*Indomptable*, we have no record of you registering your crossing at Cap Gris-Nez or Dover. What is your destination in the U.K.?"

"I am not making land. I am returning to Cherbourg tonight."

The radio went quiet for a moment and Zac began to second-guess his decision to radio in.

"*Indomptable*. Can you put in at Dover?"

*Not a chance in hell . . .*

"I do not think it is safe for me to go into a strange port in this weather."

The radio went quiet for half a minute.

"*Indomptable*, you may proceed on course but you are instructed to call MRCC Dover as soon as your workload permits or immediately upon making land. Do you copy? Over."

"*Oui*, Coastguard, *merci*. *Indomptable* out."

They weren't happy, but the coastguard seemed to be placated for now.

Navigating through the ship traffic in the sea-lanes had taken Zac far off course. The wind speed had dropped into the low thirties, but his new heading had him plowing into the face of the steep waves. White water broke over the bow with every second or third wave and he was making less than two knots toward land. Zac was battered and exhausted. He stood numbly at the wheel and tried to keep *Serenité* under control.

Neither he nor the boat could continue like this for much longer. He'd sailed so far off course that the English town of Hastings was now half the distance to his original destination in Eastbourne. The course to Hastings would also put the wind on his beam, allowing him to sail faster. He turned north and immediately felt the boat accelerate.

*Serenité* closed within ten miles of shore and the wind speed dropped into the low twenties. Though the seas were still rough, the conditions had subsided enough to set the autopilot for a few minutes. He was exhausted, cold, and sore, but grateful for the dry suit. It had undoubtedly saved his life.

Scattered patches of night sky broke through the cloud cover as the storm blew itself out. Zac yawned several times as his adrenaline rush subsided. He closed his eyes for a moment and thought of Genevieve.

"INDOMITABLE, INDOMITABLE..."

He had a vague sense that someone was speaking. He opened his eyes and squinted at his gloves. They were stiff from gripping the cold wheel. They looked more like hooks than hands. He flexed them slowly, trying to . . .

"*Indomitable, Indomitable*, this is HMS *Raider*, over."

There was that voice again. If he could just sleep for a few minutes more . . .

The glare of a searchlight became visible. It swept the surface and found *Serenité* after a few seconds. Zac snapped out of his stupor.

"*Indomitable, Indomitable*, this is HMS *Raider*. Do you copy? Over."

In his sleepy trance, Zac had forgotten that he'd told the coastguard that the boat's name was *Indomptable*. The Brits had simply anglicized it. They'd been calling on the radio and now there was a damned Royal Navy ship a quarter mile off his port beam.

"*Raider*, this is *Indomptable*, over," Zac said.

"*Indomitable*, is it your intention to make port in the United Kingdom? Over."

"*Negatif, Raider*. I am sailing close to shore only for the calmer waters, over."

"And then?"

"Home to Calais."

The radio went quiet for several seconds.

"Stand by, *Indomitable* . . ."

Zac could see the navy ship begin to turn toward him, the searchlight never leaving the sailboat.

"*Indomitable*, repeat your final destination."

"Calais . . ." Even as he spoke the word, his exhausted mind knew something wasn't right.

"*Indomitable*, we understood you to be sailing on to Cherbourg. Have you changed your plan? Over."

"*Non, Raider.* Sorry, I am very tired. I am heading back to Cherbourg. I am going to sail along the shore for a break from the big winds, and then I go home."

Zac watched HMS *Raider* approach. The navy ship turned out to be a large patrol boat. Apropos of nothing, he thought whoever was on the searchlight was doing a hell of a good job keeping *Serenité* in the beam as the two vessels pitched and rolled in the weather. Zac also needed to keep *Raider* away from his stern. The wrong home port had landed him in jail in Dubai and he didn't need the Brits reading *Serenité* from Dieppe where it should have said *Indomptable* from Cherbourg.

*Raider* pulled abreast *Serenité*, fifty yards off her port side. Zac was again grateful for the miserable weather conditions. On a calm night the navy vessel probably would have tied up alongside. *Raider* doused her searchlight and matched the sailboat's speed and course. The patrol boat was made of steel, and a little over sixty feet in length. A .50-caliber machine gun was mounted on her bow and a nest of electronics sat atop her deckhouse. For several minutes the two vessels sailed on parallel courses. Zac guessed there were night-vision binoculars and maybe even a thermal scope watching him in addition to radar. He went on with his normal routine, trimming the sail, manning the wheel, and trying his hardest to look too busy to talk.

*Raider* confirmed one more time that Zac would not be making landfall in the U.K. then slowly motored away, repeating the coastguard's instructions to call in ASAP regarding the collision. Zac cursed as he studied the GPS. He suddenly had a new and very serious problem. He couldn't dock the boat in England.

He switched on the autopilot and went below.

Zac hauled himself back on deck ten minutes later. HMS *Raider* was nowhere to be seen. He turned *Serenité* hard and headed straight for the English coastline. Each yard, each foot closer, could mean the difference between life and death. The radio chirped after just a few minutes.

"*Indomitable, Indomitable*. This is HMS *Raider*, over."

"Go ahead, *Raider*, this is *Indomptable*," Zac said.

"*Indomitable*, please put in at the marina that is two miles north-northwest of your position, and we will follow you to shore. We will take your statement there."

"Ahh, *oui, Raider*. I am still returning to Cherbourg. I turn north just now only to make the better tack for home. Over."

"*Indomitable*, please change course immediately or your vessel will be subject to search and seizure."

"Roger. I am turning now and then going below to make some dinner. *Désolé, mes amis. Indomptable* out."

He hoped the charming Frenchman routine would keep the Royal Navy off his case for a while.

The trip across the Channel had been brutal and now he was barely two miles from the English coast and forbidden to put ashore. He set course for Cherbourg. With the autopilot engaged and the wind from the southwest, the sailboat could sail straight to France on a single tack. Zac shook his head as he watched the English coastline recede slowly in his wake.

He looked over *Serenité*. She'd held up well and kept him safe during the worst storm he'd ever experienced. He owed her his life. So it was with distinctly mixed emotions that he trimmed the mainsail, stepped to the rail, and plunged into the sea.

## FIFTY-FOUR

T HE FORTY-THREE-DEGREE WATER enveloped Zac's body as he sank into the night sea. He struggled to orient himself in the black water, to distinguish the surface from the deep. The only sensations were the sounds of the splash and the feel of cold water on the exposed skin of his face. Slowly he floated upward. His head poked above the waves. Zac rose and fell with the sea, riding awkwardly atop the large swells. He watched as *Serenité* sailed on under autopilot, already thirty yards distant and moving quickly. He couldn't catch her if he tried, but he wasn't planning on swimming back to the boat anyway.

When he'd seen the dry suit back in Dieppe, its value had been obvious. Warm clothing had been the reason for his foray into the shop. The scuba gear he'd taken merely as an afterthought, an insurance policy against perils unknown, and now he'd bet his life on it. He looked over the waves toward a sandy beach and oriented himself with the compass that was a part of his dive instruments. He needed to swim due north to reach the English coast.

Zac vented the excess air from his equipment and descended below the surface. The unlighted instruments on his dive gear were almost impossible to read. Only by holding them inches from his mask could he see the glowing dots on his gauges and compass. A cold trickle of seawater ran down his back when he reached a depth of ten feet. He was an avid warm-water diver but had never used a dry suit before. He ignored the water against his skin.

The strong winds on the surface had abated somewhat, but the heavy seas had not. Each time a wave passed over him, Zac felt an uncomfortable and disorienting change in pressure. He began to feel nauseated. He would have an easier swim if he dove deeper, but he would also use more air. Because of its weight and bulk, he'd taken only a single air tank from Dieppe and it was nearly a two-mile swim to shore. He couldn't risk running out of air. Swimming on the surface in such rough seas would be exhausting after just a few minutes.

Zac descended to twenty feet to reduce the effect of the heavy swells but the additional water pressure turned the trickle of water inside his suit into a stream. The fleece lining along his back was soaked. He guessed that the suit had ripped when he'd been thrown against the railing on *Serenité*, or maybe it had already had a leak when he'd taken it from the shop, but it didn't matter how it had gotten there. Now he needed to manage the problem. He ascended to fifteen feet and tightened his dive vest. It staunched the flow of new seawater, but the cold stayed with him.

Zac kicked steadily for the next half hour, yet he worried about his heading as he swam. The absence of visual references in the dark, murky water made his survival dependent upon the gauges attached to his dive gear. When he'd decided to swim north to the beach he hadn't factored in the current. Even on *Serenité* he'd noticed it pushing the boat up the Channel. Now he feared that it might be taking him far off course. He surfaced briefly to recheck his heading and discovered that the lights along the beach were off to his left now. The current was indeed pushing him to the northeast, but because of the shape of the shoreline, it was also bringing him closer to land. He decided to keep swimming straight in. He would miss the beach, but it would be easier to walk to Hastings along the shore than to swim against the current.

Zac dove back down to fifteen feet. The change in water pressure caused the hole in his suit to open up again and icy seawater soaked most of his torso. He began to shiver. His best hope for survival was simply to reach shore as soon as possible.

Exhaustion and cold took their toll on his body and mind. He began to drift deeper into the sea. A torrent of cold water gushed into the dry suit at twenty-five feet, soaking his entire body but jolting him back to alertness. He kept kicking. He had no other choice.

A muffled crash rolled through the water. It sounded like distant thunder, but it was too rhythmic to be thunder. It might be the surf breaking on a nearby shore, but he was still twenty-five feet below the surface. Fatigued and confused, he simply swam on.

The crashing became louder and he soon felt himself rising and falling with the swells. Frigid seawater gushed into his suit with each oscillation. His teeth began to chatter around the regulator that supplied his air for breathing, breaking the watertight seal. Saltwater leaked into his mouth with every breath.

Zac desperately hoped that the breaking waves meant that he was almost to shore. In such rough surf, it was critical that he swim underwater until his hands and knees hit the beach, until there was no more water in which to swim. Any one of these waves would topple a standing man and leave the undertow to suck him down.

Still twenty-five feet underwater and kicking hard, he swam with his hands out in front, reaching into the darkness for the shoreline. After a few minutes his hands hit something, and then his mask, but whatever he'd hit wasn't a sandy beach. It was rock hard. He tried to feel his way around the obstacle but the surge became faster and more violent. Zac rose and fell several feet with every wave, but still the object blocked his path. He swam to the left and right, searching for open water, but the obstruction seemed to go on forever.

The utter blackness of the water left Zac blind to whatever it was that blocked his path. Though he'd vowed not to surface again before reaching the beach, he found himself with no alternative. He began to ascend. The water in front of his mask burst into a galaxy of bubbles with each crashing wave. The sound was deafening. The moment he reached the surface, a wave lifted him up and slammed him into the barrier. He took the hit with his shoulder and pushed off feebly. He looked for an easier path to shore but came to a grim conclusion as he looked around.

When he'd left *Serenité*, he'd planned on swimming north to a sandy beach, but the strong current had carried him far off course. Now he was staring at a cliff. A hundred-foot-high cliff that had been carved over eons by the fast-moving English Channel. To each side, for as far as he could see, the heavy surf pounded against the rock face, exploding upward with each impact. He felt faint.

A wave broke on top of him, slamming him face-first into the wall before dragging him underwater. The impact tore the mask off his face and ripped the regulator from his mouth, taking his supply of air with it. Zac gasped for air, but his lungs filled with saltwater. He kicked weakly for the surface, but the undertow sucked him down.

## FIFTY-FIVE

THE "SPECIAL RELATIONSHIP" between the United States and Britain was based on centuries of common heritage, laws, and cultural and religious values. In many ways it was a familial relationship, with America playing the part of the idealistic and headstrong child, while Britain played the wizened parent, who had gone through her own period of global hegemony before the sun had finally set on the British Empire. The two nations provided each other with balance, sage counsel, and a trustworthy ally in the best and the worst of times.

Given the history between the two countries, the U.S. ambassadorship to Great Britain was perhaps the most prestigious foreign posting in the State Department. Appointed by the president, many ambassadors were political donors, powerbrokers, or behind-the-scenes kingmakers. Walter Stephens was not one of them.

Like Winston Churchill, he was the product of an English father and an American mother, but Stephens's parents had chosen to settle in America after World War II. Young Walter served in the Marines for six years before he and his brothers inherited their father's modest machine tool shop. In twenty years they had turned it into the third largest manufacturer of military and commercial jet engines in North America and Europe. Stephens retired from the business to serve his country again, this time as a U.S. congressman. But after four terms, he became so disillusioned with the political machinations of the nation's capital that he chose not to seek reelection. Upon hearing the news, the president had reached across party lines and offered him the ambassadorship to Great Britain, stating that the country wasn't ready to lose such a gifted and principled leader.

And so it was that Peter Clements and Ted Graves sat in Stephens's outer office awaiting the meeting that the ambassador had requested. The tension between the two men was palpable. Neither knew why the ambassador had summoned them and each assumed that the other had initiated the call. As the chief executive of the American government in Britain, the ambassador wielded enormous power. He had been heavily involved in intelligence matters since he'd arrived in London and was generally a friend to CIA. Yet when the doors to his office opened, his demeanor was anything but friendly.

Stephens directed the two men to chairs in front of his desk.

"What's the status of that SNAPSHOT operation you two were arguing about last month? The one I had to sign off on because it involved SIS, a bunch of civilians, and a $400 million British airliner."

Graves spoke up immediately. "Sir, we've had some issues with the officer that was deployed. He failed to check in from either Iran or Singapore and he's blown two attempted exfiltrations. He's also wanted for a murder in Paris and another one in Singapore."

Stephens glanced at his computer monitor. "This is Zac Miller, right?"

"Yes, sir," said Graves. "He's contacted us twice. First, he claimed to be in Dubai, but we sent a team to recover him and he was nowhere to be found. We scoured the UAE, Oman, and Saudi. We even risked alerting a few of our sources inside Iran, but we came up dry. Most recently he claimed to be back in France, where he'd previously made unauthorized contact with a DGSE agent. I had a team airborne from the Paris embassy forty minutes after he called. They were in position in Antibes an hour early and there were no signs of him or any trouble. I'm not sure he's been playing straight with us."

The ambassador looked at Clements expectantly.

"The mission got fouled inside Iran and Miller escaped to Dubai," Clements responded. "He said the Iranians and the local police were after him, and there was gunplay in the neighborhood right before the rendezvous, so that's probably why he went to ground. I don't know what happened in Antibes. I was on a videoconference with the Seventh Floor at Langley when he called in and Ted handled it. I can't speak to the murder allegations either, but I've worked closely with Miller for three years, and I stand by him."

Graves spoke up again. "Sir, it's possible that the reason Miller insisted on going on the operation was because he had to skip town after the Paris murder, and when he arrived in Singapore, he committed a second murder. I think he's snapped. Having him on the loose is a risk to the Agency and the United States."

"OK. Enough of this. You two obviously haven't worked this out since we last spoke and I think I've just seen how the process broke down on our end. The reason I called you in here is that I just had a very interesting visit from a woman I know. She's a dame of the British Empire or something; not normally my cup of tea, but she's friendly with my wife and I've seen her a few times at events here in London, so I met with her. Funny thing is, she said she sat next to an American by the name of Zachary Miller on a British Airways flight out of London. She told me about how the plane landed in Iran and how Miller was taking photographs of a mountain range near the airport."

Ambassador Stephens leaned across his massive desk. "I was sitting right here, about to have a heart attack thinking that this woman had stumbled onto one of the most highly classified missions I've ever heard of, and she smiles. You know that smile when you're holding a pair of twos and the guy across from you is about to lay down a royal flush? That smile. I don't know how she knows, but she knows. Anyway, she tells me that when they finally got to Singapore, not only was Miller *not* on the goddamn plane, but there was a guy who looked like him wearing his clothes and carrying his bag. So it sounds to me as if the Iranians put a double, or a look-alike, or whatever the hell you guys call it, in his place, which means that Miller is probably running for his life and you two have him on ice."

Graves spoke carefully. "Sir, how would you gauge this woman's credibility?"

"Better than yours," said the ambassador. "You two need to fix this, now. Dismissed."

## FIFTY-SIX

I T WAS NIGHTTIME and he was deep underwater, kicking furiously toward the brightly lit beach. He looked down at his right hand. He was holding the scuba regulator that was supposed to be in his mouth, but he wasn't panicked. He seemed to be breathing fine without it. When he looked up, the cliff wall came rushing at him, moving impossibly fast and obliterating his view of the beach. It stopped a split second before impact.

ZAC WOKE UP breathing hard, soaked in sweat, and lying in a hospital bed. He had no idea how he'd gotten there. There was an intravenous drip in his arm and an oxygen tube up his nose. A battery of medical instruments surrounded his hospital bed. He could wiggle his fingers and his toes, but it hurt when he breathed. Maybe he'd cracked a rib or punctured a lung. He tried to sit up but was too weak to do much more than lift his head off the pillow. He remembered surfacing at the end of his swim. The breaking waves had thrown him against the cliff face until he'd finally gone under. He couldn't remember anything more.

He looked around, wondering if he was in a CIA facility, Iranian custody, or maybe a French or an English hospital. His gaze drifted out the window but the overcast sky told him nothing. Moving anything more than his eyes required concentrated effort. His body resisted every action, as if the earth's gravity were ten times its normal strength. The urge to sleep was incredible.

The soft squeak of rubber soles on the hallway floor gave him time to feign unconsciousness before two nurses walked into his room. If they thought he was still out cold he could avoid answering questions that might make people suspicious. Questions like: Who are you? What were you doing scuba diving in the middle of the night during a raging storm? Where did you come from and how did you get there? Little things like that.

"This one's had a horrible time," said the first nurse. Zac listened intently to her voice. She sounded older and compassionate, a mother if not a grandmother. Most important, she was speaking the Queen's English. Zac had made it to Britain. Still, he couldn't risk divulging his identity until he knew he was in friendly hands. He would call Peter Clements at the first opportunity.

"Where did they find him?" said the other one. She was younger, and sounded skeptical.

"Someone out for a morning stroll saw him washed up on the rocks just north of the cliffs. He was wearing diving equipment and a dry suit, but it didn't keep him very dry. The ambulance brought him in on blues and twos but he was nearly dead . . . had a core temperature of twenty-three degrees. The crash team downstairs took a full day to warm him up."

The younger one recited Zac's vital signs while the older one changed his IV bag.

"Is there any brain damage?"

"We don't know. He's been unconscious since he came out of the emergency department. The doctors said the cold water might have protected the brain but it depends how long he was underwater without oxygen."

The two nurses worked in silence for a few minutes until the younger one spoke again.

"It sounds very dodgy to me. Who goes diving at this time of year? I'd like to hear the story behind this."

The two nurses finished their tasks and stepped into the hallway. Zac couldn't quite hear the older one when she spoke again.

"Well, you'd better hope he wakes up soon if you want to ask him yourself. He's not going to be with us much longer."

# FIFTY-SEVEN

T HE DASSAULT FALCON 2000 rolled gracefully out of its turn and lined up on final approach for runway twenty-one. The wide-body corporate jet had been specially configured for the day's mission. Two banks of seats had been removed and a custom Aeromed stretcher had been fastened to the floor. Complete with an EEG, a defibrillator, and enough medicines to fill a small pharmacy, the air ambulance was on its way to pick up a very special patient. But those weren't the only modifications that had been made to the aircraft. The lavatory in the back of the plane held a false panel that led to a secret compartment in the tail. In a body bag surrounded by dry ice, lay the corpse of the young Iranian agent who had framed Zac in Singapore. His passing resemblance to the American had swiftly changed from a career-enhancing asset to a terminal liability.

Inspector Olivier Boucher of the French *police judiciare* shifted anxiously in his seat as a few low-level gusts of wind buffeted the jet, but it was not the weather that made him uncomfortable. Many years had passed since he and Arzaman had had their fateful encounter with Abdul

Assad in Tehran after the downing of Iran Air Flight 655. That meeting had been the cornerstone of a two-decade campaign of espionage and counterespionage operations against the West. Today Arzaman and Boucher were together again to protect a secret vital to the security of the republic, to protect the sword of Islam. If they failed, the very existence of Iran might be at risk.

Boucher stared out the window as the jet touched down smoothly on the runway. He never could get used to the gray skies of England. He was not in his element here. At least in France he carried a badge and a gun. Few people would dare challenge him there. But here . . . the British were so officious, so proud, yet their erstwhile empire and its ill-conceived borders had left the world a mess for centuries. How Boucher loathed them. He did not fear death, but he did fear rotting away in an English prison for the rest of his life. The sooner he got out of Britain, the better.

He had lived in France for many years in secret service to his native homeland. It was a noble and important job, but he was growing weary of the duplicity, of the constant paranoia and the separation from his family and his culture. In eight hours his mission would be accomplished and he would consider returning to Iran for good.

The Falcon turned off the runway and Colonel Arzaman spoke to the men accompanying him inside the aircraft.

"Today, we will recapture the spy who seeks to destroy our national security. Today, we will deliver a crushing response to our enemies' cowardly attack. We will show our strength and vigilance in the face of their arrogance. From their aggression, they will gain only defeat and humiliation. This mission is not just for the Guardians, not just for the president and the supreme leader, but for the entire Republic of Iran."

The others nodded as he began to review the plan.

"Olivier, you'll ride in the front of the van with the driver. Remember, he is one of ours, but he is not cleared for all aspects of the operation. He knows only that we are picking up a prisoner and flying back out. He has weapons in the van and has practiced the route several times, but he will remain in England. Do not discuss anything else in front of him or they will be the last words he ever hears."

As Arzaman spoke the last sentence, he made eye contact with each man to ensure they understood the implications of his warning. The plane taxied toward the far apron.

"It will take us forty-five minutes to drive to the hospital. We will obey the traffic regulations, but if for some reason we are stopped by the British police and they become suspicious, Olivier will show them his police credentials and the extradition papers. Professional courtesy should prevail. Olivier and Hafez will enter the hospital first and immediately start the paperwork. Naseem and Rashid, you will unload the stretcher and wait for Hafez to show you to the room. You both have the drug?"

The two men were dressed in the blue-and-white uniforms of French SAMU paramedics. Naseem spoke excellent English and Rashid spoke a few words of French, but the men had been chosen for today's mission because both were combat medics in the Revolutionary Guards.

They could keep the patient stable and fool an inquisitive doctor if necessary.

Naseem answered. "Yes. It is a sedative-hypnotic agent. It will leave him unable to speak or move. We will inject it into a peripheral line off of the intravenous drip. If there is no peripheral line, we will have to inject it directly into a vein, but can use only half the syringe. Too much too quickly will kill him."

Rashid added, "The drug will take effect in twenty to thirty seconds, at which point we can move the patient to our own stretcher."

"Sedate him immediately," Arzaman said. "Remember, we are snatching this man out of a hostile country. It is a blessing from Allah that he is still unconscious, but we cannot risk him awakening before we are back aboard the plane. If there are hospital staff in his room, take them into the hallway to look at some paperwork or ask them some questions, but get them out of the room. There may even be police there, but remember, they are there to keep the prisoner in, not to keep us out."

Hafez smiled at the irony. Seconded from the ranks of the Iranian Qods Force, he would be their security and their interrogator. Legend had it that he'd once cut out a man's tongue then suffocated him by stuffing it back down his throat. Hafez was a blunt instrument, but an effective one; and he'd never failed to extract the desired information from one of his prisoners.

Arzaman looked briefly at his men to see if there were any questions, but there never were. He was not the type of man who encouraged people to think on their own.

"I want everyone back in the van half an hour after we

reach the hospital. It's forty-five minutes to the airport and we will leave the moment everyone is on board the aircraft. The pilots have told me that our medical status will allow us an expedited departure."

Olivier frowned, concerned about the tight timeline, but said nothing.

Arzaman continued. "Once we are in the air we will have approximately one hour to perfect the deception. Naseem will switch the prisoner with the double and Rashid will stabilize the prisoner in the tail compartment. Remember to draw at least three vials of blood. Olivier has assured us that he has a sympathetic coroner in Paris who will test the blood, and not the corpse, to confirm that the DNA from the two crime scenes is the same. Ten minutes before we land at Le Bourget, Hafez and I will climb into the compartment with the sedated prisoner. As soon as you three are off with the double, we will fly on to Croatia, where we have a second plane waiting to take us to Tehran."

The aircraft engines throttled back and the ground crew directed the jet to its spot on the ramp.

"Be careful with the prisoner. He may be very weak. We are taking a great risk coming here to recapture him instead of simply having him killed. We must find out what he has learned and what he has told his handlers." For the first time that anyone could remember, the speaker looked worried. "The very existence of the republic may depend on it."

The plane stopped and the copilot lowered the stairs. A black Vauxhall van was waiting for the team.

Hafez leaned in to the group and whispered, "Sir,

what if something . . . *happens* and we lose control of the prisoner?"

"There is always a chance that this is a trap. Maybe the INTERPOL notice was a trick, or maybe the agent has recently regained consciousness and spoken with the authorities. We must take that chance. So if, as you say, something *happens* . . . then put a bullet in his brain, and may shit rain down upon his grave."

## FIFTY-EIGHT

Z AC HEARD A commotion outside his room. He caught only snippets of the conversation, but there was talk of transferring a patient. A smile crossed his face. Clements must have learned of his arrival and sent people to transport him to London. He felt enormous relief that he would no longer have to run and hide, that he would soon be in a place where he could finally tell the truth.

But he wasn't there yet. He kept his eyes closed as three people walked into the room. He heard a man tell a nurse about the advanced life support equipment they'd have en route.

"We'll have you out of here soon, Mr. Miller," said another man.

With his eyes still closed, Zac focused on the voice. The accent wasn't American, as he'd hoped. It sounded almost English, but not quite. It was the English of someone who'd learned the language in England but had grown up speaking something else.

The nurse recited his recent vital signs to the men. One of them asked if he could have a copy of Zac's chart and the nurse left the room to print it. Zac felt a needle prick his arm, followed by a burning sensation.

One of the men spoke quietly to the other in a foreign language and Zac's eyes popped open. The two men standing in the room were not American or English. They had Middle Eastern features. One was putting a syringe in his pocket as the other walked out of the room. Zac's last controlled act was to close his eyes.

## FIFTY-NINE

CHRISTINE KIRBY RAN down the hall to Ted Graves's office. His door was closed and his assistant said that he was not to be disturbed. Kirby ignored him and walked in.

"We found Miller."

"Where?"

"He's in England; down in Kent. I've got a team assembling right now. Let's go."

Graves hung up the phone and followed Kirby into the elevator. They emerged inside the parking garage. Two CIA security men were waiting with a silver Range Rover. Kirby tapped the thick windows with her knuckle as she and Graves climbed into the backseat.

"Anything up to a seven-six-two NATO, ma'am," said one of the security men.

"I've got a feeling we might need them."

The driver sped through the London traffic while the other man navigated. They were soon out of the city and driving down the motorway at nearly twice the speed limit.

"How did you find Miller?" Graves asked Kirby.

"I put flags on the borders, airlines, rails . . . everything you asked me to, but it was the local police in Kent who matched his picture with an INTERPOL Red Notice, if you can believe it. His status changed in the system to 'located' last night and Scotland Yard passed it over to MI5 this morning as part of their daily routine. Five called us about ten minutes before I came into your office."

"Is he all right? Why is he in the hospital?" Graves asked.

"I have no idea of his medical status but he's definitely not all right. While I was on the phone with my contact at Five he told me there was a second hit on the INTERPOL system. Apparently, the French filed for extradition last night and are picking him up today. We don't know what time. MI5 was going to ask the Home Office to call the local police and tell them not to let Miller out of their sight since he's an American citizen, but it's anyone's guess how that will go. The Home Office is usually very helpful, but with Miller's media coverage, you never know."

"Great work, Christine. Now we just need to get him before the French do."

## SIXTY

THE IRANIAN PARAMEDICS transferred Zac, with his oxygen and IV, onto the Aeromed stretcher and took him down in the elevator. Arzaman smiled inside the van when the hospital doors slid open and the group emerged.

*Ahead of schedule . . . For all their faults, at least the English are punctual.*

Naseem and Rashid folded the stretcher's wheels and slid it into the Vauxhall.

Hafez watched a police car speed up the drive and stop in front of the hospital's main entrance, two hundred feet from the van. Two constables jumped out and jogged toward the doors.

"Let's get out of here, now," said Arzaman.

Hafez yanked the rear doors closed and the heavy stretcher slammed into Naseem's ankle as the van accelerated. He cursed loudly and fell to his knees. His ankle started to swell immediately, but he and Rashid locked down the stretcher before tending to the bruised and bleeding joint.

The driver ignored the speed limit while the passengers rode in silence. The arrival of the police at the hospital might have been a coincidence; however, the Iranians were trained to expect the worst. None of them wanted a firefight, but they were ready if the situation demanded it.

Arzaman took a prepaid mobile phone from the driver and ordered the pilots to be ready for takeoff as soon as the team arrived. Burning a few extra pounds of jet fuel might be the difference between a successful mission and a lifetime spent in an English prison. They would be safe once they were airborne. Whatever the English suspected, they wouldn't shoot down an unarmed passenger plane. The van sped down the empty two-lane road as they counted down the minutes to the airport.

Olivier saw it first through the side-view mirror. A police car was coming up from behind. Its warning lights were off, but it was moving fast. The driver of the van eased off the gas and moved to the left-hand lane. Hafez opened a heavy plastic container marked "Medical Waste/Biohazard" and removed three Heckler & Koch MP7 machine pistols. He stashed two of them below the seats and kept one for himself.

"What do I do?" asked the driver.

"Just drive the speed limit," said Arzaman. "We follow the plan. If he stops us, Olivier shows his ID and the extradition papers. Tell them we are rushing only because the patient needs urgent medical attention."

The police car slotted in behind the van. Hafez's hand reflexively went to his MP7. Arzaman gently pulled the hand away and motioned for him to relax. There was no point in acting like kidnappers if they were being stopped for speeding.

The police car's blue warning lights started flashing.

"Just pull over. We'll be on our way in a few minutes," said Arzaman.

The driver was agitated. "They're armed response."

"What does that mean?" asked Hafez.

"See those yellow circles on the car? It means they're armed."

"Is that uncommon?"

"Many police in Britain do not carry weapons. Armed officers are deployed only when trouble is expected."

Hafez's hand went to his weapon again. "Nice of them to warn us."

"Did the police car at the hospital have the yellow circles?" asked Arzaman.

"I did not see them, and I would have noticed," said the driver as he lowered his window.

Arzaman acknowledged that the situation might be more serious than he'd initially thought. He removed his own machine pistol from beneath his seat. Two officers stepped out of the car and walked toward the van. Both carried sidearms but neither weapon was drawn.

Olivier stepped out of the passenger side of the van with his hands away from his body. In his left hand were his police credentials, open to reveal his badge and ID. In his right hand was the extradition paperwork from the U.K. and French governments.

The two constables stopped ten feet behind the van and glanced at each other. One of them ordered Olivier to stand still while the other spoke into the radio microphone attached to his epaulet. The standoff lasted only a few seconds until the radio dispatcher responded. Both officers drew their weapons. The one closer to Olivier ordered him to turn around and get on his knees.

One of the officers covered the driver's door while the other watched Olivier slowly lower himself to the ground. Neither was looking at the back doors of the van when they burst open and a barrage of automatic weapons fire erupted from inside.

Arzaman and Hafez were each down on one knee and firing the machine pistols. The high-velocity, small-caliber rounds penetrated the officers' body armor before tearing into flesh and bone, rupturing blood vessels and puncturing vital organs. Both officers collapsed on the ground without firing a shot.

Arzaman began barking orders. The country road was quiet but the Iranians would be asking for trouble if they left the two policemen lying on the pavement. Rashid jumped down. The officers were already in shock and nearly dead as he tossed the first one into a drainage ditch.

The driver turned around and started yelling. "We're ten minutes from the airport. Let's get out of here!"

A deafening burst of gunfire ripped into the van from the rear. A third officer had been in the car, obscured from view by glare on the windshield. Now he was standing behind the police car, raking the Vauxhall van with a fully automatic rifle. Hafez was hit in the throat and chest, but Arzaman ducked away before taking any fire.

ZAC'S EYES HAD popped open at the sound of the first gunshots. Distracted by the police, the Iranians had forgotten to administer the second half of the sedative. Zac could once again move his extremities, but did so minimally to avoid drawing attention. He spotted the straps that held him to the stretcher running across his chest and legs. They were more like seat belts than shackles. He would be able to release them easily when the time was right.

Bullets ripped through the air above Zac's head and blood splattered down on top of him as rounds tore into Hafez. The dying man slumped atop the stretcher before rolling onto the ground. His weapon fell to the floor.

Rashid yelled something from outside the van before another burst of fire silenced him forever. Arzaman glanced at Zac, then fired back at the officer, but the bullets crashed harmlessly into the police car. The automatic rifle responded instantaneously and more 5.56mm rounds tore through the sheet-metal skin of the van. The driver was grazed in the shoulder by a bullet. He screamed again for Olivier to get back in the van but the French police officer was nowhere to be seen.

Arzaman shot a few more rounds and shouted to the injured Naseem. The medic crawled over and picked up Hafez's weapon, firing off the rest of the magazine. Zac watched Naseem search for more ammunition. The two men made eye contact. Neither one said a word.

The driver and Arzaman were screaming at each other. Zac could feel the van start to pull away. Arzaman fired a shot through the windshield and the safety glass exploded with spider-cracks. The driver slammed on the brakes and stopped the van.

Naseem found another magazine and shot at the police car, but a burst of return fire forced him to dive for cover. He lay flat on the floor as three distinct reports came from outside the van and the policeman's rifle fell silent.

Olivier walked out from behind the police car with his pistol in his hand.

Arzaman jumped down from the van. "Where the hell have you been?"

Olivier holstered his weapon and jogged toward the van.

"I dove off the road when the shooting started and was just getting up when the rifle opened fire, so I crawled through the ditch to flank him."

Naseem stepped forward. "What took you so long? Hafez and Rashid are dead!"

Olivier swiftly raised his weapon and pointed it at Naseem's head. "And if the cop had seen me, we'd all be dead. Shut up and get in the van."

"Good work," said Arzaman. "Now let's get out of here before the fucking SAS show up."

## SIXTY-ONE

THE ROADSIDE TREES flew by in a blur as the silver Range Rover sped southeast along the motorway.

"What do we know about the French extradition party?" asked Ted Graves.

"Zero. I'm guessing they'll have maybe two cops and a doctor or a nurse," answered Kirby. "If we can't grab Miller before the French get to the hospital, then we're really going to need the Home Office to come through with the local police."

The man in the front passenger seat took a call on his mobile phone. He turned around quickly to face Graves and Kirby.

"MI5 says the local police just missed Miller at the hospital. The French have him."

"Dammit," Graves shouted. "Do we know where they're going?"

The man with the phone asked the question and shook his head.

"Where *would* they be going?" Kirby asked.

"From Conquest? Brighton is an hour west, Lydd is an hour east," said the driver.

Graves slammed his fist against the seatback. "Are you still on with Five?" he asked the security officer with the phone. The man nodded.

"Tell them to get police cars to both airports. Tell them to pull out all the stops. This is a matter of national security for the U.S. and Britain. Do not let Miller out of the country."

The security officer relayed the instructions and the interior of the SUV was quiet for the next fifteen minutes until he received another call. He kept the phone to his ear and pointed emphatically at the exit ramp. The driver slammed on the brakes and turned off the motorway. The man with the phone punched a new route into the SUV's GPS system and turned to face Graves and Kirby. "It's Five again. Three local cops just got into a firefight with automatic weapons. It's the same black Vauxhall van that was spotted at Conquest Hospital. It's heading for Lydd."

The supercharged Range Rover accelerated to nearly 120 miles per hour. Graves spoke first. "Do the police have the men from the van in custody?"

"No. Two officers are down and probably the third. He called for backup and was engaging the threat but isn't answering his radio. It sounds as if the police were overpowered."

"It sure as hell doesn't sound like an extradition party," said Kirby.

"More like a rendition team," said Graves. Despite the SUV's high rate of speed, he reached behind him and opened a hidden compartment in the floor, revealing suppressed rifles, vests, and dozens of loaded magazines.

He passed two vests, two rifles, and ten of the fifty-round magazines up to the front seat.

He showed one of the stubby rifles to Kirby. "Do you remember how to use one of these?"

"I trained on them back at The Farm, but I haven't shot one in years."

Graves tapped the end of the barrel with his finger. "Point this part at the bad guy, then pull this thing until he's dead." He pointed to the trigger and handed the rifle to Kirby. "You're good to go."

## SIXTY-TWO

THE VAN REEKED of blood and spent ammunition. Arzaman was back on his mobile phone and shouting at the pilot, telling him that they weren't going to wait for immigration, customs, or even air traffic control. The pilot began to protest but Arzaman hung up and helped Olivier load Rashid's body into the van. The airport was ten minutes away, the turbines were spooling up, and the cabin door was open. In fifteen minutes they would be in the air.

The devastation receded into the distance as the van accelerated down the road, the wind whistling through the bullet holes in its thin metal skin. Olivier drove while Naseem wrapped a compression bandage around the original driver's wounded shoulder. Arzaman looked dispassionately at Rashid's dead body and considered their options.

No one saw the silver Range Rover coming down the side road until it was too late. It clipped the tail of the van and spun it sideways. Tires shrieked as the van slid perpendicular to the road and tipped onto two wheels. The impact caused Olivier to be thrown halfway out the open window and Zac's stretcher to break free from its mounts.

With its high rate of speed and high center of gravity, the van rolled onto its right side, crushing Olivier's head and torso beneath the five-ton truck. The crash sent the stretcher flying through the air and smashing into the already injured Naseem. Zac screamed a string of obscenities as the intravenous line and oxygen tube were ripped from his body. The van's metal skin screeched as it slid across the pavement.

Arzaman had been thrown forcefully into a metal rack along the wall of the van, cutting his head and breaking several ribs as the van came to a halt. The original driver tumbled onto Olivier's severed legs. Awash in his comrade's blood, the driver was dumbstruck but not seriously hurt.

All was still inside the van as Arzaman pulled the stretcher away. He was hunched over and wheezing. Blood dripped down his heavily scarred face.

"How many more people have to die before this is over?" Zac asked.

"Just one," said Arzaman.

He leveled his machine pistol at Zac's forehead. The driver was shouting but Arzaman refused to break eye contact with Zac. The Iranian's finger tightened on the trigger, but the driver reached for the gun and gently lifted it away from Zac's face.

"We need the other car to get to the airport. If they hear gunfire, they will leave."

Arzaman saw the Range Rover through the smashed

windshield. It had stopped after the accident. That would be its driver's final mistake.

"Get a weapon," Arzaman barked.

Naseem lay on the floor with one eye swollen shut. Blood dripped from his mouth and ears. Arzaman handed him one of the MP7s and gestured toward Zac.

In English he said, "Kill him if he so much as blinks his eyes."

Arzaman and the driver opened the back doors of the van and climbed out. Zac heard a muffled burst of automatic weapon fire, then a louder one. He looked over at Naseem, propped up on one elbow, his gaze unfocused. The machine pistol rested perilously in his hand, his finger on the trigger. Zac unbuckled himself from the stretcher and gingerly removed the gun from Naseem's grip. The dying man's face registered nothing.

Arzaman ran past the rear of the van and fired a few rounds at an unseen target. The muffled gunfire sounded again and bullets ripped through the back of the van. Arzaman grunted loudly as he took a round in his thigh. He shouted to Naseem, but the medic had lapsed into shock. Arzaman laid down a few more rounds of suppressing fire and stuck his head inside the van.

Zac jerked the trigger of the MP7, spraying bullets through the walls of the van until he was out of ammunition.

Arzaman reached around the open rear doors and fired blind. A round grazed Zac's arm and he dropped the empty weapon. He stepped across the bloody interior of the van and crouched behind the seats, next to Olivier's severed body. The French policeman's pistol was still in its holster, just inside the driver's side window.

Arzaman seated his last magazine in the MP7.

Zac drew the 9mm SIG from its holster and wiped off the blood with his hospital gown. He peered around the seats.

Arzaman swung around the back of the van and fired. Zac cried out in pain as two rounds tore through the seat and into his shoulder. Arzaman's gun was empty in a little over a second. He looked down and saw Zac's empty MP7 on the bottom of the van.

The two men made eye contact. Arzaman knew that at least some of his rounds had found their mark. He picked up a stainless steel bar from the broken stretcher and called out as he limped toward Zac.

"Come, Mr. Miller. Do not be afraid. Every man must go down to his death."

Zac stepped out from behind the seats.

"I couldn't agree more."

He raised the pistol and fired.

## SIXTY-THREE

ARZAMAN LAY DEAD in the back of the van as Zac lowered the empty pistol. Outside, a man was shouting.

"This is your last chance. Put down your weapons and come out with your hands in the air!"

Zac looked around, absorbing images he would never forget. The interior of the overturned van was quiet and still. It was littered with bullet holes, dented sheet metal, and shattered glass. The poses of the dead bore witness to the violence of the day.

"Coming out!" he shouted.

The empty gun slid from his hand.

"Slowly! Keep your hands where we can see them."

Zac staggered out of the van, his hospital gown awash in Olivier's blood. Pain flashed through his wounded shoulder as he raised his hands in the air. Four men with black balaclavas and suppressed weapons were fanned out across the road. Three of the rifles were trained on the van while the other one swept the area for additional threats. The Iranian driver lay dead on the pavement just a few feet away.

"Son of a bitch . . ." muttered one of the gunmen upon seeing Zac covered in blood. "Who else is in there?"

"Everyone's dead," Zac responded. "Who are you?"

The man ignored the question and directed the other team members with hand signals. Zac watched as two men moved toward the van, their muzzles expertly dividing its interior. The men were professionals, but definitely not the police.

"Clear!" shouted one of the men.

"All clear!" shouted the man giving the hand signals.

Two of the men dragged the dead Iranians into the wrecked van while the other two walked toward Zac. When he was ten feet away, the man who'd been giving the hand signals removed his balaclava.

Zac recoiled as he recognized Ted Graves.

Christine Kirby pulled her hood off a moment later and Zac took a step back.

"Welcome home, Miller," said Graves. He used a medical kit from his vest to quickly clean Zac's gunshot wounds and cover them with hemostatic dressings. Zac was in a great deal of pain, but he could still move his hand and arm. Graves gave him a few acetaminophen tablets.

One of the CIA security men was busy inside the overturned van while the other one brought a trench coat from the back of the SUV and handed it to Zac.

"Toss his hospital gown in the van too," Graves said to the second security man.

Except for a broken headlight, the Range Rover was undamaged from the crash. The driver stowed his weapon back in the SUV while Kirby and Graves bookended Zac in the backseat with their rifles on their laps. The other CIA security man jogged back to the van with two small canisters.

The driver turned the Rover toward the side street from which they'd come and opened the passenger door. A siren wailed faintly in the distance. The front-seat passenger threw the canisters into the wrecked van and sprinted to the Range Rover. The supercharged SUV was fifty yards down the road when an earsplitting blast shook the three-ton vehicle. The two incendiary explosives had detonated among the medical oxygen and diesel fuel inside the van. Zac turned and watched as white-hot flames and thick black smoke reached into the sky.

From the backseat of the Range Rover, he spoke. "Where are we . . ."

"Not here," Graves interrupted.

Zac had a thousand questions, but he relented, not knowing what had transpired between Graves and Peter Clements while Zac had been in the field. The front-seat passenger made a brief phone call but the ride otherwise passed in silence as the SUV wound its way through the English countryside, passing fog-shrouded farms and picturesque hamlets for over an hour.

The Range Rover turned abruptly into a narrow driveway, where a sturdy iron gate closed behind it. Hidden cameras monitored the SUV's progress as it sped down the long gravel driveway and pulled in behind a green Jaguar sedan. The five CIA officers entered the Victorian-era farmhouse.

## SIXTY-FOUR

THE GREEN JAGUAR was owned by a septuagenarian doctor who'd been summoned on the ride over. He ordered Zac to strip down in front of the group and examined him carefully.

"You're very fortunate, young man," said the doctor.

Zac looked above the half-moon reading glasses, below the bushy eyebrows, and into the doctor's green eyes for signs of intelligence. Zac was covered in blood, had been in a rollover car accident and shot multiple times, just in the last few hours. Forget about the last month.

"How do you figure?"

The doctor gave Zac a grandfatherly smile. "For starters, you're still very much alive."

*Well, it's hard to argue with that*, Zac thought. Since his first day in Iran, his continued existence had been anything but a given.

"Also, the small-caliber bullets seem to have passed through your shoulder area without striking anything vital." The doctor wagged a finger at him. "Your recovery will be arduous but complete."

The doctor had Zac shower, stitched up his wounds, and gave him a handful of painkillers and antibiotics. Graves walked the doctor to his car while the caretaker of the safe house, a fit man in his early sixties, led Zac to a ground floor bedroom. Kirby followed with the two CIA security men.

By the time Graves rejoined the others, Zac was already in bed and under a pile of blankets.

"How are you doing, Zac?" Graves asked.

"I . . . I'm good," he mumbled. His eyes were firmly closed.

"The doctor said the combination of the painkillers and everything else your body has been through might shut you down. Get some sleep. We'll talk later."

Graves motioned to the others and they left the room. Out in the hall, he spoke to the caretaker.

"Do you have surveillance in that room?"

The caretaker nodded. "Audio and video."

"Good. Feed him, keep him hydrated, give him his meds, and call the doctor with any issues, but don't let him talk to anyone or take one step outside that room except to use the bathroom. Understood?"

The caretaker nodded again.

Graves turned to the two CIA security men. "You two stick around, just in case."

"What's the threat assessment, sir?" asked one of them.

"I'm going back to the office right now to try to figure that out, but let's leave it at 'no one in or out' until I get back. Get your heavy gear out of the SUV and the caretaker will show you where to set up. He's a man of few words but he knows what he's doing. He's ex-SAS. I'll have someone reinforce you tonight and I'll be back tomorrow."

THE NEXT MORNING, the caretaker walked Zac to a modern, windowless conference room in the interior of the farmhouse. A new security officer was outside the door and Ted Graves was seated inside, wearing the same clothes he'd had on the previous day. Zac eyed him warily as he entered.

"We've got a lot to cover and not a lot of time," Graves said. "Take a seat and tell me what happened in Iran." Graves closed the manila folder he'd been reviewing.

Zac lowered himself into a seat at the conference room table.

"I had a clear view of the site from as soon as I stepped off the plane. The camera from S&T allowed me to see each of the 'buildings.' They were all just slabs of re-barred concrete with plywood walls and roofs that were made to look like residential construction. Some of them were superficially damaged by the quake but most were intact because they weren't bearing any weight. It was all camouflage. The bottom line is they've got a dozen nuclear ICBMs in reinforced silos."

"How can you be sure the silos are operational, much less loaded with nuclear missiles?"

"Because one of the blast doors was severely dislocated by the earthquake and I was able to see the tip of a nosecone. It was a Chinese DF-4."

"While the political implications of China selling

ICBMs to Iran are enormous, that's for Washington to handle. But wasn't CIA expecting Iran to use a home-built delivery system for its first ICBM?"

"We were, most likely a variant of the Shahab-3. In fact, I wrote that assessment, but the DF-4 is very distinctive. It looks like the tip of a crayon. The Iranians must have bought them from the Chinese when they upgraded to the 5As."

"But why would they build a launch site on a geological fault line?"

"Silos are designed to be insulated from shock. That's how they retain second-strike capability, and building it in such an apparently unsuitable location probably explains why no one has found out about it until now."

"How could they have built the silos and loaded the missiles without us knowing? We have persistent surveillance over there. They're living under the unblinking eye. You said before you left that it was the satellite imagery that turned you onto the area in the first place."

"I thought about that a lot," Zac said. "Do you remember how the whole area is a 'special economic zone'? They were putting up and tearing down warehouses for years. At the time I thought they were just terrible businessmen, but now I'm starting to think that the whole 'special economic zone' was cover for the ICBM program. They built each silo inside a warehouse, then tore it down when they were finished. I'll bet if we overlay a time sequence of satellite shots, that's what we'll find."

"So what's their endgame?" Graves said.

"That's way above my pay grade, but how effective is a deterrent that no one knows about?"

"You think these are offensive weapons?"

Zac nodded slowly.

Graves looked up at the ceiling for a few seconds. "So forget the treaties and screw the sanctions, it's a fait accompli . . ."

"Just like it was with North Korea."

THE TWO MEN spent the next few hours discussing the details of Zac's arrest and escape, his evasion through Dubai and Europe, and his eventual arrival in Britain. At Zac's request, Graves entered Emma Rogers's name into a computer on the table and learned that she had safely reentered the United States almost two weeks ago.

Graves told Zac that the accusations of murder in France and Singapore had been disastrous for his credibility, and that there was an INTERPOL Red Notice out for him.

"You know I didn't kill those two women, Ted, and I'm going to need the Agency's help to clear my name."

"Don't be naive, Zac. It doesn't matter whether you're innocent or not. The police have your name, your picture, your fingerprints, and your DNA. You've already been convicted in absentia by the court of public opinion, but we'll give you a new name, some plastic surgery, and you'll be good to go."

Zac shook his head. "So that's it? Zac Miller's last act on this earth is as a fugitive double-murderer? You were right when you told Peter that I'm not cut out for operations. There's too much smoke-and-mirrors in it for me. How long until I'm back at my desk?"

"You're not going back to a desk, Zac. I have much bigger plans for you. Look at what you've accomplished. You had no language skills, no survival training, no money, and no backup plan, yet you successfully completed the mission *after* being arrested. We all thought the real risk was getting the aircraft into Sirjan without the Iranians shooting it down." Graves looked across the table with genuine admiration. "You have gifts that no amount of training can teach. There are people like you who risk their lives every day to keep this country safe. You know first-hand how ruthless our enemies can be. The field is your true calling. Zac Miller died in that van yesterday for a reason. Your new life in operations starts today."

"I don't know, Ted. I need to talk to Peter about this."

"Clements doesn't enter into this!" Graves said.

"He most definitely enters into this. He's chief of station."

"He *was* chief, until he sanctioned your little world tour and it blew up in his face. Now *I'm* chief, and before you get any ideas about whining to the Seventh Floor, remember that the police have your DNA and the only thing keeping them from locking you up for the rest of your life is someone telling them where to find you."

"That's a real nice speech, Ted, but don't pretend that Peter went down all by himself. You've been waiting to take him out ever since he beat you for the London chief of station job. I'm sure you undermined him every chance you had once the mission went south; and now that it's turned into a success, here you are trying to reap the gains. In fact, I wouldn't be surprised if it was you who tipped off the Iranians that I was going to Sirjan. So with all due respect, there's no fucking way I'm working for you."

Graves stared at Zac for several seconds.

"I'm not asking you to volunteer." Graves shoved the manila folder across the table. "This is CIA and those are your orders."

Zac caught the folder and read the name off the cover. "Who the hell is Jake Keller?"

"That's your new identity," Graves said. "This is your new life, *Jake*, and I'm in charge of it, so man the fuck up and do your job."

The two men stared at each other. Neither one moved for several seconds until Zac picked up the folder and walked to the door.

"OK, Ted. I'll play your game. But just so we understand each other, if you ever try to stab me in the back, like you did to Peter, I'll kill you."

Keep reading for an excerpt from
David Ricciardi's next exciting novel . . .

## *ROGUE STRIKE*

Coming June 2019 in hardcover
from Berkley!

## ONE

THE TWO MEN in the bed of the old pickup told the driver to step on it. They were on their way to send a man to hell, or Paradise depending on your point of view, and while they could survive a rough ride, they might not survive being late.

A wake of dust rose into the predawn air as the truck pounded over the rough dirt road. The monsoon rains usually turned the Wadi Bana into a flowing river that made life in southern Yemen almost tolerable for a few months each year, but the rains had been light this summer. The land was hot and dry.

The driver switched on his lights as he turned onto a paved road. The war-ravaged town of Zinjibar loomed in the cracked windshield. Most of the buildings had been destroyed by a combination of artillery fire, aerial bombardment, and car bombs. Abandoned vehicles littered the main boulevard, some shot up, some broken down. The air smelled of smoke and a fine dust that never quite settled to the ground.

The senior CIA officer slapped the roof twice as they passed an open-air market. The pickup turned into an alley and slowed. He threw a goatskin satchel over his shoulder and jumped down to the street. The truck resumed normal speed and returned to the boulevard. Two blocks away, the second officer stepped out. He was dressed in the same mishmash of loose-fitting pants and faded suit coat that was favored by the locals.

*Game time, Zac,* he thought to himself.

Then he grimaced.

*You're not Zac Miller anymore. Zac's dead.*

The man now known as Jake Keller stooped over and feigned a slight limp, hoping that darkness and distance would make him look to the world like one of the many old men who carried their wares to the open-air market each morning.

It was his first mission as part of the Agency's elite Special Activities Center. He and his partner were after Mullah Muktar, a quasi-religious leader who had helped plan the September 11 attacks and since become the head of al-Qaeda in the Arabian Peninsula. Two days earlier, an NSA signals intercept had revealed the time and place of an upcoming meeting between the mullah and an unknown subject.

Jake walked back to the main boulevard. He climbed a pile of rubble and entered an abandoned apartment building that was two stories taller than the ones around it. His partner was already there, standing in the dark with a scruffy beard, a scarf wrapped around his head, and a stubby AKS-74U rifle in his hands. Curt Roach, a former special operations marine, was only four years older than Jake but had worked in the military or CIA his entire adult life. He hid a battery-powered motion detector in the lobby and motioned to the stairway.

Jake unclipped his own rifle from a harness hidden under his jacket and unfolded the wire stock. The two men ascended the concrete stairs in silence, clearing each room in the five-story building until they were certain it was empty.

"Let's get set up before sunrise," Roach said. "Graves said this thing could go down at any time."

Jake hung camouflage netting from the ceiling, five feet back from the outside wall. Roach set up a tripod behind the net.

"Pass me the designator," he said.

Jake handed him what looked like a high-tech pair of binoculars. The device could bounce a beam of invisible infrared light off whatever it was pointed at and guide a weapon to the target or simply determine its coordinates.

"Run the antennas?" Jake said as he scratched his beard.

Roach nodded. "Just be sure they can't be seen from the ground."

Jake disappeared up the stairs, trailing a thin cable behind him. He returned a few minutes later.

"SATCOM and GPS are up. I'll check in," he said. *"Mustang, Mustang, this is Cobra."*

From a top secret facility halfway across the Arabian Peninsula, the CIA mission control element responded, *"Cobra, go for Mustang."*

*"Mustang, Cobra at position Alpha."*

*"Copy position Alpha. Strike package is two ships.*

*Drifter-75 and Drifter-76 are hard altitude eighteen thousand feet and orbiting your position with fifteen hours till bingo."*

High overhead, two unmanned combat aerial vehicles flew wide racetrack patterns around Zinjibar. From a distance, the stealthy, bat-winged drones resembled miniature B-2 bombers. They each carried fifteen hours of fuel and a pair of lethal air-to-ground missiles.

*"Roger, Mustang,"* Jake said. *"No sign of Jupiter. Any update on Saturn?"*

*"Negative, Cobra. You have current intel."*

The signals intercept that had alerted the CIA to Muktar's location had referenced an unfamiliar code name for the man he was meeting, and the Agency was eager to learn his identity. Each new intel target would be fed into a matrix that might one day prevent a major attack or take down a terrorist network. It was a paradox Jake was still adjusting to. They had to end a life to potentially save many more.

The two CIA officers watched the streets for hours until a battered Nissan pickup truck arrived, spewing black smoke from its diesel engine. Six men with rifles hopped down from its bed. After suffering through years of a multiparty civil war, armed men in Yemen were a common sight, but these men were better trained than most. They positioned themselves around the intersection, with overlapping fields of fire on all the approaches.

Curt reached for the SATCOM. He whispered despite being two hundred meters away.

*"Mustang, this is Cobra, we have six military-age males*

in the open at Alpha. Definite weapons and tactical movement. No sign of Jupiter or Saturn."

"Roger that, Cobra," said the radio. "Be advised we are tracking three vehicles westbound to your position."

A heavily muscled man in fatigue pants and a black T-shirt stared up at the nearby buildings. His eyes moved methodically across the openings where windows had once been, right to left, top to bottom, looking for anything out of the ordinary. Despite having the sun in his eyes, he paused as he looked at the floor where Jake and Curt were holed up.

The man in the fatigue pants spoke with one of his comrades on the street. The two men checked their weapons and began walking toward the Americans' building just as three identical SUVs stopped in the intersection. Mullah Muktar emerged from the third vehicle. The cleric waved to the man in the fatigue pants.

"Mustang, we have Jupiter at Alpha," Roach said. "He's linking up with the six dismounts."

"Roger, Cobra," said mission control. "Copy positive ID on Jupiter. Drifter-76 in range. Ten hours till bingo. Mustang standing by."

The man in the fatigue pants returned to greet Muktar and escorted him into the building across the street. A Yemeni government Land Rover pulled up a few minutes later and four soldiers climbed out. They spoke briefly with Muktar's men before a civilian wearing an open-necked suit emerged from the passenger seat.

Roach picked up the radio. "Mustang, we have probable Saturn at Alpha in a tan government Land Rover with a four-man security detail."

The man in the suit scrutinized the intersection.

"I don't understand why a government official would come into the heart of al-Qaeda territory driving that truck," Jake said. "It might as well have a bull's-eye painted on the door."

"The truck is a ruse," Roach said. "Look at how the bodyguards are behaving. They're watching the street, focused on external threats. If those were legitimate government forces they'd be watching Muktar's men. These guys are working together."

Roach looked through the laser designator's magnified optics as Saturn entered the building.

*"Spin up your missiles, Mustang,"* Roach said. *"Jupiter and Saturn are inside the target."*

*"Cobra, if you're concerned about the government personnel, Drifter-75 can target Jupiter's vehicle once he's clear of the area."*

*"Negative, Mustang,"* Roach said. *"These bastards killed three thousand Americans. It's payback time."*

The man in the fatigue pants returned to the street and linked up with the other man. They resumed walking toward Jake and Roach's building.

"You see this?" Jake said as he picked up his rifle. Roach nodded.

"Why don't you want to hit Muktar's truck after he leaves?" Jake asked. "Just in case they really are government troops."

"First, there's zero chance that those are government troops. They would have been shot on sight before they even got here. Second, the mullah has been dodging drone strikes for years. As soon as those vehicles start rolling, his goons will play a shell game with them. The odds of a successful mission go down by two-thirds the second he gets in that truck."

The radio came to life. *"Cobra, you have permission to engage. Drifter-76 is in range and holding on station. Prepare to provide terminal guidance on the target."*

*"Negative on terminal guidance,"* Roach said. *"We've got hostiles inbound. We're going to transmit coordinates instead."*

In terminal-guidance mode, the designator would send coded pulses of laser light that would guide the drone's missiles to the target, but Roach and Jake would have to stay in position for the duration of the operation, and Roach was worried about the man in the camo pants.

Roach pressed several buttons on the designator and keyed the SATCOM.

*"Cobra is transmitting coordinates now,"* he said. *"You are cleared hot."*

*"Good copy on coordinates, Cobra. Missile launch in three . . . two . . . one . . ."*

Roach's watch vibrated. "Somebody just triggered the motion detector in the lobby."

Jake took his rifle to the stairs and listened for intruders. He glanced at Roach. *Shouldn't the missiles have hit by now?*

Roach was thinking the same thing. *"Mustang, this is Cobra. Repeat, cleared hot. Execute."*

*"Stand by, Cobra,"* said the voice on the SATCOM. *"We are, uh, negative contact with Drifter-76 at this time. Drifter-75 is being retargeted to Jupiter's location."*

Jake looked at Roach. "What the hell happened to Drifter-76?"

*"Cobra, be advised Drifter-75 will be in range in one-six minutes. Maintain your position,"* said the voice on the SATCOM.

*"That may not be possible, Mustang. We've got armed hostiles inbound."*

Down in the street below, the two principals exited the meeting.

Roach scowled and keyed the SATCOM again. *"Mustang, we are losing both targets."*

The radio was silent as Jupiter and Saturn spoke on the street.

Jake squeezed Roach's shoulder. Someone was climbing the steps a few floors below them. Jake put his rifle to his shoulder and aimed down the stairway.

Jupiter and Saturn looked like old friends as they exchanged customary hugs and kisses.

Jake heard men speaking one floor down.

Roach cupped the microphone in his hand. *"Mustang, Mustang . . . Repeat, we are losing both targets."*

The voices downstairs stopped.

Two minutes later, the man in the fatigue pants and his partner appeared on the street next to Mullah Muktar.

"That son of a bitch is going to walk," Roach said. *"Mustang, this is Cobra. Jupiter and Saturn are bugging out. Does Drifter-75 have eyes on target yet?"*

The men on the street entered their vehicles. Roach banged the SATCOM with his hand.

*"Mustang, this is Cobra, how copy?"* he said as the terrorists drove away.

Roach switched off the designator and sat back against the wall. He kicked the SATCOM across the floor and looked at Jake.

"We'll call for extraction once it's dark."

---

## TWO

T HE CAMERAMAN USUALLY covered soccer matches for the Al-Arabiya television network, but the equipment today was the same, the best that money could buy. He could capture a million people in the frame or zoom in on a single face. Ultra-high-definition sensors rendered flawless images of whatever he'd selected. The control booth would occasionally tell him to take an artistic shot and on a clear night he would zoom in on the moon and fill viewers' screens with images of craters, ridges, and shadows that most people never knew existed. It was an awesome piece of technology.

From high atop one of the hotels, he panned right to catch the buses, cars, and pedestrians that were clogging the highway from Mina. They were latecomers making their way back to the Masjid al-Haram, the enormous outdoor mosque in the holy city of Mecca, Saudi Arabia. It was the last day of the Hajj, and they were obligated to enter the mosque and complete the final *tawaf,* seven laps around the black building in the center known as the Kaaba. Only then would Allah erase their sins and their pilgrimage be complete.

Covering the Hajj was easy work for the cameraman, except for the heat, which could run to 130 or 140 degrees Fahrenheit on the roof. He downed another bottle of water and zoomed in on the profile of a single pilgrim, prostrate before the Kaaba with his hands pressed up against its stone side. Tears of joy streamed down the man's face as the song of the muezzin appeared to be directed only to him. It was one of the cameraman's favorite shots. He focused on the individual for several seconds.

The tearful man raised his head and the cameraman began to zoom out. He widened the frame until it included the dozen or so people closest to the pilgrim, symbolizing the man's family. He kept widening the picture until perhaps a hundred people were in the shot, representing the pilgrim's community. The cameraman kept going until viewers could see the *tawaf*, rotating counterclockwise like a great galaxy of Islam. The shot reached its maximum width, encompassing the entire Grand Mosque with the Kaaba drawing the viewer's eyes to the center. It was breathtaking. The booth usually held it for twenty or thirty seconds before cutting to a different angle. The cameraman lifted his eyes from his viewfinder and looked out over the scene, savoring the moment.

There was an explosion in the crowd, followed by a cloud of smoke rising into the air near the Kaaba. The crying man was gone, vaporized along with at least a thousand people around him.

*Oh, no,* thought the cameraman. *Some madman snuck in a bomb. Is nowhere sacred?*

There was a second explosion on the other side of the Kaaba. And then he heard the noise, the whoosh of two objects flying rapidly through the air, followed by the noise of the explosions.

*Delayed by the speed of sound,* he realized. *Not a madman on the ground, but a madman in the air . . .*

The cameraman instinctively spun the camera toward the action. Its powerful lens picked up faint trails of smoke. He followed them into the sky and zoomed in until he spotted a dot in the distance. He zoomed as fast and as far as he could until the dot took form, the form of an aircraft turning away. The image was grainy on the hot and hazy summer day, but the cameraman had no doubts about what it was. The distinctive, bat-winged aircraft was possessed by only one nation on earth, and millions of people had just seen it attack the holiest site in all of Islam.

**COLLEGE FOR THEIR CHILDREN**

A portion of my royalties from each copy of *Warning Light* sold goes directly to Children of Fallen Patriots Foundation, a 501(c)(3) nonprofit charity whose mission is to provide college scholarships and educational counseling to military children who have lost a parent in the line of duty. The organization is dedicated to serving the families of service members who have died as a result of combat casualties, military training accidents, and other duty-related deaths.

If you have lost a parent in the line of duty, or would like to help those who have, please visit FallenPatriots.org.

Ready to find
your next great read?

Let us help.

**Visit prh.com/nextread**

Penguin
Random
House